PRAISE FOR *DAISY &*

'Michelle Cahill deploys poetry and history in the most powerful manner possible to write back to Virginia Woolf, and expose the colonial gaze that did not (does not) acknowledge the full humanity of others. This novel will be to *Mrs Dalloway* what *Wide Sargasso Sea* was to *Jane Eyre*.' MEENA KANDASAMY

'A dauntless novel of empire, and its ever-replicating costs. There are echoes of Michael Ondaatje in this novel's lush and observant prose-craft. This is fiction at its most human and humane.' BEEJAY SILCOX

'At once critically acute and narratively rich, *Daisy & Woolf* shows us that there are always new ways to read the past in order to understand the present.' PATRICK FLANERY

'Written with an essayist's precision and a poet's grace, *Daisy & Woolf* is a clever, lyrical and moving meditation on the novelist's responsibility. It is a profound comment on the stories we choose to tell, and the gaps in our choosing. Meticulously rendering Virginia Woolf's faintly sketched, sidelined characters in full vibrant colour, Cahill's sweeping novel traverses centuries, cultures and continents to deftly explore how race, gender and class have the power to shape a narrative.' MAXINE BENEBA CLARKE

Daisy & WOOLF

MICHELLE CAHILL

hachette
AUSTRALIA

This project has been assisted by the Australian Government through the Australia Council, its arts funding and advisory body.

Published in Australia and New Zealand in 2022
by Hachette Australia
(an imprint of Hachette Australia Pty Limited)
Gadigal Country, Level 17, 207 Kent Street, Sydney, NSW 2000
www.hachette.com.au

Hachette Australia acknowledges and pays our respects to the past, present and future Traditional Owners and Custodians of Country throughout Australia and recognises the continuation of cultural, spiritual and educational practices of Aboriginal and Torres Strait Islander peoples. Our head office is located on the lands of the Gadigal people of the Eora Nation.

 A catalogue record for this book is available from the National Library of Australia

ISBN: 978 0 7336 4521 1 (paperback)

Cover design by Christabella Designs
Cover photographs courtesy of Maria Petkova/Trevillion Images (background) and Glasshouse Images/Alamy Stock Photo (woman)
Author photo: Nicola Bailey
Typeset in 12.7/19.2 pt Baskerville MT Pro by Bookhouse, Sydney
Printed and bound in Great Britain by Clays Ltd, Elcograf S.p.A.

The paper this book is printed on is certified against the Forest Stewardship Council® Standards. McPherson's Printing Group holds FSC® chain of custody certification SA-COC-005379. FSC® promotes environmentally responsible, socially beneficial and economically viable management of the world's forests.

for Taron and for Sarah

'A woman writing thinks back through her mothers'

– VIRGINIA WOOLF, *A ROOM OF ONE'S OWN*

33 Tavistock Square
London

15 March 2017

I did not know the dead could speak until today, when I received a letter from my mother. It seems there is every possibility an afterlife exists. A place I have questioned. A place from where those who have departed shed their quiet, unseasonal praise, like winter leaves falling. The warm wit I have cherished in my mother's voice has returned to this earth to bring me solace. Love is a strange feeling when it is controlled by the impossibility of separation and distance. It feels like hunger, a fine vibration tapping the sheath between my heart and my stomach. My mother had started to suffer dementia in her last years; it was a fluctuating absence, although she could still write and her conversation was unexpectedly sharp, if hesitant and unsustained. She was usually wheelchair-bound. Her gaze would slowly fix on me, when I visited, accommodating its milky focus to clarity, and she would stop scratching her nose, a habit that seemed to fill time in her absent moods. From the periphery of her disorganising mind she would speak beautiful sentences. One day, as I approached the house carrying flowers, she raised her stooped head and said, in that dry, surprising manner of hers, 'Nobody could not want to keep living to see you . . .'

She had passed away in January, while I was living in London, freelancing, teaching a poetry workshop at City University and reading the novels, the diaries and the letters of Virginia Woolf.

The prospect of the trip home for the funeral terrified me. I booked the first available flight, but worried that I could not bear the trauma of travelling there and back alone, sitting in a Boeing between strangers, presenting myself through border security and customs. Muslims and refugees were being restricted by Trump's immigration ban; Theresa May was advocating an early Brexit deal, with Scotland calling for talks on a second referendum. All over the world, people of colour felt vulnerable when crossing borders. Did the same apply to the transit between life and death, I wondered, or was that zone of separation excised from all political upheavals?

I felt guilt-ridden for all the times I had been less present for her, the times when I had been stuck in routine, driven by ambition, or when I had been competing with my ego, bettering myself at conferences or writing stodgy articles to earn a living. (As I am writing this, I wish my mother was alive, and that I could call her now and listen to the ebb of her voice, the rhythmical tap, tap, tap, tap of the phone shaking in her trembling hands.) How little I could do to help her. She had gradually stopped complaining about the pain in her thigh and her leg. I could not take it away. By the time I had flown back to Sydney, slept for four or five hours in a hotel before driving a hired car to Tathra because there was nobody willing or available to collect me, I was several days too late.

A breeze entered the house like an oblique presence. It lifted the vertical blinds, filling the emptiness. My brother would have wanted to keep my mother indefinitely but, according to Australian law, once a person has been certified as having died, they may stay in their abode for no longer than twenty-four hours. Arrangements had begun for the church service, a guest list, the selection of hymns and gospel readings. The funeral directors arrived with a fold-out trolley. They zipped her body into a bag. They transported her to storage. All of this, I had been spared from. My sister sat down with me. She offered me a glass of water. She told me how my mother had died in her sleep, unattended; how she and my brother washed her, turning the board of her body from side to side, dragging the sheets from under the sticks of her legs, which were bent like the folded wings of an insect. She showed me the first photographs taken after she was found cold. Her body was covered by a sheet on the bed where she lay suffering for the last two years, ever since the exacerbation. She looked peaceful, her skin only slightly loose over the fine facial bones. Then a photograph of my family by her side, the sad beauty of my niece, and then the two Polish priests saying prayers. One of them told my sister that my mother's soul had left. How raw the grief that followed. My brother had kept the garments she wore: the over-stretched t-shirt; the shoes she sometimes slipped on, betraying the smallness of her feet; her six bangles. He removed the solitaire ring my mother wore and gave it to my sister to keep. In her wardrobe were her dresses, dry-cleaned and hung on carefully spaced coathangers. In the room, the wheelchair, facing the window where the morning sun streamed. No sign of the neighbour's cat, which was often stationed there, outside, looking in.

The dead never look pretty. On the day of the funeral they kept her body behind a screen in the church in Bega. The choir was seated but the organist was playing, and the pews were filled with family members who had travelled from Melbourne and Perth, and friends from the parish. I walked to the coffin, straight up to her. Mentally, I had been trying to prepare for the alteration. Her face had thawed after the refrigeration. A blotchiness had crept into her skin as she lay in the coffin. Her shrinking flesh was thin like the petals of native indigo I have found on the bluff growing under rocks. I bent over to embrace her; instantly and violently I wept. The wreath my sister chose was less to my liking than a spray of pink lilies, cream roses and dark green foliage I had ordered. The choir sang hymns my mother had chosen. Her head was turned to the left side as though she were facing a portal into the afterlife, and a slight frown creased her brow, not as in a gesture of resistance to dying, but to me, at least, it expressed all the pain of her parting without us exchanging last farewells, and without her dying even being witnessed.

There had been a spill of vomit on her pillow. She had been refusing food intermittently for over a year, her lips pursed when we endeavoured to feed her. The illness left her muscles weak. She often struggled to breathe but we all understood she would not tolerate tube feeds. That would have been cruel, an artificial prolongation. The hospital staff had never quite understood our cultural beliefs about caring for our elderly family members at home. Then again, I let her down. I hadn't come back, too busy writing, so what was the point of living? (How is it in life that words betray us? How can we say or write the most devastating things to people we love the most?) I kept thinking about the bile entering the stem of her oesophagus, burning the life out of her, ballooning into her mouth. My brother may have been sleeping off his boozing from the previous night that afternoon in the house overlooking Horseshoe Bay.

Our family live halfway between the old wharf at Tathra, the refurbished hotel and Kianinny Bay, where my father and my brother used to take the boat out fishing on weekends. They might catch yellowtail or salmon, occasionally a small shark. The view is deceptive; the indigo bay at dawn, the sea's corduroy lines and the trees obscuring the ragged foam and rip currents as the swell beats and pounds the shore and the rocks bite back mercilessly. The bluffs were overgrown with melaleuca, the dry undergrowth easy fuel for bushfires.

Along this looping foreshore I had often pictured the first maverick European arrivals, Robert Campbell and William Clarke, and seventeen Bengali lascars who made peaceful contact with Djiringanj people of the Yuin nation. They had left Calcutta for Sydney Cove in 1797, with the promise of trading supplies, but after being shipwrecked on Preservation Island in Bass Strait they took longboats to the mainland. They were shipwrecked again at Ninety Mile Beach in Victoria. From here they had no choice but to walk north to Eden, through Merimbula and Tathra, all the way along the coast to Sydney, a distance of seven hundred miles. Historical records written by European settlers describe the Aboriginals as hostile, even though Campbell and Clarke's party had been fed and guided through country by First Nations people. About the lascars, little is recorded in the official history, but the wiry, barefoot, hardworking dark-skinned men wearing lungis were the mainstay of indentured labour in the colonies: in Burma, India, China, Malaya, East Africa and Britain. I have been thinking of lascars on the steamer Daisy travels on; they were recruited often, from north-eastern Bengal, also from Gujarat, and were treated harshly. Like First Nations peoples, they are the invisible ink in the history of cross-cultural connections between India, China, Australia and England.

My brother heard voices, which drinking spirits helped to subdue. Through no fault of his own, Dad said. He was teased for his brown skin at school in England and he had never fully recovered from the breakdown. We had talked to doctors and mental health nurses, but they said he was not a danger to himself or to others and all they could do was offer him an appointment. He was friendly, capable and well-liked by the neighbours. The voices told him that my mother had a microchip implanted in her brain and that through a complex network of conspiracies involving rebels in Zanzibar, I was somehow responsible.

I'm not sure why he sent the letter. In the tangle of paranoia it is possible he misread the note as a threat, and more than likely he had retained it for a considerable time before posting it. Perhaps it was mislaid somewhere in the trail of South Coast mail, which is slower and less reliable than mail from the suburbs reaching the CBD's general post office in Martin Place. The road to Cooma up Brown Mountain is a very steep single lane with hairpin bends used by fuel tankers and logging trucks. Sometimes they have to swing across the other lane to take the bends, and when there's frost and ice they can lose traction. Driving the alternative coast road often means queuing behind wide loads and station wagons. In the days of the first aeroplanes and motor vehicle transport, in the time that Virginia Woolf was writing *Mrs Dalloway*, in the quiet village of Rodmell, the letter would have been bundled up and sent by horse and wagon to the old Tathra wharf at

Kianinny Bay, thence by coastal steamer with pigs, livestock, cheese, butter and a few passengers to Sydney, from Sydney to Adelaide, to Colombo, from there to Port Said and then to Italy, across the continent.

The letter hadn't been airmailed. It was written in my mother's neat handwriting, the loops and curves grown shaky. As was her habit, the tone is reserved. Two lines were all she had composed:

My darling Mina,
I hope you find in London the inspiration, time and distance
you need for your writing. Please let me know how it is going
Mum xx

I notice that the second sentence is not punctuated by a full stop, because my mother was particular about such things. Before she was married, she had been employed as a book-keeper for the Department of Finance in Nairobi. She had borne three children, nurturing them with a partiality for myself and for my brother. As Anglo-Indians from East Africa we had our misfortunes, of course. But her disposition, I would say, was contrary to mine entirely; like so many women of her generation, my mother was able to strictly govern her duties in marriage and in her professional life.

I am too upset to figure it out, or maybe I can't face accepting that I knew so little about the daily flux of Mum's deterioration. I suppose she wrote it for me at Christmas, when I didn't show. Perhaps the time it took for my brother to send it by second-class mail to England had delayed its arrival. He had been kept occupied in the last year of her life, as her dependency increased. He refused help. Often, he carried her in his arms instead of using the lifter. They loved each other, and he cared for her tenderly. The envelope lay on the patterned blue carpet. It had fallen through the magazine slot in the front door of the house in Tavistock Square, bundled up with advertising pamphlets and the rest of the mail. I am renting the ground floor flat of university housing, my hallway tucked behind the stairwell, furnished with a coat and umbrella rack, where I drape my flimsy scarves and gloves. I can hear the student tenants come and go, greeting each other in passing. Going by the thud of boots or stilettos on the steps I can tell if it is Celine, a Jamaican drama major, or James, a medical postgraduate in cardiology who lives on the top floor. He is carrying out research which he explained in technical detail; something along the lines of measuring calcium levels in heart muscle during stress testing.

I always hear the doorbell ring, and from time to time the door sweeping over the carpet, then whispers in the hallway, so already I have acquired a little skill in interpreting the words of those who speak when they are not visible. This morning it was raining outside. The wind needled my nipples when I walked to the shop run by the Bangladeshi family in Marchmont Street to buy oranges, bread and milk. Despite the blotches, leakages and spills, the pavement stones were bleached by the cold. Bags of garbage were bundled near the railings of the houses, waiting for the rubbish collection. The gusts played havoc with my umbrella, turning it inside out. Within minutes a spine snapped, and it became a useless instrument in my hands, the frustration of a wasted purchase so that by the time I returned to the flat I was soaked and for the rest of the morning I have been drying off.

But the envelope was dry, and I recognised its ethereal appearance at once. I sat down on the sofa in the lounge room, perplexed and deeply sad for the love it bears, and for whatever truth is wrapped inside, to which it is impossible that I can respond. But here it is: simple, wretched, irretrievably mine. I sit feeling trapped by life. There is no way out. I want there to be less of the future left and more of the past. How I miss being able to talk over the phone to my mother; the ease by which that liberty had been at my disposal to exercise seems to mock me now, in this stranded, powerless state. The point in time at which her dementia began and she found it hard to follow the meanings of conversation is elusive to mark, and so it just happened that she progressively lost her grip on the real. I could no longer expect her to understand my complex thoughts, my impatient demanding mind, and even her memory grew dim. Yet still, how it dawns on me now with the envelope fulfilling its destiny in my hands, that I had taken our relationship in this world for granted, expecting it was prearranged, for love feels deceptively boundless, though our days are numbered from the start.

On the table there are books I am reading: *Mrs Dalloway*, the Woolf diaries, her later Sussex novels, and her essays, including one on Oxford Street in the city and another on the docks of London, published in a popular magazine. There are essays I have been reading on Woolf and Empire. I like to have them here as a signpost to a theme that curiously beckons. On days off, I sometimes read the original digitised manuscripts at the British Library in St Pancras. Here I discover that Woolf had lively, forward slanting, at times uneven handwriting. Her words are strongly spaced, and where phrases have been struck through, the corrections have a neatness and are methodically placed above her original lines. I'm not sure what I expect to find from these readings; perhaps another interpretation of the novel, meanings that had escaped from the final draft (though what could have escaped the numerous volumes and scholarly articles of criticism on Woolf?).

I wanted some clue to Peter Walsh and Daisy Simmons: how they meet; why it so happens that she falls perilously in love with him; what eventuates after he leaves India. Does she leave her husband and elope with him? And is she as madly jealous in her moral ruin as Tolstoy's Anna Karenina? What does she think of Clarissa, if ever the two women should meet: the privileged upper-class socialite from Westminster and 'the dark, adorably pretty' Eurasian mother? They had, at least, motherhood in common. The joys and the constraints, they knew all these.

Sentenced to trip over a single word for a few moments I stare at the envelope. Till now the depths of my melancholy has not vented. I had been choking at my mother's funeral, a hot summer's day, the worst time of the year for undertakers to preserve and paint the dead. We sweltered at the cemetery as hymns were played and they lowered her body into the ground. All of us so forlorn, wearing sunglasses and black-ribboned hats. I watched the flowers disappearing with her. I cried on my return to London. It sometimes feels like I am travelling in her footsteps, a mother taking the calculated risks and measures required to immigrate. How much more difficult it would have been for Daisy Simmons to immigrate. I need to give Daisy a voice and a body. Daisy is the character whose story I hope to write, the woman whom Virginia Woolf had scarcely sketched as naive, vulnerable and wanton, giving it away too easily, pretty and young, all dressed in white.

Tears stream, running fast down my cheeks. I feel guilty about how my mother died, the gradual emaciation, the physical dependency, the spill of vomit, the way she had choked in her sleep. What had I been doing for so long? Dying my own slow death, year after year, since before my divorce. The truth is that writing has consumed me, overtaken my part-time work responsibilities, distorted my values, even my sense of harmony and proportion in friendships. Writing justifies unhealthy habits, social media addictions, tendencies and erroneous actions. It had been a slow deflation by a few reductive reviews my work had received, by 'gatekeeping'. When I had received an international prize I couldn't convince the newspapers to run it. I once read about an author who faked being her own publicist and sometimes wish I had given that a go. Never mind. None of us are special and being in London I feel protected. I have been turning over in my mind the seed of Woolf's idea of colonial India, and London. The hub of the empire she sought to question and to flag, was a place I have passed through like so many new arrivals with my mother and my father, my sister and brother. Now it is a place of temporary refuge. I've returned as an author, trying to escape from racist hierarchies, only to find myself re-entering them until I strike it lucky with a fellowship, or a festival or a prize or a publication. So here I am.

And should there be gaps in heaven, should the borders of that territory be guarded by a militia of saints, then this message has slipped through to find me floundering in my work in the stone-cold flat, where I huddle up by the radiator to keep warm. Some days I spend washing clothes and then walking to and from the shops to buy groceries, so that after peeling vegetables and ironing shirts, after cleaning and tidying the kitchen, there is not enough time in the day to read or try to write. London pollution saturates the air in the evenings and often by six, I find myself overcome by fits of coughing until I am too tired to stay awake.

Now, suddenly, this letter, like a pendulum clock chiming, from shadow time, from an afterlife. Everything will be okay, perhaps. I've felt guilty that I wasn't there when my mother died. I have left my son Sam in Sydney with his father. My extended stay being justified by the thought that, as a teenager, he doesn't need me now. Teenagers can't relate to their mothers anyway. Sam is at high school, starting year eleven. It strikes me as improbable, but perhaps my mother is sending me a sign of her approval and encouragement. Like a heavenly seal. I sniff the letter and imagine the oil of her perspiration, for there were times when she suffered unpredictably for up to an hour with erratic tremors, and when her eyes were fixed with the expression of a terrible agitation, through which she was frozen in speech, her arms flapping. Then, if I were with her, I would wipe the sweat from her brow, and I would wash her with a flannel and French soap lathered in warm water. The perfumed candle burned slowly in her room. During her illness hours were spent as I bent over her trembling body, her frowning face. She became fixed in my mind, her skin browner from failing kidneys, like the English patient, not dying in a ruined monastery, nor in the desert, but by the sea on the South Coast of New South Wales. She was like some ancient still-breathing artefact locked in a long glass cubicle in a dusty room in the British Museum – before it became corporatised, before they added the café and the souvenir shop – and I was her attendant, her scribe.

I keep thinking about the envelope, which bears the certain knowledge that she knew she was dying and, with it, an unbearable intensity of joy and sorrow. She wanted to say goodbye. My gaze moves from the letter to a framed photograph of my mother I have on the desk, in which she is wearing a satin dress, radiant with warmth, and I find myself watching myself reading the words, searching the reproduction, questioning myself and my feeling: is it real, this grief? Or is it shards of memory, is it nostalgia, is the bereavement spliced with fantasy? Is it my mother? Is it the idea of her, or something or somebody else? (At times I find myself thinking for hours about my ex, as if it were him I had lost.) And all of it in my mind, in my mind?

Days are followed by dark nights, a darkness that seals my windows and sweeps under my bed. So dark I cannot tell the pavement stones from the sky; so dark that the bars of the cast iron gate begin to fade, and my eyes strain to recognise the sharp edges of the desk. I draw the curtains and unfold the blankets. I lie in my bed as the clock ticks and occasionally the fridge creaks, as the wind rasps against the windows, or it howls like an animal gone mad trying to tear down the plane trees, deeply rooted in the square while traffic on Gower Street rumbles and whines. Memories creep into my dreams, the present swirling vertiginously with the past: a chink of light reveals exposed rafters, the sound of waves endlessly rolling, breaking themselves, little wrens chirruping and flies buzzing. Were it not for this porosity of my mind the darkness would bring an end to each day's sorrow, regret, confusion and anxiety but these entities blur and I am sleepless for hours, and there is history waiting to fault me, and there is a story I have been trying to speak without contradictions, without censorship or belief being suspended; a story that is mine to tell and not Virginia Woolf's, and yet not entirely mine, because it is within me, of my people, the Anglo-Indians, while also beyond me. And so, the darkness comes and goes indifferently, the leaves tremble in the square and the wind shrieks, waiting for the future to show.

33 Tavistock Square

London

22 March 2017

I have been making preliminary notes about the novel. How does one get to the crux of race in a character like Daisy Simmons? What was it like to be Eurasian? Does Daisy live near the synagogue in the grey zone, or the white zone? And only a decade after the end of indentured labour. I try to picture Garden Reach. I check the maps. I imagine its dockyard warehouses, empty where once it had been over-crowded with recruits, waiting for their departure to the Caribbean or to Fiji.

Yesterday, I walked to Westminster, retracing Clarissa's steps from Mulberry's, the florist in Bond Street. I took a turn through Green Park, the trees bare and bending, the grass tussocky, blown flat by a cold windstorm ripping through the meadows. My hair became strings to be pulled, summoned by the wind, my heart too. It was hardly ideal to be walking out here, though a group of men were cross-training and a man was running his dog. I felt the force of nature control me.

I gave myself over to be pummelled by grief, my thoughts and feelings at the whim of weather and its vicissitudes. A thick branch may have snapped from its trunk and broken my neck; twigs might have flicked in the gust and scratched my eyes, my hands, a reminder to me that it was not without risk to be outdoors walking that morning. I took a selfie with my phone capturing the wind towing my hair and my scarf. Taking selfies has become a habit, a way of recording how I seem to be in the world. By taking a selfie, it is almost as if I might become what I see, or I may find in the image a mirror for my soul. It is not simply narcissism; it is therapy, the disturbed therapy of a writer.

I've read how Virginia Woolf also liked to photograph friends, and that she often wrote letters to them, requesting photographs. Her first camera was a box form magazine with a peculiar handle. In 1931 she bought a Zeiss, for twenty pounds. Her sister Vanessa and her great-aunt Julia Margaret Cameron were photographers, and the visual was always present in her writing.

After she lost her mother at the age of thirteen, Virginia began to hear Julia, her mother, speaking almost every day for more than thirty years, to the point that it became oppressive and she turned to fiction, raising Julia from the dead in *To the Lighthouse*. Writing is reviving, purging the past, and bewildering as our real lives. Only after writing this novel did the voices of her mother stop haunting Virginia. They came from different worlds but in some ways, Julia was like my mother. She was gracious, quietly brilliant, subdued, dutiful, sympathetic to others, an angel in the house dying quietly during the night, unobserved, not making a fuss, with no messy excretions or malodours. The smell of my mother was never acrid or fermented even when she was incontinent, when she had been sweating in her bed for hours and was too tired to sit straight for a shower, her head falling back, the greyness messy, like steel wire. She would lapse into moments of authority over her mind. I believe there is firmness in the angelic disposition, no matter how dominating a father may be. My mother hated discontent, she hated quarrels, and I remember her swiftly drawing the curtains, whispering, 'Hush, what will the neighbours think?' whenever there was a sign of discord.

Beholding her letter, reading between her lines, perhaps there was a residue of resentment that I had left her to die with my brother, selfishly, for the sake of my work. I had abandoned her for several months when my books were being published. I, also a mother, struggling to survive the daily grind with my son. My mother wasted, she stopped eating, she was tired sitting in the wheelchair, not really piecing together everything around her, but nonetheless calm and patient, trembling, frowning as the daylight spilled into the room and the fan droned and the movies that she watched replayed or the radio blared. And whenever we spoke over the telephone, her voice was like sunlight. Whenever I visited, her eyes would shine, and her face would light up.

Walking from The Mall towards the fountain in St James's Park, I crossed into Birdcage Walk, the trees casting shadows variously in the afternoon sun. There was no Hugh Whitbread or Peter Walsh to detain me, there were no minor characters, no old beggar woman singing of eternal spring, no little girl in pink collecting pebbles, though there were plenty of richly attired Arabs and immigrants of all nationalities strolling with me. The palace and historic buildings invite appreciation. As always, London felt different to the rest of England; gritty and spirited, pulsing and prosperous. Young and old, from all walks of life, seemed to be enjoying a lull in the storm, the gusty winds having subsided to a cool breeze. A young couple wheeling a baby in a pram and one or two joggers. I thought of the drunks in Hyde Park, Sydney, who played chess with giant pawns and who slept on the benches in crumpled jackets, brown paper bags and an empty bottle spilling from their hands. And all the while I imagined what the parks of London would be like in summer; garden beds blooming with yellow, red and burgundy tulips, with geraniums and daisies, people reading newspapers in deckchairs by the lake, the pelicans on parade, the blue herons basking in the sun.

I walked further along, past the Guards Museum and the military buildings to where the road was being widened and partly barricaded, on my way to St Anne's Gate. At Westminster, I found a vantage point from where I could imagine Clarissa, setting out to buy the flowers for the party she planned to host that June evening. I was standing where she would have most likely passed, not long after leaving the house, because the day beckoned, and she had decided to buy the flowers herself. I took a photograph with my phone using a black-and-white filter and, though there were taxis and buses and pedestrians, Big Ben commanded the intersection now as it would have done in 1923. Later, I tweeted the photograph for modernist allies and Sydney followers who liked it. There had been no explosion in Bond Street, no mysterious VIP car, although there was an ascending aeroplane, leaving its cloud trail. And hemmed in the eaves and parapets of buildings, pigeons hovered and roosted.

Strange how in life there is always some catastrophe imminent. How was I to know that the very next day Khalid Masood would drive a car into pedestrians on the south side of Westminster Bridge? It spread over social media within moments: his eighty-second attack ending with him being shot dead at the gates to parliament, a policeman was fatally stabbed, four others died and fifty were wounded. There was conjecture about jihadi influence, about Brexit. He was born in Kent in 1964 to a British teenager not much older than my son. A decent chap and a footballer at school but convicted of shoplifting. He began hanging out with the wrong crowd, taking drugs. Had spent time in prison for assaults; had three children. His body, large, dead and sagging, seems vulnerable in the photographs.

And all this would happen within the space of a day and a night, while birds sang and scattered, and branches swayed, and purple crocuses bloomed through tissues of frost, after dark and cold, rain and snow the buds of spring leaves exploded like my mother's words in my mind, and her no longer being able to hear my reply. (So it persisted unspoken.) 'I hope you find in London the inspiration, time and distance you need for your writing.'

But standing where I was, by the statue of Abraham Lincoln in Parliament Square, imagining Clarissa setting off to buy the flowers, there was no sign or premonition of the impending catastrophe.

Garden Reach
Calcutta

10 February 1924

Dear Peter,

I stepped out today into the dark, leafy street. It was before dawn, but I was not able to sleep for thoughts of swallows and redwood, the raked meadows and tall hedges which you have described to me with such fondness. Do you remember that afternoon we sat, sheltered a little from the hot sun, beneath the dusty mango tree after strolling through Eden Gardens? Having wanted to show me photographs of Oxfordshire, your favourite haunts at Magdalen. Having evoked the twittering of small birds and the finest pattering of rain at Bourton, so unlike our tropics, and having mentioned her – Clarissa, of course – her splendid parties, with all those fine people, all the slippery years between us, my heart furtive as an eel in the moss-green river?

On the corner of Park Street, the sweepers were gathering yesterday's waste in black mounds. Crows swooped, jabbing their sharp beaks into the road to pick out worms and other appetisers from the rubbish. The streets were silent. Drivers curled and cradled in their carts, and the low-caste men lay dreaming in their dhotis on mats or sheets of cardboard. James, dare I mention, was snoring, recovering from a malady kindled by our marital discord and his addictive temperament. Charlotte and Joseph were safe in their cots, their dreams kept cool by the spinning monotony afforded by wondrous electricity, and discipline, discipline, discipline! We must have order in our households! With all the recent disruptions they struggle to keep up with their lessons. They read mostly in English and are better schooled in science and arithmetic than the Bengali dialect.

Joseph gets enthused by mechanics – trains and automobiles – while Charlotte is absorbed in the study of insects and is partial to biology. She entreats me to arrange another visit to the zoo, so I have set aside a date. Mrs Burgess has engaged a new munshi to teach the children Hindustani and Urdu since we speak only English at home. But that will not do. Little angels! My darlings! They must weather the winds of change in India. English will not stand them in good stead. You warned me of this. I think you guess I prefer sunlight and clear summer skies to bayonets and battlefields. How I would watch the sun slip into a distant patchwork of hills while the kettle steams and a line is cast into the river. How I would speak with you in one tongue and be cured of my homesickness.

Lately, there is always some rumour of a protest, or a Maoist gathering. A train strike brought the mail from Shimla and Varanasi to a halt, and one reads about the Swarajists and Gandhists. The country is swept with riots, flared by Hindu republicans falling out with the Moslem league. Mama and I witnessed an incident only last week when we drove past the village of Durgapur. It had been raining heavily and the roads were treacherous, having been muddied by the wheels of carriages and cars. We were proceeding well until a para-wallah stopped the traffic flow. Hindered in the rain, and hemmed in by bullock carts and dog carts, water began leaking through the bonnet of our carriage, at first as drips and then a steady trickle until it poured, and we were soaked. Mama regretted not wearing a hat, and Charlie kept whimpering and shaking, though every now and then he licked our faces dry. At last, the downpour eased. Beyond the traffic, about a hundred yards ahead, we could see a crowd of people and what seemed to be a riot unfolding between a band of poor aggrieved Hindus and choli bedraggled in their wet attire, their thin limbs brandishing sticks and knives. Some were throwing stones. Mama was typically reserved, though I could feel her anxiety when she asked the parawallah in Urdu what was going on. He explained that the licence tax has deprived the shop stores of grain and flour. Many of the shop owners are Moslems. They had been observing the month of fasting but that was coming to an end, with a new moon rising in the heavens.

Having starved for weeks, the Hindus turned against the Moslems for serving the local English collector, Mr Clarke, a stout, moustachioed gentleman wearing a topee. He was at the mercy of the crowd, unable to quell the hostilities, which draw their source from deeply entrenched rivalries. A swarm of officers soon arrived for his protection. They fired shots into the crowd, disbanding the protesters within fifteen or, at the most, twenty minutes. In the scurry, several bodies were trampled, and the screams were heart-rending, then silence afterwards. The sky was bruised, purple and black. Fat droplets of rain hugged the casement, wind swept through the trees. We heard thunder and rivulets of monsoon rain. I asked myself how miserable life must be for those whose cries signalled escape. My heart pulsed tenderly for all the poor in this city; those who camp in makeshift dwellings along the railway, the women especially, who labour barefoot and wear the same gaudy saree. When, finally, the disturbance had been cleared, the traffic moved slowly past the troubled precinct and it was horrific to realise the dark glistening pools running into mud and rain along the roadside were blood.

The whole episode was a shock to me, and how I longed to see you that day, and all last week your arms were missed. I ache for their comforting strength. When I told James what had happened, he simply grimaced, muttered something about the natives needing to be corrected, and carried on carving the pork. I did not say a word to Joseph or Charlotte, but the serenity I hoped to bring to my maternal duties and affections has been for me a considerable strain. Still, it is true to say that there are many concerns weighing on my heart.

We are following the trial of Gopinath Saha. People are protesting his arrest, but I doubt he will be pardoned. Though his attempt to assassinate the police commissioner failed, everyone expects a severe punishment will be imposed. Papa says the British must make an example of him. He does not like to talk about it much. Rumours spread and we live in fear of surveillance. Some even seek his execution. I think that would please my husband. Revenge is cowardly. One man's life does not make up for another's. An eye for an eye, a tooth for a tooth, perhaps. The Bengalis are as proud a race as the British. Some sneer at us for wearing dresses. They will not visit our homes. They eat with only the right hand. But the Loreto nuns taught us to sit at the table, to pray, to use a knife, fork, spoon; these are our normal ways. All our communities have been woken to the politics and economics of the times. As a woman, I do not feel immune to these incidents. Do you remember our mayor, Mr Deshbandhu? He has been burning his European clothes; Swaraj and Congress, it seems, are not in agreement about the state.

Why does it trouble me? My mother has never cast a vote and politics is peopled with men, yet I feel strongly that these are equally the affairs of women, for the sake of our children. There is widespread unease about what the freedom fighters are saying in the Punjab. Papa says that after the massacre at Jallianwala Bagh, life in British India will never be the same. I have heard there is a young Sikh revolutionary, Bhagat Singh, who speaks feverishly about the republic and has travelled across the seas to Germany and to Berkeley, California enlisting the support of passionate and liberal-minded students.

Sometimes one is cowardly, one struggles for autonomy over the day while the sun burns. I often take a nap after tiffin and housekeeping, or after a morning ride across the Maidan with friends from the gymkhana. I like to undress in the heat. In the evening I may write. I may venture out to visit my cousins, the Prescott girls, in Railway Colony. We take a plate of carrot halwa. Mrs Burgess comes with me and we go in the horse cart. Surely you have not forgotten? Three of them, so pretty, very fashionable: Sarah, Jane and Nora, and their father Lloyd, second engineer at Howrah station. It is an odd thing, I know, but after the children and you, it is dear Nora whose company I most desire. A delightful creature, though not in the least bit conventional. Her heart can be quite stern, aloof at times, but also forthright, calm and strong. We have romped about a fair bit in conversations about the nation, about poetry, about religions. Although she is twenty-one and has been introduced at balls, she has confessed to me that very recently she declined an offer of marriage. The suitor, Mr Pettit, is a handsome, well-mannered Parsee who owns one of the thriving shopfronts in Chowringhee Road, quite a catch for Nora, really. Her mother and father have been shocked by her decision and are trying their best to restrict the spread of rumours for fear of it affecting Nora's prospects and her sister's. I believe she is a lucky girl to have parents who are forgiving. Listening to my heart against propriety and many personal obstacles has strengthened me but it was you who first led me to question dominion.

'If I had loved him,' Nora said, 'it would have been an entirely different matter.' This was much to my surprise as I believe Mr Pettit to be most genial, and there are so many young women in search of eligible husbands, the times being difficult. We read about the war wives in faraway Europe, but here we have our own crisis. And even though Nora tells me she has rejected his advance, my imagination got the better of me, and I envisioned a fine Parsee wedding with Mr Pettit's entourage, his handsome friends and European foreigners. The women dressed gaily in embroidered silk sarees serving trays of Gujarati sweets and sugar loaves. My dear Nora dressed in white georgette with gold-embroidered Chinese silk. Alas, it is not to be at all . . . except for love, love that weaves with the rickshaw man turning into alleyways and lanes, becoming a veritable, self-disclosing presence; love that is furtively escorting a wife who is also a mother en route to the tailors or returning from the orphanage, how it pulses through her veins like dhaki drumming, rising to second- and third-storey rooms in the grand houses of Park Street, which sometimes in her dreams are engulfed by jungle; love that infuses her heart tenderly, insistently, when she kneels to pray in the cathedral in Synagogue Street. Love itches like a breeze that cools her burning skin. Her sweat evaporates, the little boats are moored, the ferry chugging across the Hooghly River downstream from Howrah. Like the flow of time, love is tidal . . . for though it is boundless, all its forces and demarcations are imposed by family, by church and by society. Where shall it find a home?

There are so many refugees from the provinces in Calcutta. Entire families have lost their personal belongings and their property in guerrilla mutinies or other acts of sedition in the Punjab and in Allahabad. The mood of the times is desperate, with prices and taxes being high and produce being scarce. Here in Calcutta, at least, we are fortunate. There is food in Hogg Market, vegetables and fruit, eggs and fish, goat meat for the Moslems, but fuel for the barges and naval ships is scarce.

The war has drained our economy and led us away from dominion. It is dangerous to walk through the villages alone. I am cursed and ridiculed by Brahmin boys. They call us 'eight annas' and 'blacky whites'. Some dare to throw stones. They hate us because our sons earn two hundred rupees a month whereas they are paid one hundred rupees. They say that the British tell lies, and we are their 'bibis'. With the civil unrest, James is stationed for long hours at Fort William. Nowadays, we scarcely see him. I miss your protection. For Anglo-Indian women, Calcutta may be a dangerous place. There are so many broken-spirited soldiers and unfortunate widows after the war. Men who are no longer welcome in their villages. Poor souls thought of as traitors for serving the Empire. Morale is so low there are misplaced hopes, even rumours that a visit from His Royal Highness may be imminent. It is thirteen years since King George V visited as far north as the Himalayas. We hear that the Viceroy, the Earl of Reading, has invited him for game hunting in Shimla. We hear the construction of the Gateway to India memorial is almost finished in Bombay. There are caves at Karli and tigers in Khandala, so is it surprising that the wildness of the Sundarbans or the northern state of Sikkim attracts far less attention? Papa has been talking of a new Labour government setting up office in Westminster. Dearest, do send news of the happenings in England, so, I may share it with these brave and tragic sepoys! Truly, they are martyrs for an imperial cause that all Indians are beginning to question.

By train or by boat, these men arrive in such a state, suffering from trauma and destitution, for what horrors they have witnessed in the trenches of the Somme, in Ypres or at Gallipoli. Some were stationed in Mesopotamia and East Africa. One lad, an amputee, told me how all but one other Indian in his entire regiment was killed, slaughtered in a river of blood, in the stinking mud, by the Germans. It is heartening that these men find care and solace here. There are several charities and halfway houses in Dum Dum. The wounded officers spend months in rehabilitation hospices and farmhouses. Nora and I have been visiting one such hospice to keep company and spend a few hours with veteran soldiers and convalescents. We read them stories, or we sing if they like in Italian or French, or we help the nurses by sponging them down, changing sheets, or we bring them clothes. The time passes very well there since it is rewarding to volunteer. I have had Elsie prepare special treats like strawberry sponge cake and chocolate boats, and I like to bring a bottle of sherry or gin for their nightcaps.

Yesterday there was a special ceremony for the lascar veterans, mainly Hindus but also Moslems, Sikhs, Chinese, Arabs, Eurasians. The Governor, Lord Lytton, unveiled a handsome memorial at the southern end of the maidan, less than a hundred yards from Princep Ghat. There he was. Very stately. The figure of Britishness surrounded by an entourage of men in bright shiny suits, batons chained to their tails, wiping the sweat from their brows with their immaculate handkerchiefs. The tower has a gilt dome and four small minarets with the prow of an ancient vessel projecting from all its four sides. Few attended to commemorate the lives of these lowly sailors and soldiers. It was a pity since the colonialists and administrators have not yet fled to the hills to escape the heat of summer. Still, it was a memorable affair, with the regalia of full brigade, with elephants and Australian horses. Three brave subalterns received the Order of St Michael and St George. It was a pleasing sight and when drumbeats struck solemnly, instinctively my thoughts fled to you in London. Please do send news of some progress with the lawyers of Lincoln's Inn. I would like to persist with them despite the delay. Do they need me to provide any more papers? When you were here, Mrs Burgess cautioned me that the stigma of divorce can ruin a woman's life. Sometimes I think my unhappiness has turned my nerves to steel.

We had dinner with my parents only to learn of an accident. My father's aide de camp, Mr Khan, a senior officer with BWTC, had been visiting his relatives in one of the outskirt towns. The nearby village is predominantly Hindu. As it was Ramadan, Mr Khan was crossing a field on his way to worship at the idgah when he was shot by one of the landlord's hands, simply on a presumption of trespass. The incident was fatal, causing a bleed in his brain.

A furore has erupted in the village. Mr Khan was a promising administrator. He left behind a young widow, Rukmini, and their six-year-old son, Ali. The case is to be heard in the district magistrate's court and there has been a piece in the newspaper. Papa and my uncle Jeremy were discussing the growing hostility between the Hindus and Moslems, the situation only briefly appeased when the Mahatma called for cooperation with Sunnis. But now the Khilafat movement has collapsed and is not expected to recover. The accused farmer did not have a gun licence and is likely to be severely sentenced, let us see. I felt very sad, having met Mr Khan when he came to our house for dinner parties. Mama says very little on these matters, but I sense my father's concern. We have heard that Gandhi has been released from gaol for a surgical operation. Hard to believe that he who had supported the war is now advocating disobedience. And who is to know what will happen here, what lies ahead . . .

And yet, for all this, February has arrived with such gaiety it fills my heart and delights the servant girls, our neighbours and compatriots. The heat has not yet reached its greatest intensity. Pilgrims will soon flood the city from as far away as Chittagong, Dacca and Allahabad for shopping and leisure. Hindus arrive for the celebrations and for puja to their goddess of poetry, Saraswati. Mothers and children come from every village to the markets to buy sweets, sindoor, silver and the lavishly embroidered sarees for which, you may remember, our district is renowned. Every sweaty and exhausted rickshaw man, every tiffin carrier and porter, even our favourite chai wallah and coconut wallah, every crooked vendor forgets their troubles and their debts and revels with the crowded, bustling city of Calcutta, her war wounds licked clean for these weeks, though not quite forgotten.

You are constantly in my thoughts. It's as if I'm driven by a need to stop whatever I am doing or trying to do. To sit down. To write. Even now I am struck by how bleak reality became after you left me in the dusk last August, pleading on the dusty road that I would do *anything, anything* . . . So much for leavings! Remember how Charlie sat on my lap, cocking his head? Sweet Charlie, he whined and moped late into the evening.

What do I really know of the world? Though I am burdened with the weight of desire, I am not blessed with the light of patience. A year or two after Charlotte's birth I had stopped railing against motherhood, but now that I am possessed by want, it torments me. So does guilt. How encumbered I feel with darling Joseph and Charlotte! He will turn ten in April and she will be eight in June. Should I be unhappy for the next eight years till they are old enough to be independent? I cannot fathom what the future holds. Calcutta is changing rapidly. One loses one's nerve at times, for the Hindus despise us. Should the Empire collapse, I do not know what might happen to my children.

The mail for England leaves on Sunday evening. Mrs Burgess suspects our private correspondence in these typed pages, though I have told her I am responding with my reflections on the books you sent me. I fear she may not approve, though there is nothing that she wishes more for me than true happiness. Ten years of married life, my heart and soul bolted, and not once have I known even a fraction of the joy that you stirred in me from the first day we met. Ten years of being marshalled. Living with the coldness of his embrace, even his bigotry, of which I am ashamed.

This evening after supper, James adjourned with colleagues to play cards. It is likely in the merriment he shall drink heavily and lose. But even in his sobriety I find myself drifting more and more into the shadows of my own self; sometimes it feels as if you are here and I find solace, and either I am never alone, or you are my sole companion.

Yours ever,
Daisy

Garden Reach

Calcutta

16 March 1924

Dear Peter,

This is where I begin. This blank page draws me nearer to you, the day sweltering, my courage quickens, the curtains billowing and the punkah swaying, the punkah rattling as I sit at my writing bureau . . . it is a soothing sound. I have spent the day at home, stagnating, for the heat, though I walked by the foreshore before breakfast with Mrs Burgess. Charlie is curled fast asleep in a shaded patch of dirt under the lemon tree.

News has arrived of another riot in the east. James has taken ten officers from his regiment to Roorkee for training. He expects to be away for weeks. As Bunny helped him and as the car left, I felt a throb of relief. Quite suddenly the pressure in my chest eased; lightness filled my lungs and I sighed deeply. I do not believe the children shall miss James if I am to judge by their response. Like me, they have grown accustomed to his absence. I used to fret in the evenings but that was boredom, the consequence of too much leisure and being domiciled. I have been reading the novels you sent, and must thank you, Peter. I adored Mr Forster's romance, *A Room with a View*; particularly the moral challenges posed by Mr Emerson for dear Lucy Honeychurch, the way he counsels her to be free of her deepest fears and muddled thoughts: 'Let yourself go' is his theme, which is entirely the kind of bold extravagance I needed to read. I daresay that was your intention, your mission? And is it true that you are acquainted with the author? For at least the first hundred pages, I could not put down *Crime and Punishment*. It affects me the way Raskolnikov finds it difficult to be loved by his mother. To fall in love is exclusive; it is to read the beloved as a sign in all things.

You always hover in my mind – the thought of you, poking about in the Bodleian, wanting to write a novel. Though you are a master, and I have little expertise, perhaps we share the same compulsion to narrate. Only your trust in me and our hopes override this fear of rejection. Speak to me. I cherish what we have and crave to learn more about the fleeting incidents you describe; the party in Westminster, the little girl you bumped into in Regent's Park, and Clarissa. Clarissa, carelessly basking in her brilliance as English ladies do. Here in Garden Reach, we have lived in their periphery, accustomed to their scowls, skirting the favour of memsahibs only to be ridiculed.

But, equally, your letter roused my pity and concern for the welfare of that unfortunate widow. I try to picture her for I feel akin. We are like peasants among these English women with their cool conventions. Still, to think in Italian, a language of beauty. A woman from the continent. Lucrezia! I do love the texture of her name! Having rolled it on my tongue, indulgently. And Sally, with French blood, and her ancestors going back to Marie Antoinette and her ruby ring and talking back to Hugh Whitbread about women's rights at Bourton! Pardon my curiosity about her, too. Perhaps I mentioned that Aunty Rita lives in Birmingham with her husband and three boys. He is in textiles. How perfect it would be if destiny forever altered our lives, our fortunes woven as one. To be with you, to dream, even simply to hear of these marvellous companions . . . and although you hint at, however fleetingly, an air of disappointment about Clarissa, it is impossible for me to imagine a woman more absorbing.

I hope that day approaches. I live in the shadows. If it is true that you cannot bear to think of me with another man, you should know that you are the only man to enter my dreams. I cannot seem to forget you. What is proper? I try to undo a desire that may ruin us, but the feeling burns with every felt word. So, writing advances me from my private sentiments to small acts.

Does it matter if my intention is not to harm? And is this wrong? Shouldn't I be thinking of my two children? Heavens! What will become of us?

By the time her child reaches the age of five, a mother, having endured the sleepless state of those first years of hunger, producing tears and a husband's coldness, loses her protective instincts to fatigue. There is a little spill in her heart. She is torn and open to supplemental feelings. Over time the feelings may take seed. They may find roots. They may strengthen and bloom, fragrant and soft and thorny, like the rose you have planted in my heart.

Yours ever,
Daisy

Garden Reach
Calcutta

20 March 1924

A few days ago, I visited Nora in Railway Colony, and we had cha. She said she had met an officer by the name of Roland Wharton at the Anglo-Indian Railway Institute dance. She showed me a photograph. The youth is a handsome and well-mannered bachelor, but low in rank, on three hundred pounds a year. With so little, their prospects would be grim if they marry. Nora was teary so I hugged her. I confessed to her in confidence that I have also fallen under a spell and felt an urgency to pray to Kali. She frowned a little, gesturing disapproval, but saying nothing. Kali and Durga are the devas of our Bengali blood, I said. If I am to trace where I come from, going generations back, my great-grandfather John Fay married my great-grandmother Rani, a woman he was introduced to through the Bengal Military Orphan Society. He fell in love with her and was a loyal husband for the twenty years that he lived in India, fathering three children, two of whom were educated in England. But even before him the infusion of foreignness brought new gods to our shores, and it was Jesus who touched the souls of my school friends in St Thomas'.

Yet, there have been times I have felt different from the AI's. I envy the Hindus bathing in the muddy brown river, glitteringly lit, downstream from the jetties, the ghats further north from where the budgerows and the shipping liners are moored. I've watched pilgrims float their pujas in candled baskets, festooned with pink lotus, hibiscus and bel leaves at sunset. At dusk, the sun swathes the darkening clouds, turning the river blood orange. My heart is bursting, I told Nora. She promised to keep my secret and to accompany me if that is what I wished.

We walked downstairs to the street where rickshaw wallahs were asleep on the pavement or squatting on their footrests with shut eyes. Some were awake. A thin man with ropey arms dressed in lungi with a towel wrapped around his head signalled us. We asked for a cart to take us to Jagannath Ghat. The man ran to call for one and then came back to wait with us, along with two other men. It was uncomfortable to have them standing there in the heat, waving fans, regarding us as if enthralled by the prospect of an excursion, however trifling, perhaps a few spare annas, but, oddly, that discrepancy in our kind heightened the feeling between us. (This is how the lowly have a way of getting to me!) Soon enough a cart appeared. Though it was five, the sun was still fierce as we weaved through the traffic. I felt my heart lighten for having shared its bursting secret with Nora. We passed St Aloysius Church and, closing our eyes, we made the sign of the cross. The awning provided shade, filtering the bright sights of the streets, the salt barges at Tolly Nullah, the hawkers, shopfronts and hotels, the cows, dogs and cripples, the monuments, squares and equestrian statues in the distance.

We drove along Strand Road, past the jute factories and the empty depots near the dockyards, infested with mosquitoes, where coolies were housed until a few years ago. I thought of those miserable women and men, stripped of their sacred threads: the cowherds and the goldsmiths, the weavers, whose hands were never destined for calluses. I thought of the untouchable women being used, being offered puddings, sleeping on sacks with the pigs. How they drowned. What lives awaited them? Girls beaten in the plantation fields not unlike the slaves from Senegal. How they were slashed with cutlasses by cane-cutters jealous of drunken overseers. How they vanished from their villages and from the story of Calcutta across the dark waters.

They say those who dared return have no memory, no village to call home. The chaplains and charity workers say they are broken men and women, living in refuges or the crowded slums of Babu Ghat. It is less than five miles from the docks and jute mills. Some of the girls sell themselves. The lucky ones are recruited as nannies.

At Jagannath Ghat there was a crowd of people streaming towards the temple. We bought sticks of sandalwood and bright yellow marigolds before entering. Inside the circular foyer, there were garlands of flowers draped from the bell tower, swaying in the breeze. Children were being lifted by fathers. I saw the bangled hands of women reaching for the clappers, the bells ringing in tones brassy and deep. Crouching in the temple alcoves were groups of soothsayers and sadhus and an old woman. She was singing a folk song. The clear notes belied her frail appearance. One of the soothsayers stood before me, taking hold of my hand. He had liquid eyes and very dark, oiled skin. This sadhu's hair was like rope and his hands like leather. He told me that I must prepare for a journey, to speak less, not to follow books or maps, and that only then would the truth of my journey come to me as it comes to the Rishis. Running his fingers over the brown creases in my pale palms he said the lines of my destiny were like stumps as if they had been divided. He said that I was carrying unnecessary doubt and that I should give offering to Kali-Ma and recite my prayers daily. I wanted to believe his counsel, perhaps because we were so close to the embankment, to the pyres and the naked boys immersing.

On the steps going down there were tents and shade cloths pitched. Tea was boiling and pilgrims were eating sweet lentils, some under the cover of colourful parasols, and a poor cripple was kneeling on his stool, begging. Women were sitting on the ground, displaying flower pujas, holy cards and mehndi. We walked down the steps right to the water's edge. Despite the splashing and wading around us, and the noise and clamour from the temple, when the river crept up and licked our ankles and then rippled back into herself I felt this as a whisper, a summons. A deep peace filled my heart as if a curtain had been drawn, as if I could divide the light from shadow. Nora and I set our flower pujas on the surface of Ganga. We watched as the offering pulsed further away with the receding tide towards the ships moored in the distance. We did not talk much on the way back to Nora's home. When we parted I wept, having made my decision not from the quickness of reaction, but from someplace else; a still centre.

I worked quietly that evening tending to the children's needs, and found that for the first time in weeks, my thoughts were clearer, and I was listening to them. Charlotte had been to the zoo in Alipore with Mrs Burgess and was terribly excited about the panda bear they have acquired from Peking, and Joseph stayed at home with Bunny to work away at a diorama he has been making with model trains. We had supper and talked more and then played a game. Afterwards, I tucked Joseph into bed and kissed his brow and, as I held him in the darkness, I shed tears quietly. A breeze stirred in the coconut trees, breaking the heat. The moon was bright and drew me into the garden. I walked awhile, taking in the night's fragrant airs, aware of the moon's varnish preserving stones, leaves and branches.

33 Tavistock Square

12 April 2017

With my back to the window, my neck stretched, and my eyes shut I've taken a selfie. I want to see my face with writer's block. Minutes become hours, then days. Opening files, browsing online, down rabbit holes is recursive. It escapes the loneliness of the writing life. Depleted of inspiration I can't seem to get past the first few chapters. I need to bring Daisy to London, but how does Daisy feel about leaving her son behind? How will she cope with the journey ahead, with Charlotte to care for, with Radhika? Can I be assured that this is the right story?

Mid-morning, as it is not raining or too cold, I walk outside to have coffee at the kiosk. Sometimes I meet Cathy, a writer from Auckland, and we chat about our frustrations and our challenges. My heartbeat slows as I walk through Tavistock Square, itself a survivor of terrorist bombs and the Great War. Today, it feels a little shabby, with loose leaves and weeds, softly lit. There are peace memorials here dedicated to the war victims, a statue of Gandhi, of the gynaecologist Louisa Aldrich-Blake. In the south-west corner, facing the Hotel Taviton there is a bronze bust of Virginia Woolf. It was built on the bombed ruins of the house that she and Leonard rented in 1924. From their basement at number 52, they operated Hogarth Press, publishing the likes of Sigmund Freud, T.S. Eliot, and corresponding with many writers, including the Chinese modernist Shuhua Ling. The statue has an air of melancholy, the eyes deeply set and wide. She could almost be floating past, writing in the mind.

It helps to take a break from my desk and catch a few bars of some random conversation. Somehow the sparsely furnished flat I return to is comforting, also. Though the walls are bare, it is spacious. There are empty cabinets and bookshelves in the lounge room facing Tavistock Square.

In my bedroom there is a chest of drawers and a chair over which I have developed a tendency to throw my clothes in layers. A bag of laundry has been sitting on the carpet untouched. I need to buy some kitchen utensils. There is only a frypan, one saucepan, a toaster, an assortment of crockery. The dishes need to be washed. The sink in the bathroom frequently gets blocked or the lights fuse, and I have to call maintenance. The grout has chipped away between the tiles in the bathroom floor. Being in the basement, I wonder if the rooms above have been waterproofed.

We lived in a Georgian terrace like this when we first immigrated to Britain. My father was teaching at King's

College and Mum was breastfeeding my dainty four-month-old sister. She had such slender arms and legs. In a certain light, she had grey-green eyes and fine brown hair. For an Indian baby, even an Anglo-Indian, this was considered unusual and Mum was quite besotted with her. Serena was kept wrapped in a stretchy muslin shawl the colour of lavender.

'See how fair she is, and what pink cheeks,' my mother would say sometimes. This admiration lasted into adulthood. Mum was very colour-conscious, like most of her family. When I travelled back with her to Nairobi, the fairness or darkness of a child's complexion was often spoken about. My mother did not like us to spend time in the sun, since our skin darkened so much faster than English girls, whose skin, when it burned, became the colour of strawberries in their cheeks. Like Miriam's skin, for instance. She was our New Zealand neighbour, but we never played much together, and one day she sided with the boys who teased us.

I heard my mother scream one morning. I ran into the bedroom to find her shuddering with my sister at her breast. The ceiling above the bed had fractured and water and gyprock dust were raining down. The tenant in the ground-floor flat above us had been taking a bath and the weight of the water caused the rotten joists to give way. After that day, my memory lapses. My mother was taken away, suffering from stress. We moved to a ground-floor flat with peeling cornices that made interesting patterns. The rooms drew light but were soon cluttered with our boxes of books and cured animal skins. The curtains were an unlikeable mustard and the window frames had warped and splintered from dampness and been fixed cheaply. I knew that my mother was altered when she came home, tired and depressed. I think it was January, the coldest month.

It was cold and it was cruel living like that, being poor. But the cold was numbing. There were snowflakes and tulips, the tip of my nose and the tips of my fingers.

Sometimes, even wearing a coat and gloves, it was too cold to walk in the streets. Spring was joyful with its daffodils and primrose buds pushing through the dark earth after winter. My favourite season was autumn. I loved the rich russet browning of leaves, the way they would sometimes spiral and flip like helicopters or be scooped upwards past our rattling windows, up, up above the trees, caught in eddies. My companions were the wind and the sound of branches scraping the window. We played soccer and hockey. We kicked the crisp leaves which had swollen in orange and yellow piles beneath the giant trees. Walking to school we were sometimes teased for being coloured. I avoided other children, living instead in my own world, peopled with characters I'd read about or imaginary creatures.

From the late 1900s there was a legacy of poverty among Eurasians in India caused by their living in tenements and in railway colonies. Many had been schooled in hill stations under a British system that imported a curriculum and teachers from England, taught them to assimilate and to behave in all ways as if they were English. But the social stigma of mixed ancestry persisted; made worse by the barriers to employment, careless resettlement. There were poor whites, as well, in colonial times, once the Suez Canal was opened and the passage to India became a possibility for those beleaguered by the British class system. But those lives have been washed out of history.

Our food, our dress, our names. We were Anglophones, betrayed by our own words. I felt ill when I was growing up encountering some Indians: the ridicule and scorn they heaped on us. My father had English friends, Steve and Rosemary from the university who were kind to us and would come for dinner. Sometimes they took my sister and me to the playground; or we had tea and cakes. A social man and a creative thinker, Dad was at ease with travel and taking risks. As times got harder, I could tell he became weary. Little by little the seed of difference planted in us grew. I learned not to talk about who I was and where I came from. If Indian girls did not understand, how would English girls? How was it for Daisy? How was it for Peter? And isn't all this what I know, or am I supposed to feel it through the voice of an English novelist?

How it irritates; the blankness, the emptiness that immigration caused. Yet it never leaves me entirely. The past twitches, hindered by rehearsed lines. Did things happen the way we remember? The urn overspilling with rain, the weeds spreading untidily, the small, bright daisies, the shoes with no feet to fill. 'Ayah, she can't come anymore,' my mother explained one day. Did the hens stop laying eggs? Were they nesting when the wind swept through, their bones picked clean by eagles? I remember dusty roads, tulip trees and nut trees, grass cutting my ankles. I remember boys fishing and swimming, the sound of the river. We were lucky, my father used to say. There were many books and furnishings in our flat, trunks shipped from Nairobi.

I loved hearing my mother talk about the days before trouble came. Her face lit up and she looked the prettiest I had ever seen her. She was a striking woman with stylish hair and beautiful hands. It's strange how I resisted her composure. She held herself distant from us for many years, a formality that became less rigid as we grew older.

Maybe I hope objects like photographs, furnishings and clothes will fill the gaps. Maybe memory has no function when life is perfect; when life is warm, secure and charmed. In one of the albums, there is a photograph taken of my brother and me at Victoria Falls and another from a safari in Archie hills. They seem strange and familiar. I have often wondered if the past can speak its own story in the same way the wind's presence shapes the dunes, sculpting acacia and saltbush, making the leaves whisper and howl.

Garden Reach
Calcutta

30 March 1924

Dear Peter,

I slept strangely last night. I dreamed I was in your arms. We were lying in a boat floating upstream to the delta, and out to the Bay of Bengal. The moon was still and summoning. When I woke this morning, the world had changed. I felt immeasurable joy for a few hours.

The children moved about the house after breakfast. They played hide-and-seek in the garden. I have told them to watch for snakes, since it is mating season and last week Bunny found a cobra in the stables. Before long, I began to feel guilty for escaping into the dream, for my selfishness – Mama always warned me to beware of the vanity of desires. She is right. Ideals can be treacherous and love corrupts – there are hopes and wishes I've sublimated for months. Still, at least I am not paralysed with anxiety. I am less bewildered and possibly numb to my decision. It appears that I have found a way to numb myself, not realising the extent to which I shall feel the consequences for months to come, and even longer once the numbness wears off.

Uncle Robert has recently purchased shares in a ten-acre parcel of land in McCluskieganj. He dreams of keeping a rose garden and hunting in his retirement. The community are longing for a mooluk. A year ago, you mentioned Whitefield to my husband after your visit there, and it seemed promising with its schools and post office and churches, but the climate in Mysore is dry and the difficulties of recruiting labour have thwarted the ambitions of many settlers and agriculturalists. I have been patient, waiting for an opportunity to speak to James about the trouble posed by our distinct ancestry. My heart is brimming but I have kept my true feelings concealed. A few months ago, as promised, I suggested that we ought to apply for a passport. At first, he grumbled and rebuffed me. I let him brood upon it over winter until he came to believe it was an idea of his own. Last week a Christian boy died in a skirmish. After supper, James asked to read the application, so I asked Radhika to fetch it.

'We need to think about the future, Daisy,' he said.

'Yes, dear. With all the riots and strikes it might be wise to have proof of our birth right,' I replied, and James agreed. He read the form which Radhika had placed on the table and signed it. It was that simple, and the civility of the process rather surprised me. I expected him to complain or apply for a passport for himself. He did not seem to care about the past.

'*My* loyalty is to Bengal! What could possibly be left for me in Devon? Mother's bed-bound, my brother has moved to a village in Oxfordshire.'

Didn't he miss them? I wondered. But he was so young when he left England. They would not recognise him now with his leathery complexion and beard.

I still remember his pale hands and blue eyes when we courted. Now his hands are stubby and rough, his skin darkened.

Quite sternly, he said something about having no wish to frequent the Royal Asiatic Society or the Oriental Club in London, nor to spend his days mastering Sanskrit. (I remember that part!) Then he drained the claret in his glass. I believe he means not to return even though he would be granted leave of service.

Bunny accompanied me to the Labour and Emigration offices in Dalhousie Square. We took the completed application, birth certificates from the hospital and two small square black-and-white photographs and lodged the application for me and the children. By marriage, I should be classified as a British subject. The interviewer, a humourless, spectacled man, measured my height and weight, and recorded the colour of my hair and eyes, all of which made me feel nervous, but in the end he decided that my skin colour is too dark. (Mama has always said that I am 'a little dark'. I used to think it was petty of her to scold me whenever I played in the sun without a bonnet or a parasol.) He did not use the word 'half-caste', but he said I am classified as Eurasian. I tried to persuade him by mentioning my great-grandfather, John Fay, but it failed to impress him. He said something about taxonomy, that it was a clerical issue, and not to worry since Mr Mohandas Gandhi, also born in a princely state, is classified as a British Protected Subject. But it didn't console me.

Still, all that matters to me is that I have the dispensation and purchased tickets on the SS *Ranchi*. We are leaving for Southampton on Wednesday. I have decided to bring Charlotte, for I cannot leave her in Bengal with the riots and the famines, but Joseph will stay here. He will be safe with Bunny and Mrs Burgess. And I have met with the headmaster at St Lawrence's and arranged for Joseph to board in Ballygunge. Though I know Charlotte and Joseph will miss each other, they have had these years together and more shall come. It thrills me to know that you have spoken with Mr McGregor in Lincoln's Inn and that the news is good: that he can proceed to have my present marriage annulled.

At last, and not soon enough, I have procured a passport for myself and the children. We may be country-born but we are British Protected Subjects in the Indian Empire! The price: a mere one rupee, small change for a licence to take leave. Some may speak of love's voyage in measures of ambition; I believe it is my destiny. Of course, I harbour anxieties, but we have a purpose, a vision and not least the blessings of Mother Ganga. Already, I am thinking what to pack and trying to make arrangements for Joseph. I try not to dwell on how sad I'll be to kiss him farewell. Mama and Papa are alive, but I am too young to accept the trauma of separation twice. The future enthrals and terrifies. Whether she is a Hindu or a Christian, a mother's future is a heavy cargo. My heart quickens; having for too long been resigned to duty, it refuses to be oppressed. Freedom ripens like the tamarind, without abstraction in my thoughts and on my lips. The entire nation dreams of nothing but freedom. There are prisoners dreaming of freedom in Mandalay and in Port Blair. I cannot wait to board that ship with Charlotte – am counting the days and nights – to embark on our voyage, to be with you, in your hemisphere.

All my love,
Daisy

SS *Ranchi*

Kidderpore

17 April 1924, Thursday evening

It was dark when Radhika woke Charlotte to dress. I could hear her small feet creaking on the floorboards upstairs. A feeling of excitement for the adventure ahead had para-doxically subdued her, and throughout the day she showed no signs of irritability. Our trunks were packed and had been carried on to the front verandah while Bunny prepared the carriage. I had made a checklist of the essentials: coats, bonnets and gloves, petticoats, remedies for minor ailments, a selection of photographs, my box camera, my diary, my fountain pens, my pendants, my pearls and my bangles, Charlotte's books, our tickets and our passports. Indeed, we were modest travellers. We had a tiffin of parathas, dhal, curry and mango chutney to take for the journey as there is no cook in Calcutta who can match Tulsi. How I shall miss her sorpotel and cutlets! Charlotte came downstairs with Radhika, who was holding a lantern. She hugged me, clinging to my waist. I praised and encouraged her. 'We're going to have a wonderful time in England,' I promised. 'It will be such an adventure. There's nothing to fear, darling.' My voice a whisper affected confidence.

Charlotte had already kissed her brother goodbye the previous evening after supper. We would be returning soon from the visit abroad, I promised him. We would bring him back a fine present from Harrods. He was going to have a marvellous time with Mrs Burgess, and Bunny and Daddy would be home in two weeks. And what a sterling semester he would have at St Lawrence's. I'd left Grandad and Granny's home for school in Darjeeling when I was the same age as him. 'You're going to make so many friends!' I assured him cheerily. Before we left, I tiptoed into his room. He looked angelic, distant in sleep, his eyelids the colour of seashell. I held him in my arms and broke down. I was trying to muffle the sobbing, to hold it down with the knotted feelings of fear and confusion . . . what a monstrous feeling, compelling me to choose between Peter or my son. I kissed him, saving the image of his countenance in my memory. Mrs Burgess hovered in the doorway, and I knew it was time to leave.

The SS *Ranchi* was moored with river and mail steamers at the dockyards in Kidderpore. We arrived after dawn had broken, an amber flare spilling through the clouds, exposing the half-naked men asleep on charpoys outside the indigo depots and warehouses. The river was silvery and sleek, the network of masts and riggings gradually becoming visible.

Bunny fetched a coolie to help him with our suitcases as we hurried along the wharves and dry docks. Porters carried our trunks past gantries, bales of coal and grain, and crates being lifted into the holds. We had to wait for two hours while provisions were loaded and luggage was stowed, and the first-class passengers boarded. The sun was gathering intensity and the smell of oil cake, wood smoke, chickpea flour and tamarind wafted from upstream, piercing our nostrils as the shift workers started to prepare meals. The gharry wallahs and tikka gharry wallahs, the drivers of victorias and automobiles, had dropped off passengers and the riverside was soon teeming with industry and people: officers, cadets, coolies and lascars and those unfortunate men and women – six hundred and ninety, it seems – travelling in steerage. From the lower and middle deck, the scrape and heaves of thin, muscular men throwing ropes, wheeling barrows, lifting and stacking crates in the dry dust.

My mind was churning. Despite the battery of sights, noises and smells, foremost was the dread of leaving Bunny and Mrs Burgess. I was determined to be strong for Charlotte and not to weep. I could shed a few tears, but the knowledge that I should protect my children and not allow them to gaze too deeply into possibility was never lost on me.

We set off from Calcutta after nine that morning, piloted by a smaller vessel through the treacherous sandbanks. The rapidity by which ships and foreign sailors had been lost to the quicksands was common knowledge, so our cautious progress came as no surprise. The wind blew and the sun burned fiercely on our faces. There was much to admire in the vista of Calcutta's spires and country boats, the villas and fine palatial homes owned by British civil servants and merchants gracing the foreshore, the Botanic Gardens and the spectacle of domed roofs, the High Court tower and Company buildings. We passed sugar and jute factories and mango orchards. Downstream was a very different sight: single-storey bungalows sprawled out along the mud banks. We saw vultures perched on the remains of the dead, floating in the river. Dhows carrying stacked hay from the fields ploughed the turgid water. Embankments were strewn with washed clothes, pegged with small rocks, magnolia trees and lone palm trees bending in the breeze. Soundings were taken at frequent intervals by the first officer as we steamed past mustard fields and the occasional temple towards the delta of the dun-coloured Hooghly.

It was very hot near the boiler room where the lascars worked hard, dressed in dhotis and headscarfs, stoking and feeding the furnaces. Two lascars stood with legs astride behind the steering wheel on the main deck. They were handsome in red-embroidered kaftans, khadi pants, and matching red turbans. Charlotte had discovered there were many children on board (the steward had told me there were upwards of ninety). She had already made the acquaintance of Wilhelmina, a girl travelling with her parents, who are returning to Port Adelaide. They live on an outback station, so

I guessed they had been on vacation in India. Wilhelmina has piercing blue eyes and a most cheerful disposition. Charlotte pointed out to her the dome of the post office and other landmarks that she recognised as we left Calcutta.

The river widened, the sand shifts and streams causing clearer, shallow water as we approached Haldia. We were now in the Sundarbans channel which would take us to the Bay of Bengal. With the current we started to see white caps, and porpoises playing in the clear, sparkling water as it slapped against the hull. A two-day stretch across the horizon to our west was the palm tree-lined coast of Chittagong, Cox's Bazar, and Akyab in Burma, where another great river flows. The company my father runs has been issuing licences to the steamships. They ferry mail to the landlocked villages and towns as well as exporting rice and other provisions. We stood on the deck gazing at the white sands lined by palm trees, imagining beyond to its prosperous fields of fattened crops, blessed by rain and the goddess Lakshmi. I thought of friends who had left India for other reasons than mine, but with no less risk. Some, like my grandfather, had landed small fortunes. He sometimes reminisced about the years he spent in Chittagong. Perfectly lovely scenery, the deep gorges and wooded hills, the orchids and wild turmeric. Even now, I can picture the outlook from his plantation home, the pretty sight of sailing vessels docked in the river, and the ocean farther still, beyond the woods. Too many insects and the servants were lazy and overpaid, he once complained to my father. But he told us a different story, conjuring in my mind an idyllic country: pagodas, butterflies, missionaries, emerald moss-covered waterfalls and the blue distant hills. Even if the jungle has perils, I was captivated. It was like being charmed, the way he described Burma.

Bengali immigrants had been arriving in Rangoon for decades to work in the rice mills along the Irrawaddy River, or to man the ports and stations, or serve in the banks, even to pull rickshaws. But there are also revolutionaries in the Mandalay prison as there are in the Andaman Islands. Forgive me for saying this, but the British are brutal with their taxes and prisons. This is how they have governed and prospered. This is how they weaken the Indians.

We were warned that a few miles into the inlets we might catch sight of tribesmen. Naked, rowing sampans, I pictured them staring at us through dense vegetation with their dark insurgent eyes. Preparing for departure from the mouth of a muddy river, the unknown exaggerates our apprehensions and plays upon our fantasies of fear. I pray for courage and determination, and all that is required to keep my mind and moods in balance.

We passed through a strong current. The steamer began to pitch and rock and the wind grew more turbulent. Radhika looked pale from the abrupt effects of nausea. By now it was far less pleasant on the deck; a few passengers had vomited, others had retired to the forward cabin. As the motion sickness increased, I felt limp, and so I had Radhika fetch Charlotte and told her that we must all rest a few hours.

Our cabin in the second class is more modest than I could have imagined. Two bunk beds, a desk and chair, a few shelves and hanging space built into the casements, leaving space for a rug and a bucket for water, our quota of which is rationed daily. The small window caked in the flaky residue of salt allows some daylight to enter the room, but the jalousies are stiff to open. There is much congestion around these basic quarters and men who show signs of drunkenness loitering near the washrooms. It is no small relief that our door can be locked with a key. I brought with me some fabrics: several yards of silk and pashminas to keep us warm. On our bunk beds, Charlotte and I each have a pillow. Radhika sleeps in the space beneath the beds on a mat which we pulled out from under the desk. She is only nineteen, married at eleven. She seemed afraid to sleep in the between-deck steerage, where the women and men are cramped together. How they sleep there is a wonder with the unbearable heat, and all of them in a heap near the stalls where some cows, hens and goats are kept.

We know very little about Radhika's family, except that her husband was schooled by Methodist missionaries and is now teaching the low-caste children in their village in Bihar. It was through the mission that she came to us. Her parents are Christians.

They live a good fifty miles from Patna, where famine is rife. The poor girl has suffered from rickets for most of her life and is very short. Once, during the monsoons, when the ayah's room at home was flooded, Radhika rolled her saree above her knees to sweep out the rising water and I was shocked by how spindly her legs were. She is a diligent girl; she speaks a little English and understands more. There is nothing of the tinge of contempt about her, nothing like the abrasive glances of high-caste women. Yet, like the beautiful servant girls who come from the upstream villages, those who know innocence as if they were soulmates, she has not a pinch of personal ambition, nor does vanity mar her character or her countenance. This gives her a sweet disposition, even a simple dignity. Of course, I made sure her family were paid in advance for her return journey to England, though very likely I shall not want to send her back. She and Charlotte are close, and she will be an asset to me, to us. But I am skipping ahead. Let us see how she fares, how we fare. My mother taught me this way; to treat the servants with respect, as our own. They are part of a system of rank whose effects we have known in prosperity and adversity.

By supper time I was hungry and curious for company. Charlotte had been fretting, though Radhika kept her distracted with amusements and stories. We found the dining saloon towards the ship's bow. It was a little crowded but convivial with claret and English food served. At our table was a Mrs Eliza Prynne, a fair-haired woman of pleasant appearance who is travelling alone with her maid. She gave account of the difficult circumstances caused by her husband's malady, a sepsis of the blood which colonised his lungs, proving fatal. He died only six weeks ago, and as she spoke, she wept a little. She had friends but felt rather dejected and was now hoping to live with her sons in Hampstead. Wilhelmina's parents invited her to join our table. She kept us entertained with a story about a real Australian bushranger.

We took a stroll on the deck, the night sky clear, a streak of moonlight on the water, the ship rocking. Our bodies cooled with the breeze against our faces.

I felt teary, thoughts ruminating from the moonlit river to Joseph, my parents, my dear cousin, Nora. Yet I have no regrets about leaving James, having bent the force of my will towards our future – how glad I am that Peter wrote to me. Had he not entreated me to leave Calcutta and marry him, perhaps I may have lived out my life vicariously, resigned to misery, though it is a blur, and too much for the mind to hold.

London Victoria

27 April 2017

I am on the down escalator at Green Park, changing from the Piccadilly line to Victoria to get the southbound train. Nicer to go up and down rather than using the corridors which get so jammed I miss the marketing and succumb to buskers. Excited to be finally going to Lewes! And Rodmell! I always feel even smaller on the escalator, and it reminds me of childhood, going to concerts with my father. There's something mesmerising about the digital posters displayed on the shiny white tiles. They entice the eye because of the illusion that makes them appear to be moving. Covent Garden musicals, theatre shows, Czech films. I stand neatly tucked behind the smart business types and London lovelies, who clutch their handbags.

I check my phone to find an email from Luke. What bad timing! He can't possibly want me. Not genuinely. He knows I am travelling, must have read my blog. Still, there's a bit of a rush, a shock, a small, private pleasure. Because I've read him here, on the escalator. Because the chronology of the heart is more circular than linear: Luke, then my brother's harassment, then losing my mother, then the intensity of my brother, then Lucille, the girl I fell for, when I was broken, the girl who might break me more. I met her at a pub after a queer poetry open mic gig. We talked about books; her favourite writers. She is at RMIT in a Masters. I could tell she liked me, and it was mutual. That girl with her uneven fringe, awkward grammar and churlish indifference. Not the girl I knew at school who suicided, nor the socialite type who likes wearing hats and baggy trousers with her calculated, supremely superior attitude. Some girls make a habit of hovering in the mind, don't they! Makes me ponder how the triggers to one's emotions often happen in the wrong order, so it is impossible to distinguish the effect from the cause.

In her diary in 1923, while writing *Mrs Dalloway*, Woolf writes, famously, 'I dig out beautiful caves behind my characters: I think that gives exactly what I want; humanity, humour, depth. The idea is that the caves shall connect, and each come to daylight at the present moment.'

I want that too with Daisy, with Lucrezia. But what about Radhika, the servant girl, the nanny; have I fixed and limited her? How does she speak if she is illiterate? If she cannot write to her parents from England? Is it ever possible to tell stories which are not in some way partial, appropriating? How did Virginia Woolf justify sacrificing Daisy's entire life for a single day in June 1923, the day of Mrs Dalloway's party?

Not just the author Woolf, but the critics that came after her? They shorten the novel's action. Like bouncers at an exclusive venue refusing to let Daisy in. I guess it takes courage for a critic to contradict someone like Virginia Woolf. She had a fraught life, but she was also fierce. Woolf champions white women, she argues brilliantly against their subjection in *A Room of One's Own* and in *Three Guineas*, but she uses her genius to slay Daisy Simmons.

I check the time on my phone. The train takes an hour and ten minutes and leaves from platform 18, stopping at Croydon and Haywards Heath along the way. Plenty of seats. The ticket sets me back twenty-eight pounds. A few cyclists on the train; families, a laid-back feeling. Not the peak hour crowd. I have brought *Mrs Dalloway* and *The Voyage Out*.

I was planning to read but my eyes drift, scanning the grey suburbs and graffiti. Email also from a publisher, John, wanting to have dinner when I get back to London; mentions some nice Italian restaurant in Chelsea that he's been to recently. Wants to meet when he's there for the London Book Fair. Signs off with 'love'. Really? Isn't he married? But his wife is in a home. Does that count? Oh yes, right. I write back something in the affirmative, but the email doesn't send. Or maybe it does but it doesn't show. Blast, that's Bigpond for you. Still, it's rather amusing how I fret about these electronic faux pas. Decide to use a different address re: the dinner. Tentative acceptance. Nervous about using the word 'love'.

The day Mum died Luke sent an email to thank me for my latest book, which he said he would devour. The word devour is predatory. Grammatically speaking, it contains a semantic seed, the invisible word, 'our', a possessive, plural pronoun. Perhaps it is neurotic to mention this, but the meaning of the word 'devour' varies from 'to read', or 'to regard with great enthusiasm', 'to consume', 'to destroy', or 'to wolf down'. Wolves are totemic and mystical messengers of the spirit world in some cultures. Outsiders, they are kin to the jackal, the coyote, the wild dog, the dingo. Surnames like Wolf, Wolfe, Woolf derive from the Hebrew Benjamin whose father Yaacov blesses his tribe: 'Benjamin is a ravenous wolf, in the morning devouring the prey and at evening dividing the spoil.' In Virginia Woolf's London Clarissa's Englishness dominates, and others like Daisy Simmons are marked, a shadow devoured in the imperial closet.

Wolf: the word is fierce and assertive, almost a challenge. That Luke took so long to acknowledge the book I sent, which was a gift, made me feel ashamed for sending it. There are ethical conditions for giving and receiving; and there are coded meanings for offering or expressing gratitude. As I recall, that was my observation at the time. For Luke it was a sly joke we shared; a little thrust of erotic energy that he controlled, not entirely without risk. How did he expect I would feel?

Months have passed. Months of confusion, despair, emptiness. I have woken up most mornings afraid that with Mum's passing I have no family, no companion on this one-way road. They don't understand the writer's life, the hard choices made and how that changes one, ever so gradually. Virginia Woolf wrote about the phantom woman, the angel in the house who comes between oneself and one's writing. Because each day we are losing. Writing our lives at the expense of the real. How has Sam coped? How could I have mistaken his trauma? A writer forms an exquisite intimacy with language, but what fruits does writing bear? Nothing to show except for a few books going out of print, and rarely found on shelves. I have often thought the fault lies with time; my chronology is flawed. The books came after Sam was born, but before Luke, and before the fatigue of my brother nursing my mother eventually taking its toll. A death premature, yet hard-won. Mum might have lived longer with a blood transfusion twelve months prior; she might have suffered less, or it may have been more, if we are going to do the measurements.

'How about a short stay in hospital, Mum?' Serena had asked.

'No,' she said, quietly and firmly, sitting in her wheelchair, thin legs crossed, her wiry hair lifting with static, her breasts sagging in a scoop-neck polyester/cotton-blend dress. She spoke audibly without slurring or hesitation. My sister rephrased the question and got the same reply.

I was relieved. I didn't think she could go through hospital again, and I didn't want her to die in a nursing home. It was not our family way. I wanted her to die with the sound of the ocean in her mind rather than the hum of a ventilator or a chorus of neglected pensioners crying for a bedpan from their private rooms. But towards the end, things that had been familiar became foreign: the pink film of sunset on the horizon, a pod of humpbacks breaching, the prime minister smiling despite the disastrous mess of the party, the magpies carolling, the breeze in the leaves of our lemon tree where my niece and nephew play hide-and-seek. My mother as distant as an ocean liner on the horizon that cannot turn.

From its stonewashed cover, the binding of my journal comes loose, the pages are almost swimming. Two square black-and-white portraits of my mother fall out when I go to tie it with the leather string. One, dated 1965, was taken in Victoria Gardens; she is wearing a floral print rockabilly dress. Her smile and her assuredness, almost coy, bore no sign of alarm about citizenship. Maybe because there was a lifetime stamp on her passport. Nairobi's state of emergency had ended. Kenya had been independent since 1963; imports and exchange rates were being regulated. My brother was at school in England. They called him 'elephant boy' and 'darkie'; the weather was miserable, and the food bland. A mood of immigration had swept through East Africa's Indian communities. In Stonetown, Zanzibar, while on his way to church, Mum's brother, Peter, was shot by Maoists. He had been taken to a hospital in Dar es Salaam.

My father left home unexpectedly to test the waters abroad. He telephoned my mother saying that he had been offered a position and that we should live in England. My mother packed our trunks. Her lips were quivering, though her hands were steady. Those days I would find her sullen, staring out of the window in the room where she retreated. Life became complicated. She made all the necessary arrangements to leave the country.

Falcon Wharf

Lewes

29 April 2017

Bluebells and violets and the sun slung low. The last blows of winter, a grey smudge of rain, clouds drifting across the sky. My room is in a refurbished warehouse at Falcon Wharf in Lewes. I'm sitting at my desk. These past few days, light has been lingering after dusk. I am not waking through the night crying anymore, but I am waking earlier.

On 30 April 1926, Virginia wrote in her diary that her mind was wandering, and she found it humiliating to walk and wander down Regent and Bond Street being notice-ably less well dressed than other people. She remarks on the general strike, the miners' strike, the polarised politics of the unionists and the royalists, some problem with her cook. She had been writing furiously and freely, having finished the first part of *To the Lighthouse* and having made a start on the second with a fluency that surprised her. It was not like the struggle with form that she had with *Mrs Dalloway*.

I am struck by her description of entering the abstract, the empty featureless house, the absent people 'with nothing to cling to', so she writes.

And this is the daunting task with Daisy. Not having lived in Kolkata, I need to travel there. Spend a few weeks, even a few days. How to sew a garment from the rags? For the sake of reading. Reading is as important as writing. When asked what books I am reading, I think of the unwritten pages. How to believe in the scraps and scrapings? Because each morning when I wake to grief, to the workplace, to history's abrasions, I rise and tell myself this is my work, this historical restoring of my community that I should find ways to rejoice in. Our struggles bleed into family life. I've tried to protect Sam from conflict, but the tissue that separated my inner and outer lives is permeable. I suppose it was the same for Daisy Simmons. No pencil scribblings, not even rubbed-out, crossed-off ones. Mrs Woolf had kept Daisy stunted, and on purpose it seems. Her intent was always to centre Clarissa Dalloway, setting her in flight. Drifting and timeless, she is a hallmark achievement: Clarissa, the stream of Virginia Woolf's consciousness. I stumble across the many iterations of her, in journals and in broadsheets. She surfaces a little callously, making her debut in *The Voyage Out*. She is bird-like in *Mrs Dalloway* ('what a lark! what a plunge!') and there she is again in the short story 'Mrs Dalloway in Bond Street'. She is even a guest in two novels written by men, *Mr Dalloway* and *The Hours*. She's Vanessa Redgrave and Meryl Streep on screen. A modernist heroine with all the trimmings. Am I inadvertently repeating this?

It doesn't take Virginia Woolf's body to be blanched and stippled in the river, swept downstream for three weeks after her disappearance . . . Daisy was already lost. There's barely a critic who is aware of, let alone interested in, poor Daisy Simmons. How to rescue her from the cubism, the pointillism of Clarissa's mind? Daisy is not a rewrite or a burlesque inter-poem, she is not a footnote to be championed and exampled.

Outside, a blush of sunset in the darkening sky. I think of my mother lying paralysed in her bed in Tathra, while day and night the sea spilled and swallowed sand, implac-ably. It sucked into sea caves, spouting from their cavities; the swell often came with the ferocity of a distant arrival. At Horseshoe Bay after storms or bushfires, I would find oyster shells, pine needles, ash, folded Coke cans. The orange track markers stapled to trees may eventually loosen. Bits of broken glass on the forest floor were remnants left by teenage boys who hung out there, drinking at night, fishing for squid. Beneath streetlights the ghostly kangaroos watched my mother breathing as she slept by the window. If a car approached, its headlights shining, they would spring to life and vanish into scrub.

Delicate are these strands from which stories are woven; time creeping, retreating back and forth like the pull and push of waves, churning memory, being shaped by desire, by home. I'd heard my thoughts whisper the story of our lives, well before my mother died. Many times, she and I spoke about writing, intimately, and even through the vagaries of her dementia, she never doubted my work. Writing is like scouring time, sketching patterns from correspondences, a kind of oracle. Cutting velvet, twisting threads, all the things that cannot be deciphered and have no substitute, like pieces of shimmering glass. Birth and death rammed into each other. Deep, deep in my grief, I am the broken sky searching for the words as the light fails. They are her words too. Restless, I try to stay aroused, then doze in my chair for half an hour, or on the floor, my neck bent, strained, the phone falls out of my lap, then I wake in panic, mostly with no clue.

I dream that a man attacks me in Russell Square station. He is wearing glasses and has a trimmed moustache and toffee-coloured skin. He is puffy eyed, one side of his lip hitched. I see him clearly. He wraps tape over my mouth. My legs are being tied up, pressed firmly so the rope burns. People are walking hurriedly towards the lift, appearing not to notice. They button their coats preparing for the blast of cold air that will greet them outside. Things start to blur. The man's face is featureless and no longer distinctive. He could be any man. I can't breathe. Not able to kick or to scream, I force myself awake. I reach for my phone, but my fingers pinch the sheet and the pillow. I am here, lying lopsided across the bed. I roll back to the right side and take the phone from the bedside table. 5.30 am. So early! Well then! At least it's not 3 or 4 am. I get up and open my laptop. I start searching for flights to Kolkata, browsing travel noticeboards, listing hotels and homestays. Then, stupidly, I open an email from a hostile colleague and feel the pull of disgust, the push of defence. Sometimes, it helps to be angry.

I remember what I'm about, I don't feel sleepy.

Talking to myself again!

Next to the jug there is a small stainless-steel teapot. I make a pot of the Assam tea with calendula and violet which a student had given to me as a gift. It comes with a gorgeous handwritten label. Black tea, a dash of honey and soy milk, without the bitterness. The bittersweet is more complex, however, like the mind, or a thought teased into opposing strands: *I hate thee, and I love thee at once. O stranger, whom I praise sweetly and curse, bitterly!* Like Peter and Clarissa, the racist judgements cleverly disguised by Woolf – appalling, really, though what a genius she had for prose. What daring! And all of it hers. Property. Territory. Dominion. Dreadnought. Empire. A room of one's own, for Englishwomen exclusively: Charlotte Brontë. Dorothy Osborne, Lady Winchilsea, Aphra Behn . . .

Something extremely pleasing: my bedroom is nicely positioned in the north-facing guesthouse. Now it is light I can see outside. The window frames a delightful garden. A magnolia is in bloom, crocuses and bright orange azaleas. Two starlings are perched in the apple blossom tree. Their glossy dark plumes catch my attention like a perfect sentence. Spells of wind and rain as the weather turns, the birds hopping across the lawn, swallows in the skies.

At breakfast I meet Claire, an Australian from the mid-north coast of New South Wales. What is she doing in Lewes? I ask. For the last two months, she has been staying with a girlfriend, Anne, and her sons. But they had a falling out. She tells me that six months ago her mother died in her home in Heathrow and there have been problems with her older sister, who has been unscrupulous as the executor of their mother's will. So, Claire had to leave Australia to come to England to sort things out. A ridiculous business. Solicitors and so on. Claire sips her tea. She is pale, her mousey brown hair pinned back by a headscarf, tied in a knot. She is wearing loose raw silk trousers and a keyhole smock. Her eyes have secret sorrows, like bits of blue china. I like the indirect way she talks about these circumstances. I scrape the burnt layer from a slice of toast and butter it, then add a thin smear of marmalade. I tell Claire about losing my own mum. I don't tell her that my mother's name was Claire.

'So, you understand,' she said.

We slide into a conversation about the freelance marketing work she is doing with a friend in London. We talk about visiting the Saxon church in the village of Southease, the museum at Charleston and Anne of Cleves' House. Outside the sky is bright and clear. There are bees hovering in the weeping cherry and a pair of wagtails picking at the scraps of pastry on the bird table.

Later that morning, I set out, walking along the South Downs Way to Southease railway station, a zigzag through the metal gates to the level crossing. Two men on the platform are talking quietly as I pass, following the railway line and then turning right towards a straight stretch of rough farm road. There is a footbridge over the River Ouse. Beyond, I can see the gentle slopes of Mill Hill. The signposts that guide me are pleasingly unobtrusive. To my west, breaking the stillness, there are machines and cranes carrying out maintenance to the old cast-iron swing bridge, a reminder of the seagoing barges. A few cyclists pass. Shortly, there's another signpost with a confusing number of arrows. I ask a woman walking her labrador for directions. She tells me to look out for the spire of St Stephens and then take the bridleway to Rodmell.

A little exposed to the wind, I walk up on the embankment, safe in my smallness under the immensity of sky. The river cuts its mineral way through the chalk flood plains and sandstone beds like an aquamarine ribbon. Walking here over ancient escarpments, layering battlegrounds and bones, it's not hard to imagine that a writer could be driven to the furthest reaches of madness. I cannot help but think of Virginia; was it here, right here, that she succumbed to the quarrelling voices, in her hat and her fur coat? Were these the very stones? A rawness of memory is unexpectedly laid bare, and I lie down on the damp grass (I can feel it now, soaking into my leggings) and face the life-giving sun, reflected in the life-taking river, as if the day has summoned me here, alone, for this reason, to choose.

A simple choice: to preserve. I'll let the river carry my voice wherever the story leads; the river itself being tidal rising and sinking as it runs past Lewes emptying into Newhaven.

I send Lucille the photographs I've taken on WhatsApp and she replies, all the way from Fitzroy. I say that, if only she were here, we could have a drink by the river. I'm raw about Luke's email, waiting to hear from him, but who is a substitute for whom? How to decipher this? Submissively? Relationships like splits, like scratches on the surface of the mind. Does writing ever satisfy the desire running through our bones? Is it like destiny, turning over the lumbering apparatuses, issuing over river stones, hard and cold, the politics that target and determine our lives, and so invisibly? A pair of swans spin slowly like medieval dancers and for a while I am alone with them, swirling in their stream, clouds stretching thinly above us, and the placid gaze of Sussex cows watching from the meadows. A cluster of concrete pipes and a few powerlines along the river flats signal industry and commerce. The grass is windswept and glittering, silver and gold as the sun breaks through the skies and I come to the second kissing gate.

From here I turn left, taking the bridleway towards Rodmell. There are brown cows standing very close to the path. One or two are kneeling. A girl walking her dog exchanges greetings with me. I'm aware of a silence that folds in around me, away from the river and the spine of the hills. Fields are planted with crops; the water meadows shimmer, rimmed by nettles, and a farm cottage on one side. Further along I pass an elderly couple wearing raincoats and gumboots; they are smiling. The sun pours like treacle through the foliage of a large mulberry tree as I approach the village. The flint-walled cottages and the church steeple are in sight. I sidestep the puddles, and imagine Virginia walking here, on her way back from Charleston, and I'm struck again by the quietness of the hamlet.

Shaded by shrubs and trees and set back from the lane is the weatherboard cottage Leonard and Virginia Woolf purchased from the miller of the village in 1919. They renovated the kitchen, installed a water heater; they pulled down the granary but kept the walls, which make for interesting features in the garden. To preserve their view, they bought another parcel of land.

Inside, I'm struck by a certain ambience in the sitting room. It is rustic, with exposed beams, lime green walls and slate floors. The rugs, handmade furnishings and ceramics have more than a touch of Charleston about them. In Virginia's bedroom, the guide tells us that the tiled fireplace painted with a lighthouse was designed by Vanessa. There are artefacts and pottery gifted by Vita, Lytton Strachey and other Bloomsburians before she died. I am in luck: there are not many visitors, so I have the opportunity to enjoy the garden's display of tulips and bulbs. I sit and read for a while on one of the benches in the orchard, overlooking the downs. A few people arrive. They inspect the studio where Virginia Woolf wrote and the verandah where she entertained.

Nearby, beneath the elm tree, her ashes were scattered. There is a bust and a plaque that Leonard had engraved, quoting from *The Waves*: 'Death is the enemy,' it reads. 'Against you I will fling myself unvanquished and unyielding – O Death! The waves broke on the shore.'

When I get back to Lewes, I make a pot of tea and carry it on a tray with milk and sugar to the lounge room at the front of the terrace. Claire is sitting facing the garden with its views out to the canal. She is holding a handset, with her laptop on her knees, long pauses in her conversation, so it is not difficult for me to catch the drift. She is enquiring about hotel rooms in London: doubles, interconnected rooms, does it have a gym, is breakfast included, is it cheaper on Trivago, Expedia, Agoda, Hostels Combined? I try not to look conspicuous in my eavesdropping, scrolling through the photos on my phone, deleting some. She needs a room to sleep for one or two more nights. The guesthouse is fully booked. She tries the youth hostels, too, and a few other guesthouses but they are booked out. Some opera apparently in Lewes. She wants to extend her stay and go back to London the day after tomorrow.

The day after tomorrow I am going back to London. It seems only natural; I offer her to stay in my room. We are working through the logistics and she is calmly thinking it over. I do not know myself; but I am drawn to her. It runs through me, a current of feeling, or maybe it is energy. Whatever, it cannot be controlled. Let it flow like the river, Mina; perhaps you are meant to meet this woman, Claire, this stranger who has lost her mother and is in discord with her sister. You don't even know her, Mina, you might say in different circumstances, but here you are now, and you want to visit Charleston, and you want to talk it over, talk about love and grief and Luke. Damn him! He's got under your skin all right! What does he mean by asking where I am and does Daisy go to Lewes or is it just me?

So, and so, we are talking over dinner, drinking wine, and Claire – who used to be a life coach, it transpires – is advising me. Her sweet sadness, her skin pale, she doesn't need this burden. But I can't help it. I'm selfish.

There are many kinds of lovers; friends and rivals, Peter and Clarissa: is it platonic? Is it passionate, sadomasochistic? And is the love between Peter and Daisy paternal? How can Peter love two women? Is it obscene for two women to love each other and also love a man; like Clarissa and Sally Seton, both being married? We're talking like this long into the night in our beds, the light switched off. Claire is crying, telling me about her mother and how she wasn't ready for what happened . . . but I've fallen asleep while she's talking in the darkness, alone but not unheard; my dreams listen and soundlessly answer. I am deeply under; not an anaesthetic, but the most beautiful slumber I have had in months and, for once, I wake feeling rested. I hear myself say, So, it's agreed then, Mina. She has considered, she is offering you a lift back to London the day after tomorrow.

SS *Ranchi*

Madras Presidency

20 April 1924, Sunday afternoon

Yesterday, after twenty-four hours at sea, we sighted the man-made harbour of Madras. The SS *Ranchi* entered the breakwaters to drop anchor near an impressive iron pier. Massula fishing boats made from mango wood lay beached on the shore and fish had dried on nets, glittering in the mid-morning sun. Pedlars and porters moved through the crowd and plied us with offers of snacks, train tickets to Bangalore and Ooty in the Nilgiri Hills. Others offered tours through the city, to the cotton fields. Charlotte was delighted by the young boys displaying their talents of rope walking and trapezing on the beach. Women walked along the road in bright sarees, carrying jars of salt on their heads; the fisher folk were thin and very dark, the men wearing headscarfs knotted into loose turbans. They were crouching on the sand, some of them watching us.

It was exceedingly hot, so we retreated to the shaded colonnades and gardens of Fort St George, also known as White Town. We saw a group of Anglo-Indians in shiny automobiles and victorias, the men in topis, the women in dresses and hats or carrying parasols. They were on a leisure trip, perhaps to the Madras Club, where Wilhelmina and her parents had gone to take tiffin.

I took Charlotte and Radhika to see the cathedral of St Mary's, and here we lit a candle and kneeled for a while in the perfumed teak pews to pray for our safe journey. The tall neem trees provided shelter and the city felt languorous, fragrant with jasmine and frangipani. In the Armenian Street, there was much to absorb in the bustling sights of bazaars, English, Portuguese and French-style architecture, churches and synagogues, and the ancient, elaborately carved and vividly coloured temples, festooned with garlands. Many of the houses are rendered in buff or pink with green jalousies, the gates and front walls displaying signage in elaborate cursive. It was foreign to us. The city was bustling but less dusty and hectic than Calcutta. Of course, like most cities, the administration was suffering from resistance to taxes, causing poverty and famine for the poor. The low-caste people work arduously in the salt pans. In the villages, there have been epidemics of cholera. But the British have built schools and hospitals. We are told there is an infirmary for lepers.

I sent Radhika to get tiffin from a nearby bazaar as Charlotte by now was too tired to walk. We waited in the gardens near Fort St George. I was concerned that Radhika did not speak Tamil or that she might get lost, but she is reliable and astute; she returned after thirty minutes with a flask of chai and tiffin: idlis and fish deliciously steamed and wrapped in banana leaf, which we call paturi, and sweet curd cooked in coconut milk. We relished this meal after the food we had eaten on the ship.

On returning to the pier, the harbourmaster advised us that we are to spend the night in Madras Port as there had been a riot in the salt cottaur; one of the customs officers shot a native who threw stones at the officer's band-ghari, breaking the side mirror, and this caused a skirmish. The captain would have to arrange legal exemption for the officer. We were taken in an overcrowded jeep to a hotel outside the presidency where the Indians lived. Charlotte seemed out of sorts, and I discovered that she was running a temperature. I asked for some hot cocoa and honey to be made. They boiled the water and used dried milk sprinkled with nutmeg. It tasted insipid, but she drank it nonetheless. I could see through the window how clear the night was outside; a little less than a crescent moon and a few bright constellations. My heart is burdened with responsibility, with uneven measures of reason and desire.

I left Radhika with Charlotte, who was asleep, and walked downstairs. There is a single step between the hotel entrance and the market. The street was bustling with the industry of weavers, leather makers, vendors, chettys. A very dark woman squatting over a bowl was pouring and grinding millet. I could hear the rhythmic slicing of the coconut vendor, a fat man whose rotund belly protruded over his lungi. Crows were digging into scraps, the rickshaw wallahs called out teasingly, asking where I wanted to go (do I wear the unmistakable look of being lost, as I am these days?). The bheesties were returning to the chowk after watering the maidan, where pandals and circus props are being built for the puja. Was it safe to walk far from the hotel? I carried nothing much of value. I cannot live constantly fearing the dangers of my skin colour or my sex. A woman traveling alone with her daughter and a servant . . .

The day you left India it felt to me that the world would end, until you wrote to me and my loss diminished, even though by this correspondence we are made incomplete. If I receive no reply, if there is no destination, no one to read my letters or my diary, should I feel compelled to keep writing? I would feel every part of my loss as something permanent. I am afraid this has become my whole.

SS *Ranchi*

22 April 1924
Tuesday morning

We have been fortunate with the weather, but as we steamed south away from the coast, entering the open sea we encountered a cross swell and ran headlong into squalls of rain and strong breezes. The waves came in sets, causing the ship to pitch, and many of our fellow passengers were afflicted with seasickness. Those in steerage had no other place to rest than the planks which form their shared bunks and they lay huddled together. The smell brews in their fetid quarters, rising from the shaft into the underdeck where they are housed, many of them young ayahs whose duty it is to dress and feed and wheel their charges on the main deck in perambulators. Charlotte is still running a temperature, all the colour drained from her face. The ship's doctor advised a restricted diet of free fluids, but said he could offer no other treatment.

We endured a terrible night in our cabin, which is unbearably humid, though by morning we had passed through the storm. Charlotte's fever did not ease. I did not sleep well, hardly two or three hours, as Charlotte was whimpering and waking to use the bucket. No Bunny! No Mrs Burgess! It occurs to me that I miss their company most during the evenings, when I retire from the dining hall early, not wishing Charlotte to sleep alone. This is often the time when I read my diary and write.

Radhika arrived tired from steerage where she often sleeps now with a friend she has made. They speak the same dialect. Her saree was crumpled, but in her quiet way she started to clean the room and fold clothes. She soaked a cloth in tepid water and placed it on Charlotte's forehead; she sat by her pillow and every five minutes offered sips of boiled water. At the doctor's request the steward had arranged for us to receive a supply of the freshest water brought from Madras. At nightfall, many of the sailors and passengers drink wine with their meals, but this leaves also a strong smell that seeps into the furnishings and under their skin. Even now, I can smell it as I write. Charlotte is sleeping, her tongue as dry as sandpaper. She is very poorly and has passed only bile and mucousy stools that pour out like water. The last two stools were almost black with blood. The ship's doctor will be calling in soon, but he seems young and a little vague when I ask questions. I am worried about her as she has lapsed into listless fits, talking very little, burning with fever. I have been saying novenas, hoping that the Lord will hear my prayers.

We reach Colombo the day after tomorrow. Surely, with landfall, there will be reprieve! Dear Lord, bless Charlotte! That she will be revived, talking to us and smiling by the time we arrive. I cannot promise myself that I will be less distracted.

Tonight, I am pondering your letters word by word. It is curious, this pairing of disquiet with delight in my heart. A glass of claret helps to drown the day's preoccupations. You say your writing has slowed, and you are going at a leisurely pace. That is sensible. I wish words would not exercise power over me rather than the other way around. Hearing from you is quite possibly the most beautiful and the most devastating thing that happens to me and I don't want it to . . . stop . . .

SS *Ranchi*

Colombo

24 April 1924

Thursday afternoon

By day the sea sparkles, reflecting hard, endless light. It is mesmerising to watch the waves, dark curlicues cresting, disappearing, as if pulled by invisible strings as far as the horizon. Seeing is obfuscation. Sight absorbs and transfixes, it loses and disorientates. I turn to the sky's compass, the starlit night sky, steady and vast. The drifting, panoramic blue interrupted by its own cadence; water lapping against the prow, the creak of gears, the random cries of seagulls. Closer to the engine room the noisy whir of fans feeding the boiler is a constant drone.

Daylight breaks in radial streaks of light, crimson and gold, the clouds furl, gliding by. This morning I was standing with Mrs Prynne on the starboard side of the middle deck, our arms covered in shawls. The captain had promised an early view of the island of Ceylon. There in the distance we could see rows of coconut trees, the dense jungle beyond, the breakwater, the clock house and a thick, dark streak, the port of Colombo. It is said to be the busiest in the Orient after Hong Kong and Singapore.

The harbour was, indeed, a hive of activity, steamships and sailing vessels, the din of men shouting. Coolies were lowering passengers into bumboats, carrying casks, crates, chairs, portmanteaus, gun cases. We were told that we would have to spend an extra day at port because the China mail had not arrived. Some of the passengers decided to spend the evening in Cinnamon Gardens; others took the train to Kandy. I wanted to send Peter a telegram but Charlotte has shown little sign of improvement and remains confined to her bed, though at least now we have a supply of fresh water. The captain was concerned she may need to be quarantined. He arranged for Dr Shivaratnam to attend, a distinguished, slender man schooled in Western medicine, dressed in grey drill trousers and a blazer, and carrying his doctor's bag. After examining Charlotte's belly and her tongue, taking her temperature and blood pressure he recommended a remedy of quinces and a bland diet. He said she would not need to be transferred to the hospital ship. He advised me to wash my hands thoroughly after any contact with her, no matter how slight. This seemed like good advice.

Her condition did not worsen, and she even managed to keep down water. By the second day in port, Charlotte was able to sit up on the main deck for a few hours in the afternoon. There was a pleasing view of the southern embankment from this vantage; it was sprinkled with lights. Unsparing in her attentions, Radhika combed Charlotte's hair; she sponged her, applying cool flannels to her face and fed her the sliced, unripened bel fruits.

Amelia Prynne and I were able to go ashore. We had been invited to afternoon tea with an old acquaintance of Amelia's departed husband, a plantation holder who had been living in Ceylon for ten years. She was still grieving and prone to melancholy and reclusiveness. I was happy to accompany her. It was an opportunity to see the sights and step on soil, for the ground beneath one's feet is eagerly anticipated whilst at sea. I had hoped to make a trip to the general post office; to read the local news, perhaps enquire at the poste restante. It even occurred to me that, in the course of Peter's travels, he would have surely been to this gracious tree-lined city with its wide, tar-sealed streets, colonnades and whitewashed houses. I confess as a measure of his influence I was a little resentful of having to postpone disembarking till the last day, even for Charlotte's sake. (What a dangerous feeling love is when it outgrows the past; even the present's responsibilities like an unruly child.)

The captain arranged for an outrigger to row us to shore. Seated low in the frame of the tugboat we were closer to the water as it swirled and foamed. The trailing tentacles of jellyfish were adrift and the colourful darts of fish swimming around the boat. We tried not to get our ankles wet but without success. There was sand on the ramp where we were put down with ropes and crates and barrels, much to the consternation of Mrs Prynne, who is quite the proper lady. It was very odd to observe that there were no coolies; fortunately, we carried only our beaded reticules and were not burdened with bags or luggage. Mrs Prynne suffered from a little *mal de débarquement* with feelings of unsteadiness and nausea. There were several drink stalls by the landing platform, so we stopped to take a lassi, letting the sea breeze dry out our water-splashed skirt hems and stockings, stamping the sand off our shoes.

The driver we hired was instructed to take us to see Colombo Fort and the Galle Face. We walked along the beachside promenade to the sea wall. We saw the Governor's stately residence, the newly built mosque and passed the Dutch hospital before heading south along Galle Road. How pleasurable to take in the sights! The thriving commercial district seemed inviting, with its scalloped awnings providing ample shade for pedestrians. About a mile from the Fort, however, we passed an expanse of tenement slums. A rank odour was abruptly apparent, the traffic slowed, and we were soon surrounded by dirty-faced children selling magazines and bouquets of fresh flowers, wrapped in brown paper. A multitude of workers were brandishing signs, shouting in the Tamil language, a few through loudhailers. They were coal coolies, protesting their shift work conditions by non-cooperation. What brave men, to rally for their freedom!

To place the welfare of their families at risk! Mrs Prynne did not approve. She reminded me of how the coolies from Assam were punished; some were even shot by Gurkhas in Chandpur. But there were coolies, I have read, in many of the Indian provinces, in Natal, and, some report, as far as West Australia.

The driver turned into a tree-lined road that followed a canal. A tributary of Beira Lake, it was emerald green, fringed by palms and suriya trees. Yellow blossoms dispersed in the salty sea breeze. We turned again, approaching parklands and the stately homes of Cinnamon Gardens, and at last came to our destination. Set back from the street and shaded by a banyan tree, the white-pillared house had a red gable roof. Among the sandalwood trees there were trails of jasmine and hibiscus. Our hosts, Ellen and John Peechey, came to the porch to greet us. John apologised for not being at the port to meet us. The coolie strike had caused repercussions for their recruitment agency. A hundred and fifty cinnamon peelers not showing up to their kanganis! Wanting a minimum wage, medicines and rent-free housing on the estate! Those thin, deft fingers, all those mouths to feed. The stained walls of empty huts, the aromatic shavings, quills and scrapings of bark. Bundles of cinnamon needing to be stored and dried. The cart road being carved out of the thick forest now mired. But did we have a pleasant afternoon on Galle Face green?

He led us through a finely appointed drawing room out to a verandah set amid a row of palms. We sat on rattan chairs, the table covered in damask. Presently the maid brought us masala tea and an elaborate tray of shaddocks, mangoes, pineapple, banana, sliced cake, almonds and cashew nuts. Ellen is a fine-boned woman of middle years. She was dressed in understated fashion, wearing a long string of pearls and a cream-embroidered chemise. Mrs Prynne, of course, was in mourning. I felt rather drab in my long skirt, but I found my gaze peeling away and disappearing into the trees, which were alive with bees, blossoms, lizards and birds. So we spent the afternoon, very leisurely and very politely, in the heat of the jungle, drinking tea, talking about transport, the harbour breakwater, coffee prices, anti-British riots in China, all the goings-on in this corner of the world, radiating outwards.

Poona Airport

20 June 2017

Today would have been my mother's seventy-ninth birthday. When we lived in London, on family birthdays we would receive a visit from my father's aunt Queenie, who lived in Hounslow. She was very fair-skinned, a little rotund, with permed grey hair which, on occasion, she dressed in hats. She would bring a gift and a cake and her very own brand of warm-hearted kindness. When we visited her, she cooked English food – roasts and puddings – as well as halwa and other Indian sweets. Her husband was a softly spoken public servant who was always very proper and sweet. They were my favourite relatives.

The day my mother was born always seemed beautiful to me; the twentieth of June, the brightness of the first month of summer; a numerically balanced date. The rest of our family had birthdays in a cluster during the first months of the year; my mother's birthday stood apart. On this day, Poona Airport seemed such an official and unfriendly place to be stranded. It is a civil aviation facility used by the Indian army and isn't set up for commercial purposes. This explains the lack of passenger facilities: no lounges, only two shops and a few vending machines.

Kumar is travelling to Oxford to study business for a year, leaving his wife and child in Kolkata, but brimming with optimism for his education. We find two seats in a row on the ground floor, against the glass wall. Cold, rigid seats, the long stopover. Perched here with nothing to do but wait, we talk. We compare our leather hand luggage, purchased in Kolkata – mine a fake, but such a good one I am half convinced it is real.

Kumar is stocky with henna-dyed hair and a quirky sense of humour. He says he's left his accountancy practice; I mention that I'm writing a novel then feel a pang of remorse that I have so little to show for it, only ten thousand words. Kumar is not a literary buff, but he's heard of Virginia Woolf.

Daisy came alive for me in Kolkata like a dark fledgling, a literary half-caste in the city of despair and joy, loosely set and shadowy. She ventures from the splendidly camouflaged paragraphs of *Mrs Dalloway*, a young encumbered wife whose dreams and character and inner voice are longing to be written. Psychological realism indeed, I thought, walking an overgrown pathway through the Medan, where a thin rat grazed on nettles. Undoubtedly, it's an upper-class novel. Fantastic how a working-class psychology breathes life in the shape of Miss Kilman, Elizabeth Dalloway's teacher, in her resentment of Clarissa. (Why is Clarissa the victim?) Yet still, we learn nothing of Daisy's children. We aren't invited into her lounge room, nor do we see her at church or shopping or being invited to lunch.

At Diamond Harbour I sat on a coconut vendor's chaise as he skilfully peeled the green skin and pale flesh with his curved knife, right down to the nut, so I could drink the refreshing gauzy milk. Students were walking past. Under the sun's radiance the morning heat became suffocating. I walked the banks of the Hooghly River, past the boat builders' wharves.

For half a mile I walked, stepping across the railway sleepers, past the weeds and the slum dwellings, following the train tracks till I reached a poor man's ghat. Skinny, half-naked boys were bathing, and dogs kept watch, pulling at their leashes.

On my way back I was followed by an overweight man who assumed I was a sex worker and offered me a lift. I felt cheap. His stare devoured me. When I got into a taxi he tapped on the window. In the lurid daylight there were orphans asleep on mats at the intersections of roads; children who suffer as much from the clichés of poverty as from poverty itself, starvation in the sunken eyes of infants sitting on stools at the entrance to the underground. Near a saree shop I caught a flicker of life in the eyes of thin-boned beggars, barely visible in the dirt and the darkness. They were piled in a bullock cart parked opposite St Thomas' church.

One night, I ate at a food stall in a street market then became sick. An adolescent boy was serving, dressed in coarse cotton, scratching his legs and his rump through the loose trousers. I bought sarees and a leather bag, and recall now with nostalgia sitting on a stool drinking tea and talking with the leather goods vendor as the sun blazed into his shopfront on Chowringhee Road.

Not speaking the same language means that something is bound to be lost in the process of translation. Sometimes, even though we are global, I, the Westerner, was the one who was exploited; other times it was they, the subalterns. The engineer I met over breakfast working in Sikkim on developing a One Belt, One Road project said we should go out in Park Street. He seemed fine, he spoke good English, but then sent a crass, lewd text, so I deleted him from WhatsApp even before we were supposed to meet; a lucky escape! And the beautiful Muslim woman, a merchant's wife from Patna, who was noticeably tense because she was locked out of her room with her baby while her husband was out at a meeting. Veiled, yet vulnerable. She was afraid of the housekeepers. It was too risky to wait alone in the corridor, even with her young and slender body covered. She feared the heat, the sweat stains it left on her kurta. She was so grateful when I invited her to stay in my room till it was sorted out. I gave her bottled water and she breastfed her son. Coming from the West, we forget this kind of gender hatred is being normalised. The women from Patna and Bangladesh stayed together, catching taxis, finding protection from the sun. How strange it was, I thought, that we should meet like that, the writer and the young married mother from Patna.

My return flight to London from Kolkata was scheduled to stop in Mumbai, where I was going to visit my cousins, but when I arrived at Kolkata Airport – after a harrowing ride along the congested freeway – I discovered that Air India flights to Mumbai had been cancelled owing to the monsoon floods. A smart, well-spoken businessman helped me transfer to an Emirates flight going to London, with a twelve-hour stop in Pune.

After we exhaust several topics of conversation, Kumar works quietly on his laptop and I read a newspaper. The front page is filled with news of Grenfell Tower, London and the world in mourning. People are confused and community anger simmers over the missing people, many of whom remain undocumented because they were 'illegal' immigrants to whom the flats were sublet. There are calls for amnesties, inquiries. News articles focus on the bungles: Theresa May's failure to speak to the victims; the firefighters who'd told victims to stay in their flats; the fact that traumatised children and adults must walk the streets of the estate in Notting Dale inhaling the smell of charred humans. A grim reminder, the shell of the tower looms above Latimer Road station, the building itself cordoned off. The bulletins show drone photographs of the building's facade, seared and cracked, loose wires dangling, the warped debris of frames, empty windows through which occasionally the masked figures of forensic contractors are visible. At Notting Hill Methodist Church, there are hundreds of bouquets, testaments, cards and a night-time vigil; people have gathered to mourn and to pray for those lost lives. The residents want the tower to be covered in tarpaulin, but that would compromise the evidence.

It's hard to fathom the scale of the tragedy. We're the watchers, now, online, aware there's a voyeuristic instinct in tabloids, in social media. There's also a desire to witness that every writer knows: to better understand, to feel as if we belong, as if we carry a very small part of the shared burden of grief. Even as visitors, we inherit the consequences. Londoners pull together in adversity – the volunteers donating shoes and cardigans; the ambos, medics and police – though there are trolls and haters calling for the closure of mosques, and the shock reports about extremist clerics, which Sadiq Khan tweets about.

I turn from the news and try to prepare my class on narrative poetry, the 'lived poem', but I am distracted. I observe other passengers: students in jeans and jackets, businessmen, couples, a slender woman in a turquoise saree talking with her husband. Are they from Pune or another city? My boredom is soon interrupted by announcements: 'Indigo Flight 221 to Delhi now boarding from gate two.' 'Final call for Mr Anil Deshpande, Air India Flight 87, boarding gate one. Final call for Mr Anil Deshpande.' What was stalling Mr Deshpande? Was he suffering a cardiac arrest? The moment intensifies – as some moments do – returning me to Peter Walsh, how Virginia has him wanting to do away with that insufferable Anglo-Indian habit of not crying, or not laughing when he should. She makes him unseemly; what a clever stroke! Loneliness has made him indulgent. Is that human nature, or Peter's habit? Or is it Clarissa's monstrous judgement?

I start flipping through my copy to find the exact paragraph – page 150 in the Vintage edition. My cherished Penguin copy has finally fallen apart, the cover ragged, the pages loose, the way a woman comes apart if she is overused and abused because she is considered surplus and therefore less, if the patriarchal world exhausts her labour and her body, her slots, even her skin. (Hard to believe this fetish practice that my friend Lindsay has researched; how the skin of outcast women from alms houses was used in the binding of scholarly books!) That a poor woman's skin should serve the scholarship of the elite! The hierarchies. A kind of horror! Like pages from *The Heart of Darkness*. Always Empire. The Queen's speech. Her Majesty's English. The horror! To come to this entry point. Here's Peter Walsh pondering an ambulance, one of London's civic triumphs, so that life can be salvaged: the carts, carriages, omnibuses giving way along the road. Not just any ambulance, mind you, but the one that's about to pick up the mangled body of a war veteran, Septimus Warren Smith.

A friend's cancer has returned, and she's had an operation to remove part of her bowel; she gave a concert while I was in India. She had to sit down while performing. I am failing her – I wasn't able to go to her last concert either – and time is running fast. Sam seems to spend a lot of time gaming. Is he dating, while my energy is poured into this novel? I have tried to think of Daisy. And Lucrezia, the Italian immigrant, the milliner who has been widowed in London. She is described as appearing foreign and dark, in that casual way that the upper class allude to difference. Is it because she is sitting in the shadows, or is it pejorative? She is described as being prone to losing things. For what good reason is Rezia's future sacrificed in *Mrs Dalloway?* For some reason the word 'immanence' sits like a globe on my tongue, the word clear and cold. The immanence of Clarissa and her creator. Like Daisy, I am in her midst, in Bloomsbury, Virginia Woolf's London, our words shared, yet partial, marginal, invisible.

It's becoming increasingly costly to rent in Bloomsbury. I've used up my grant and my reserves are rapidly depleting. Residence is fraught, made vulnerable by the movement of people through the city. The house in Tavistock Square is undergoing restorations, a process that requires approval from the Heritage Trust. We have been told that it could take eighteen months to complete and we may sometimes have to be moved.

For the next six weeks, the Student Centre at the university have relocated Celine, James and me to flats in a terrace in Taviton Street. I'm on the top floor, looking out over the rooftops and chimneys. There is ample light and it is closer to the British Museum and to Euston station. Dreadfully noisy, though. I am a light sleeper and even with earplugs in I get woken frequently by the stream of buses and trucks. In desperation, I've tried sleeping elsewhere; once, at a poet's house, a mistake. An Orientalist. Imprudently, I was taking the advice Luke had given me after my divorce. 'Enjoy the lessons of recovery,' he'd said with the force of a prophecy.

But the lessons left me weaker, softer than flesh.

It's hunger that makes us take the bait, the narcissistic trap; the loneliness of writing makes us vulnerable. Writers are not so different from other professionals, really; it's simply such hard work and not the healthiest lifestyle. No ballast. You have a pile of laundry to wash, clothes to sort, little food in the fridge but still you keep dreaming the writing game, drinking coffee, dandelion tea, cooking scrambled eggs, noodles, a glass of wine occasionally. One is bereft of self-care. One benefit is that you can live very modestly. However, what little you earn is never enough, so you may find yourself devoting disproportionate energies to freelance work that pays or to binging creatively. At these times you are most defenceless.

I get four hours' sleep on the Emirates flight to London, though I'm hardly refreshed by it. A mother trying to settle her baby is seated beside me. With her patience she attracts my sympathy. I'm not acutely missing Sam though I haven't forgotten him. Am I taking him for granted?

'But this is your career, it's your time,' Serena had said after Mum's funeral when I told her I'd be returning to London.

I want a quiet place to sleep and simply can't face clamorous, shabby Taviton Street, so on arrival I go straight to a room I've booked in Kensington, close to a conference where I've been invited to read on a panel with three other poets. Nearby is the Victorian terrace where Virginia Woolf lived before her father died when the family relocated to Bloomsbury.

St Thomas' School

Kidderpore House

4 Diamond Harbour Road, Calcutta

14 May 1924

Dear Virginia,

I pray this reaches to find you and Leonard in good health. I am writing from my classroom at St Thomas' (formerly known as the Calcutta Free School), thankful for the Lord's love. He has preserved me, so that I might return safely to carry out his work. My journey back to India was both gruelling and enthralling. Indeed, the Orient never ceases to intrigue me, though I have seen the great pyramids in Egypt and spent already two years in Bengal. The journey itself provides the opportunity to meet such a range of men and women not usually encountered in society, which is to say those far removed from the security and insularity of our hamlet. What happy memories of Sussex! I miss my walks by the river to Lewes, and across the downs. I miss our mulberry tree, our humble church and our little school, our pear and apple trees, the little grebes that swim in our river and flocks of partridges in the fields. Aunt Jane and I were so thankful to have paid you a visit at Monk's House before Easter.

I have been pondering what you describe as Mr Kipling's 'masculine orthodoxy'. I do not find his novel *Kim* very readable at all; and it is all to do with boys. With boys and with men and their dominions, where there is no room for a woman to serve her own brethren by her actions or by her words. Indeed, his stories are like little notebooks, though I had not thought of it that way until we spoke.

From my desk there is a view across the school lawns, where boys are playing cricket; there are thrushes singing and sharp-eyed crows in the fields. Beyond the tents, there are establishments of education and governance, paper mills and factories. One is able to catch a glimpse of the holy river where pilgrims will have gathered to immerse.

I was very sorry to hear that the rector has taken ill with blood poisoning. Please do send word of my good wishes and prayers for his speedy recovery. It does not help that the cottages in Rodmell are so damp and in such a sorry state. We face similar problems with the crumbling walls in Calcutta when the rains come. And how I pity the poor natives and immigrants who live in the slums and railway colony. Leonard would know about these public concerns from his years of service in Ceylon. The miseries of poverty, hunger and disease for which we try to provide relief are distressing. But our faith in the Lord and in suitable education does count for a little, and I am only grateful to be offering my labour here and now.

I have a clear picture in my mind of you sitting at your desk in the shed by the chestnut tree, dipping the nib of your pen into the inkwell, blotting paper to hand, magazines, books open, words brimming, the tranquillity of the garden, Mr Woolf planting seedlings. I trust the days are fine, birds are feeding in the hedgerows and the apples, cherries and pears are ripening.

Yours most affectionately,
Winifred Myra Dean

SS *Ranchi*

1 May 1924, Thursday noon

On leaving Colombo we passed a shoal of whales that kept us company for miles, rolling and breaching in the silvery breakers. There was a school of porpoises, too; Charlotte was in raptures. A mass of foam carried by the current was teeming with fish, the peculiar conditions having arisen from eruptions in a volcano on some nearby island. The crew wasted no time casting nets into the swell, collecting mackerel and flounder. Rainbow-like and wriggling in a pile, the more vigorous of these acrobats jumped and flipped, gasping, in flashes of silver and blue. The spectacle was exhilarating.

The cook's assistants came quickly with buckets to carry away the catch. (A charge to the tastebuds will be welcome, for although the bill of fare in the dining saloon shows variety, the food often lacks freshness.) It was one of those days when the crew seemed to have an easy time, a group telling yarns, while in the saloon the stewards were polishing glassware and sweeping floors. The sun sparkled on the sea and smartly attired gentlemen sat in view around the deck, lolling, reading and smoking, while the ladies took a turn under parasols, relaxed by the sunshine and the shimmering sea.

Charlotte and I strolled in the evening when the clouds performed their gorgeous draperies, the horizon indigo, then crimson-veined. Stars rose, first one, then another until they had jewelled and studded the night sky. A strange phosphorescent lump landed on the deck, its glowing tail converting to the crew who handled it up, illuminating the surface where it jiggled. We soon realised this curious object was a flying fish, the likes of which we had already witnessed from afar. These blue sparks in the waves, orbs of orange and green are like Diwali candles offered to Lakshmi and Durga, ornamenting the coral beach near Trincomalee. This writhing iridescent alien made a deep impression in our abstract minds, in much the same way that hope and wonder come to be a real presence.

When I close my eyes at night, after such a seemingly endless day at sea, I see nothing but the undulations of sea-green, rhythmic and glittering blue, hear the sound of slapping against the prow and fish gasping. Then it becomes a kind of opaqueness, divested of detail before the darkness of sleep gathers and dreams entangle me, ordering their fragments in spurious clusters that nevertheless carry their own murmurings of destiny.

SS *Ranchi*

2 May 1924, Friday

We woke to a change in weather, the ship rolling in rough seas and the south-west monsoon. News has spread of an outbreak of dysentery in steerage and the loss of an elderly woman and two child passengers. All is very sombre. This evening everything was sliding in the cabin, the salt and pepper shakers and dinner plates skating off the table. The stewards were struggling to serve meals, and drinks were sloshed about as glasses tipped. In Colombo we had parted company with Wilhelmina and her parents, who boarded the *Commonwealth*, a handsome ship with buff-yellow hull and funnels, headed for Albany and Port Adelaide. Mrs Prynne is still with us. We did not see her at supper; I hope she is not ill. She may be resting after our excursion.

Our ship has been loaded with 480 tons of coal – all night before departing Colombo they had been coaling – for the long journey to Aden, which we are told is 2000 miles. It sits low, pitching, and the foul smells of passengers being sick is beyond dreadful. Up on the deck, water was sloshing about, and we almost lost the lifeboats, which had loosened from their moorings. With the ship rolling, some of the coal stowed washed overboard. The lascars were drenched, sweeping and mopping away the waters that spilled over the bulwarks. I saw the captain make a dash to the lifeboats in a valiant effort to secure them. Working contrary to the violent squall, he injured himself and afterwards was in great pain, nursing his arm. The first steward called for the ship's doctor and then a few men came to his aid and he was carried away. I believe that his shoulder joint was unhinged, and one can only imagine that the pain must be acute like childbirth, though transitory in comparison, and without the joy of new life.

It is hard to think of life as I struggle to put down these words, thankful for the electric bulb's incandescence, shedding ample light in our cabin. A fault in supply has left the public rooms in darkness, and the engineer has been called to attend to the problem. We hear doors clanging, people spitting and retching. The scurry and shuffling is quite a distraction. Charlotte has become ill again. She is not speaking, and her face has lost all colour, even as I am writing. In the pit of my heart I am trying to calm my disquiet, with no one to console me. I question my judgement, now, in bringing Charlotte on this voyage and have grown quite gloomy and pessimistic. The ship's doctor has given her a remedy of creosote. Still, she has been throwing up in the bucket and has stopped sipping the sponge that we press to her tongue. Radhika is cooling her skin now with wet flannels and wiping away the mess and I must help . . .

Kensington

23 June 2017

The hotel is an indulgence beyond my means, but I need
some pampering. I try to sleep for a few hours to refresh in
snatches. To travel is to lose one's mind. There is a psychedelic
inventiveness in jet-lag, the re-circuits and transits, the ramps
and gates. What is left of it all is the rat's tail of the writer's
life. Less than the little I bargain for.

Virginia Woolf read Greek, Latin and History at the
Ladies' Department of King's College, London in Kensington.
It was here that she met feminist educators Lilian Faithfull
and Clara Pater. Prior to that, she and Vanessa were home
schooled while both her brothers went to university. Virginia
lived in a Victorian terrace with her sister Vanessa, two
brothers, her father, the author and critic, Sir Leslie Stephen,
and her mother, Julia Prinsep. By her own account, it was
also the house where she was molested by her half-brother,
George Duckworth. Her essay '22 Hyde Park Gate', hints
at sexual trauma but withholds disclosure until the final

paragraph, when it is powerfully revealed: 'Yes, the old ladies of Kensington and Belgravia never knew that George Duckworth was not only father and mother, brother and sister to those poor Stephen girls; he was their lover also.' The essay was delivered by Virginia as a speech addressed to the Bloomsbury Memoir Club in 1920.

As inspired as she was to see women's fiction uniquely reimagined, Woolf also knew that women's bodies are exploited and pursued. She has Peter Walsh trifle with impropriety, to fall in love with Clarissa and Daisy, as if they are abstractions – or with a random woman walking along Regent Street, simply because she is wearing lipstick and a red carnation pinned to her thin cloak. But how much of this is Peter? There's Woolf, letting it happen. She uses racial scorn to blame India for his sexist whims and fantasies with everywoman, *even the poorest, happiness from a pretty face, down-right misery at the sight of a frump.*' One can easily overlook the offensive stereotypes prompted by India on page 70, in my copy. The whole book bears the scratching of Peter's idealised passions, sublimated on to Daisy *and* Clarissa, and there's Virginia having it materialise all the same, so that it is hard to know if she sympathises with his awkward ways or if she holds Peter in contempt. I understand her quandaries, the pressures placed on novel writing as a prism for a post-war, modern world. In her diary, she admitted the psychological burden of crafting this new form:

One feels about in a state of misery — indeed I made
up my mind one night to abandon the book — & then
one touches the hidden spring. I've not re-read my great
discovery, & it may be nothing important whatsoever.
Never mind, I own I have my hopes . . .

V. Woolf, 15/10/1923

I have my hopes too! Buried in my inbox, an email from a writer in Cairo, describing her weekend in the Black and White deserts: the oases, the shooting stars and the 'epic silence'. (I want that!) In Kolkata, there was clamour, insistent rhythms, cries and traffic, the night pulse that propels the dreamer into dawn as it traffics the dreams of barefoot, sleeping men, taxis drivers, recruiters, outsourced personnel. The same noise dissolves as stillness found in lush, over-grown gardens, a colonial past echoing passive mockeries. The locked, decaying shutters and brass-knobbed doors; a past that brushes against the folds of sarees, with their particular smell in the sun-poured rush of river crossings.

My thoughts skid. Kaleidoscopically they shift from deserts to map reading to drowning, to Charlotte's death from cholera and the sea burial that follows. How will this alter Daisy? It's not something I have experienced. Do I understand, or is it speculation? Such gravity can be implied; it doesn't need to be polemic. It is factual; it is history – children were more likely to die on ocean voyages until the mid-nineteenth century, after which refrigeration of food and water led to a decline in infectious diseases and better hydration.

After leaving Colombo, Charlotte's condition deteriorates, and she dies before they reach Port Said (and, psychically speaking, I am her assassin!)

I make a note to myself to research the ports of Aden and Cape Guardafui. I consider a research visit to the Suez Canal, to include a brief stay with the Cairo-based writer. Accidentally, I have discovered letters in the National Archives from Harry Beaumont, a quartermaster sergeant serving in Aden in 1917, and there are letters from a Franciscan missionary voyaging along the Port Said to Calcutta routes which may be useful. Research seems to work when I'm stuck, turning history, allowing the creative nexus to thrive, to flower, for Daisy to intone leaving her husband, her son and her household behind. But am I writing the novel in my mind if so little of it is committed to words on the page?

Never mind. I can do the writing later, I persuade myself. But what about the editing? The structure and tenses? Should Daisy's story alternate with Peter's? So long as I know what I have to do: tracking her voice, channelling her vibe; that is what matters. A commonly held belief is that talking to a plant helps it grow even as much as water and light. I imagine having to nourish Daisy. I imagine talking to her as if we are two women speaking a secret language. Except it's her voice that matters, her story, her life. Going by what I have written so far, I think Daisy Simmons is someone I would like in real life. And Daisy's suffering is not entirely strange to me, no stranger to grief.

For there she is. No longer shadowed in the pages of *Mrs Dalloway*; the negatives of Daisy illumined against the light, having left Colombo, with her son in Calcutta and her daughter dying in the ship's cabin.

SS *Ranchi*

7 May 1924, Wednesday

A grace it would be if what I am about to write were a grave misperception. I have lost my darling Charlotte. What was I thinking, bringing her with me to this hostile realm of water? The seas are corridors of Empire where few can sleep restfully. Violently gendered, always shifting. Bittersweet, that word which desire singularly composes. All the maps, the world's harbours, the skirts of its shorelines appear only to tease the mind.

Where is a lover when needed most? (I imagine him riding an omnibus across Piccadilly and down Regent Street, Clarissa by his side with little treasures from the Caledonian market.) Oh, Clarissa! With all her finery and whimsy, for one must always invent a little; and I imagine there are daffodils blooming in the square near his lodgings in Lincoln's Inn. Or was it Bloomsbury? And, he will show me the bushy black and tan hairs of the English squirrel's tail. I forget so much the memories blur. Our actual meetings loosen in my mind like strips of bark or the peel of a snake.

This grief. I am filled with sorrow. A few words on the empty page and my body sinks. I feel mute, utterly dumb. No more hopes or promises; nothing of consolation, though I know everything, mystery and misery . . . that the sea is a vast territory, a carrier and a border. She tears us apart like a wolf feeding, and we are powerless.

I struggle to write. Writing is death. A second death.

Three days ago, after twelve hours more or less – I cannot say, for I have lost proper count of time – she passed into a stupor and could not be roused. And then the English clergyman came and said prayers. For a long time after the clergyman left, I sat holding Charlotte's small hand, watching the rise and fall of her rib cage under the bedsheet, feeling her thready pulse until it stopped. I knew it was over by the coldness of her hand, limp in mine. And so, her spirit left this world.

So unexpected, the force of my reaction was hysterical, my bones quaking with grief. I needed my lover desperately, I cried for Mrs Burgess, the outpouring of tears unstoppable. Radhika says that I fainted, and she called for help. The captain and first steward were in attendance; they took Charlotte away and sent for Mrs Prynne. She and Radhika have been stalwarts. Something about a service discussed. Then the doctor returned. He checked me thoroughly and administered a sedative with his further instructions.

I must have slept for a few hours. I'm utterly alone here and can't describe the desolation and despair I feel. Fleetingly, my thoughts have even turned to James, and the burden of guilt, the self-loathing I feel.

We buried Charlotte yesterday at sunset. The sea was folding upon itself, baubles of fire glimmered across the horizon as the sun dropped. They had wrapped her in light sailcloth because of decomposition. It was a solemn service. A small congregation sang, the hymns buoying my spirit a little. The English clergyman read from the Gospel of St Mark, 'Let the children come to me, do not hinder them; for to such belongs the kingdom of God . . .' He spoke of how St Mark says Jesus took the children in his arms and blessed them, laying his hands upon them, and at that moment Mrs Prynne and I wept. I wished only to hold my darling Charlotte, but hearing this gospel eased the burden of letting her go. Then we consigned her to the deep and as they lowered the casket that held her small bones I broke down.

Dolphins had been following the steamer, their blue bodies visible, rolling, the intelligent eye and the nose almost seemed sympathetic. It was a strange sight; we had seen jellyfish and porpoises since leaving Colombo. They seemed to have arrived to accompany dear Charlotte as the water washed over the casket and it disappeared. The lapping sea sounded like knocks. I thought of water seeping into the simple casket and through the sailcloth, soaking her dress, her eyelashes and her nails. She has gone to a watery kingdom that knows no distinction between Europeans and Indians, between mammals and fish, kings, servants or clowns.

Dark blue clouds feathered the sky, gathering intensity. The air was very still. Our party of a few mourners began to disperse. I gazed into the whorls and curly streaks of blackness in the waves, details I had not cared to observe in past times. A bell chimed. Captain Findlay approached, saying, 'I'm so very sorry, Mrs Simmons.' Then the first officer, Mr Alexander Carmichael, accompanied me to the saloon, where a funeral wake had been arranged. Some of the crew had been drinking already. Everyone was very kind to me. I was offered a glass of claret, which I drank without hesitation – the beverage made no difference – and then we had supper.

How wretched I am. My nights empty, the days too long. I try to stitch pieces of calm into a pillow. My eyes are filled with tears and confusion. Why did God fail me? I cannot cross the gap between raw grief and the reprieve that sleep might allow. Nothing can prepare a mother for the loss of her daughter. She fears this happening from the first night they spend together, mother and child. I recall feeling afraid that Charlotte would stop breathing. I recall watching the movement of her ribs as she lay curled on my breast, a thread of my milk dribbling from her mouth: in, out, in, out, in, out . . . all those years ago.

SS *Ranchi*

the dark continent

12 May 1924

Seven days have passed since we buried Charlotte. I barely sleep and have not been able to write from my cabin, but today I am on deck, lulled by the calm, shimmering sea. I miss seeing the lustre of sunlight in trees. I miss the small creatures that hide among the leaves: the slinky lizard, the inquisitive squirrel, the rainbird with his forlorn song.

We are approaching Africa. Another continent, the entrepôts between England and Italy and the waters of the Arabian Sea. Apparently, we are soon to pass the coast of Somalia, or what they call the Horn. When we encounter storms, they comfort me. Perhaps the heavens are lamenting my loss. (I believe this is how God abandons us, and then reminds us of His existence – it is not unlike a man, or so I felt in my darkest hours.) The kind-hearted first officer, Mr Carmichael, said the inclement weather was the south-west monsoon. He promised we would leave it behind within a day or two, and he was right. Mrs Prynne and I have been sitting with him at supper. He's awfully handsome, clear blue eyes, ginger hair, a broad-chested Scotsman. His family are from the coastal town of Leith, and he said he would love to show me its quiet bays and cottages. The day we buried Charlotte, I told him that I needed to send a telegram to her father from Aden, and he immediately offered his service.

Think of a mother who has lost one breast; a mother disfigured, with a scar that won't heal in her heart space. She tells the story of the death of her daughter on a journey to elope and meet her lover in such a way that it lessens her guilt. She fails to recount her obsessive desires, or how she neglected her daughter's illness on board the ship. By these omissions, the prospects are improved for the wound in her heart space to heal. Or perhaps it works the other way: that because of her wound rotting, being unable to close, she is prone to extreme psychological discomforts. She is distracted, becoming forgetful of the details of how and when her daughter dies at sea, on the ill-fated voyage to meet a man who matters most.

Already, she has shattered her life for him, and if the story alters from truth, does that make her faithless? Does it make her irresponsible? Does it establish a flaw? And if so, by whose judgement? A pinch of poison, a dash of salt in the mixed lines; so truth and errors are bound in the telling of stories.

The edge of the 'dark continent', Cape Guardafui, appeared starkly before us; all sand and low rocky headland. Golden by daylight, abstract, like a mirage. The promontory is said to resemble an elephant's head (and how this makes me home-sick). Except for scatterings of grass and acacia trees, the Somali coastline is barren. Mr Carmichael says there has been rebel fighting and the Italians have completed a light-house only a month ago. While turning, the ship steamed closer and we sighted it, a simple metal frame supporting a dome-covered construction for the lantern. It has a temporary look about it, suitable for such a desolate country, a modest symbol of Italy's ambitious young leader Benito Mussolini and his army. But a statement, nonetheless.

My resolve to tell James has dwindled. He is entitled to know; he should know, but I fear James would immediately convey the news to Joseph and it would cause my son great sorrow. Not a day passes that I do not think of my boy and how he is adjusting to boarding school. With his gentle temperament I hope he is making friends. Better that I break the sad news to Joseph on my return home or when he visits me. I must plan for this. But how long will that take? Even for a seasoned traveller this distance across the Indian Ocean before it meets the Gulf colonies, the seas, canals and ports, the settlements and island states that join the subcontinent to England is a considerable journey. All of it mapped by men. All these places bearing the names of nations and explorers, surveyors, kings, statesmen!

He may not recognise me. From my appearance, yes, but perhaps not from within. He once said I was beguiling.

(Does he remember?) I fear I am like the island of Socotra –
shrouded in mist, bleak and unapproachable.

Radhika moves around our small cabin, folding clothes,
washing and dusting after me, loosening the tangles from my
hair. Were it not for her, I would be sleeping with vermin
and mice. No clean slips or dresses to wear. My hats would
be buried in bedsheets and my stockings and bath sheets
would languish with the cockroach droppings on the floor.

I have come this far. Hysteria. Midpoint. Equator. Wreck.

I've discovered Charlotte kept a secret journal. She drew
pictures of sad-faced girls with scorpion tails, some with
dragon wings. Lost her. Sweet mouth, that fed from my
breast. Neglect what you cherish most in your life and you
will know suffering. Never to see her blossom into a fine
young woman. Never to show her London Town. Nor to
meet *his* Clarissa. One lives with discontents that failure
cultivates. They multiply. This past week I have begun to
realise something about the heart; how it is more complex
than we give it credit. Lacking the perfect language for its
desires and anxieties, how well it senses danger, like a red
scarf. (When I saw him at the Tollygunge I always knew it
would undo me.)

Let it be known there are lessons in peregrination. The
seaborne mind aches for a patch of soil, for the rustle of wind
in the leaves of a tree. Sometimes I imagine hearing that
sound only to find it is the wind creaking in the deckchairs.
I miss hearing from you, lover. Keeping this diary, I have

only my unruly heart, my indulgence to blame. Snap back, I tell myself. But I cannot. At home, in Garden Reach, I was impatient, waiting on his letters. With casual reproach, Mrs Burgess presented them on a salver. Now I understand. The journey from Colombo to Aden, Aden to Port Said, from one harbour to the next, makes it simply not possible for him to reply. I have often felt that his preference is to muse, to ponder the words till they kindle. This silence exerts as much power over me as the English language. It leaves a doubt in my mind which the sight of his handwriting will instantly calm.

Instead, I have become this monologue, tedious, problematic, demanding and obsessed to the point of losing everything: my daughter, my son. On the other hand, he continues as one reified, fabulous, a phantasm lingering somewhere between postponement and possibility . . . Talking to him in this one-sided way has altogether taken over, and it isn't simply random thinking or a voice in my head: it's a whole destiny. At other times, I convince myself that perhaps only the destination counts; that it becomes a measure for the strange tale that has become my life.

I know it is selfish, but I cannot stem the tide of my imaginings, even in this state of mourning. The vista of a striking isthmus along the coastline, as it shifts and alters, helps me to recover a little. There are curiosities, anxieties, part-feelings, murmurings. Let them pass through me, then let them go.

Then there is the outrage I could not anticipate experiencing when our ship turned the Horn of Africa, where merchants and slave ships have trafficked in centuries past, and the barbarity, the prejudice of that oppression dawned on me.

SS *Ranchi*

Al-Tawahi, Aden

13 May 1924

We entered the Gulf of Aden, to replenish water and to coal. From a distance the silhouette of low brown hills and the harbour is dominated by a grand admiralty vessel of maybe two thousand tonnage. Our ship anchored half a mile from the station, where the coaling hulks were berthed. The bumboats, steered by dark-skinned Africans they call Abyssinians, manoeuvred out to greet us. We were rowed ashore to Steamer Point in the stifling heat. The boats had no awnings. We saw camels cooling off in the turquoise shallows. Alex accompanied Mrs Prynne and me out to the Aden Tanks. From the water we could see the dry, dusty barracks and outposts set against stark, pyramidal hills.

Aden lives up to its reputation for ship bunkering though I'm not sure about shopping. The tanks are a system of reservoirs built by the Phoenicians which lie about four miles from the harbour. Mr Carmichael offered to take me to the poste restante first, so I could send the telegram. Along the way we were called by the street vendors selling all types of exotic souvenirs from China, Arabia, Egypt and India, but they were not especially fine, nor were they discounted.

'The Abyssinians are very black,' I overheard an Englishwoman say to her husband. It made me start. I was not immune to the pang of their indifference, their tendency to scorn or deride those of us who are less fair than they. 'How dark you have become,' I remember my mother chastising me after I had spent a few days in the summer heat. And not simply do the English scorn us, but in bestowing their gaze they place us in rank, for what difference does it make if playing and revelling in life has made some of us blacker than others? Does it make us less human? My mother would have scowled if she were here. She secretly despises the British for their prejudices. How I must have disappointed and shocked my parents! Without Charlotte to hold in my arms, to return to theirs, I miss them more than ever. How could this have befallen me?

The Arab men watched on, a half-smirk written on their faces, their boys dallying in the shade of a few trees. They wore turbans and vests over their loose gabardine tunics. Mostly these vendors were reluctant to bargain. They gave the air of superiority, not caring if we bought their overpriced wares, an assortment of carvings and curios as one might find in the markets and emporiums of Calcutta, Madras or Colombo. The dhobis had draped wet garments on the hillside rocks to dry at the outskirts of the cantonment. Though it was not far, we took a cart to the poste restante as the noon heat was fierce. Even though Mr Carmichael had accompanied me, I could feel the leering stares of the local men. Mr Arora, a man of medium height and thin build, wearing square spectacles and churidar kurta, served me. At his request, I presented my passport card. I asked if he could check for any letters delivered in the name of Mrs Daisy Simmons of Garden Reach. He proceeded to fill out a form which he asked me to sign. Then he disappeared to check the mail.

After fifteen minutes in that crumbling edifice, cooled by stone floors, inhaling the dust of boxes bundled and tied with string on cluttered desks, Mr Arora came back with a folder. He opened it and inside were several letters. I recognised Peter's handwriting on one of these and must have been blushing, showing more than a little embarrassment at this private delight.

'You must excuse me, Mr Carmichael, for reading this letter from my uncle at once,' I exclaimed, pretending, again, that we were relations by blood. From his countenance, he appeared not to doubt that you could be anyone else.

'Yes, of course, Daisy, but not in this horde. Let me organise a room for you to sit in.' Then he spoke to the attendant, explaining.

'Madam, sir, please come.' Mr Arora spoke softly, guiding us through dimly lit hallways to a small, private room with a desk, chairs and cabinet.

'Do you need a drink?' Mr Carmichael asked. 'I'll go and see about some refreshments.' And off he went, leaving me to absorb the letter, the words, to ponder their doubts, little poison darts, tender feelings. The room was simple, with bare walls and wooden shutters. I found myself immersed, the silence washed by people speaking in the corridor and from time to time the chirping of lizards. These geckoes were beady-eyed, their toes like green cloves clung to the walls.

Some time passed. I heard footsteps approaching. It was Mr Carmichael. He had a boy serve iced water, a plate of dates, melons and cubes of pink sweets, heavily dusted with icing.

'Thank you, I am thirsty . . .' I said, but barely was I able to concentrate. I wanted to drink tea but the rose water refreshed me. I noticed him staring at me as I drank. He spoke about visiting the Phoenician tanks. His hair was moist, curled, and a little darker in this heat. I could feel beads of sweat collect on my forehead. I reached for a handkerchief in my purse; the one with blue beading.

We were thirsty for different things, blending into the day's semblances. I found myself ruminating over this later, as we cast our gaze across the valley of tanks chiselled out of the rock in terraces so that rainwater spills down the tremendous slope and through splits and crevasses into deep wells. Camels and donkeys carried water in skins back to the township. There was something innocent and forlorn about the tinkle of their bells. Though the skies were overcast, the heat was still oppressive.

I felt I was swallowing the past, and it tasted like sun-ripened melons; the sweet rinse of words with grief on my palate, thinking and feeling dissolving into the molasses of my tongue.

Kensington

24 June 2017

It is midday, going by the digital clock on the bedside table. Some of the guests at tomorrow's conference are meeting this evening for dinner. I get dressed and open my laptop, check my emails. A few bills; an email from the P & C committee at Sam's school: a message from John, my publisher, about our dinner, asking me to call him as he can't reach me, signed 'love' again. I can't face it, really. On Facebook, a note from a friend who has been teaching creative writing at RMIT to ask if I'd like some sessions. Feel dull with fatigue and this raspy throat. I close the computer and head out to the Boots near South Kensington station for headache pills and cough lozenges.

The girl at the counter looks vaguely like Rihanna, with an eyebrow piercing, dreamy mascara-coated eyes and a sleeve of tattoos spiralling up her right arm. I ask her where I can get a SIM card.

'There's a Vodafone shop on Kensington High Street. It's a fifteen-minute walk,' she says in a clipped voice.

Outside the pavement is bright and wide and there are people on their way to the museums, the village like a grand, leafy theme park. I walk back to the hotel to get my cardigan and instead lie down on the bed and fall asleep. When I wake it is 4 pm and my head is aching. Woolf suffered from 'nerve exhaustion headaches' brought on by a viral infection or the vexation of wearing a ridiculous hat. A day and a night could be easily ruined simply because Clive had laughed or Vita had pitied her. 'What a weathercock of sensibility I am!' she wrote in the summer of 1926. Gyrations and revolutions troubled her sleep, and Leonard was the linchpin.

Two Panadol will have to suffice for the headache. I comb my hair, throw on a beret, my cardigan, my sling bag and take the lift downstairs. Outside on the street, a group of guests with suitcases are looking for where they can check in. I offer directions. I walk in the direction of Queen's Gate, Hyde Park, turning into the wide, pleasant bend of Prince Consort Road, where a young violinist is hurrying to her performance and couples dressed in evening gowns and suits are gathering.

Is it odd, is it strange, to be taking in this city in gulps of air, the rich Arabs near Belgravia, the Italians and Romanians near the palace, the dog walkers and cyclists, the pony riders and the rowers in their lycra shorts, the honeymooners, the rich Indians at their Mahiki cocktail parties and rooftop soirées with live bands, the thickly moustachioed roti chefs serving the city's finest chicken burgers. I walk past the Dutch embassy, Sony Music, department stores, H&M and Eau-de-Vie. A blonde woman in a blue dress suit is walking her ginger-haired cavoodle near the gate to Hyde Park.

The Vodafone shop is blindingly fluorescent as I step inside from the late afternoon light. A dark-skinned guy approaches me. He recommends a £35-a- month plan, unlimited calls in the UK plus data. He is handsome, though his face is stippled with acne. Going by his accent I think he may be from India. He asks me what I'm doing in London as he takes my ID, my payment and sets up the account. I say something about being a freelance writer just returned from Kolkata. He tells me it is a city that he's visited. Where's he from? 'Dhaka in Bangladesh,' he says. Apparently, all his family live there. He's taking a course in business writing; he wants to work in human resources.

His name is Ahmed, spelt with an 'e', and he lives in Brick Lane. 'Have you been to Banglatown?'

I nod.

'I see you're Australian but you sound English,' he queries. He asks about the spelling of my name, and we talk South Asian origins for a few minutes. The part of me that is tired and simultaneously curious wants to talk to him about Dhaka, a city I envision is globalised, over-spilling with refugees, river slums and hedge funds, flame trees among the flourishing ruins of Moghul gardens, caravansaries and forts; but another part of me is reserved. Before I leave, he writes his name and number on the receipt and assures me I can call him if there are any problems.

I pop in to Uniqlo to buy some lightweight thermal shirts. The phone dings with an introductory SMS from Vodafone. It dings again with a text message from Ahmed; a link which asks me to rate the service I've received. I respond to all the questions positively. Not a bad experience. Fine, I'm thinking, if it helps to rate his employee performance highly.

Aware there's a few hours to kill before dinner, a surge of energy pulses through me. I enjoy the purchases, the assortment of lovely garments in the store. How late it seems when I step outside. People are walking past; women in dresses and shorts; an Arab walking his corgi. The traffic wheezes by, the shiny cabs and double-deckers, lorries idling in lower gear, the occasional car horn.

Standing near a bicycle rack, there's Ahmed. He looks different outside in the dimming light; I notice the stubble covering his jaw. We smile at the coincidence. He tells me he's taking the train back to Liverpool Street station. Ahmed is wearing jeans and a t-shirt with green piping. I notice he's carrying a backpack slung over his shoulder. It occurs to me that he's a different kind of immigrant to me, and how can I write about the working class of the global south if I don't talk to them?

'Would you like to have a drink somewhere?' I ask.

'A drink,' he says. 'I don't know any places here.' He frowns, quickly scans the street. He pulls out a water bottle and offers me a swig. The metal spout cools my mouth. He lights a cigarette then inhales, passing the packet to me. I take one from its flimsy wrapping. The sky is darkening. Exhaustion and head spin hit me at the point of inhaling. I have so little of the story, I think. Is he an extra? Who is this working-class boy from East Bengal? What can he bleed for me? Is there something he can tell me about Daisy? All the outcasts, the poor taxi driver who hurried through the smog and traffic jams of a city belching with poverty and overpopulation as a man gets run down, so I won't miss my plane. That's what I remember, and it burns my soul, but only when I think about it. We in the West are accustomed to brushing off our complicity and our guilt at the crimes of poverty, injustice, exploitation. Nothing much on paper, nothing in the history books, the official records, just the smoke of words, the daily crossings of pedestrians through parks, the vomit-stained paving stones of the Royal Borough.

We walk down Kensington Church Street where a gay couple sit on a bench and the occasional tourist takes photographs of the War Memorial and St Mary Abbots church. The playground of the Anglican charity school is empty now, and there's a peaceful feeling as we pass. I think of my primary school days in Holborn. I wonder about Ahmed's schooling and how different our lives have been. Or is that a presumption? The gnarly tree roots have caused breaches and buckled the stone path. Inside the church there are commemorative plaques to the men and women of the Empire. It strikes me that we are walking over their bones, the bones of Scottish historian James Mill, who wrote *The History of British India*. It serves to remind me that the Empire siphoned India's precious gems and gold. Grains were exported and high taxes imposed, spreading famine and poverty, leaving my ancestors and their descendants a legacy of debts and suffering.

'Let's walk through the park,' Ahmed says as we approach the gates and, recklessly, I follow.

It is quite dark now. I know how easy it is to be carried by the breeze under the cascade of these canopies. The birds dart in the bushes, singing shrill and sharp, and the wind lifts the skirts of the trees. We are nowhere open; not near the lake with its rippled currents, the ducks astride in pink stockings, and the flapping canvas of deck chairs; we are nowhere near the Broad Walk, the Albert Memorial, the Peter Pan statue. There are just the trees and the breeze lifting, and then Ahmed, closing in. He kisses me and I feel his hand touching my breast. A feeling I've forgotten. I haven't been touched. Now I can feel the growing bulge in his pants, his wet mouth, his cold tongue, laced with nicotine. I can feel the bristle of his stubble against my face. He is pushing me down and I feel I'm choking.

'No,' I say, 'no.' What is happening? My body feels swollen, my breath is quickening, my pulse races, my legs are sore.

He parts and pulls my hair like a rope. I'm choking on him. Why don't I resist? I'm backed against a tree, he reaches under my cardigan for my nipple, my zip. Snaps it undone. 'No,' I say again. His cold fingers grope. I'm like clay, wet and smooth. I can smell jasmine in the grass. The grey light beyond the sweeping branches and the cold air, too cold, after Poona, after Calcutta, like a trance fuck. Unready. Unprepared. It hurts, the cold, wet smell, is it pleasurable? I feel like I want to leak.

From the grass where I'm lying I see the ranger's lights glare then fade. The the truck passes, kicking dirt. He does not see me. 'You bastard,' I say inside. I'm not crying. I feel raw. He is not gone. He is here, zipping his jeans, pulling on his jacket. The ranger drives back. Headlights glaring. I'm ashamed. I've got my phone, my bag. Grass seeds have stuck to my cardigan. He says the gates are closed. The park is closed. It's an offence, he says. It's an offence. I'm zipped up now. My cheeks are hot. My cheeks are flushed. Did he come? That bastard. That fucking bastard. Pond water. Is that me?

The ranger takes us to the nearest gate, a bumpy drive. Nip in the air. I don't run at first. I walk away fast. Ahmed is calling me. I can hear his sharp voice, piercing the air: 'Mina, come back.' Asking something dumb. How dumb am I? So angry with myself. What did I think would happen? I've never lived in India. Never dealt with the violence women face every day, their arses slapped, their nipples pinched in lifts, their faces scalded on sidewalks, in the bazaars. But that's not in the diaspora. That's not in Britain – so I thought.

When I get back to my room I shower twice, trying to get clean. I'm crying. It's late by the time I get to sleep. At 1 am my phone dings with a message from Ahmed. *Gr8 night, LOL. Emoji. Laughing face.* I block him and try to get back to sleep.

Next day, getting dressed, getting a coffee, I think about going to the hospital. But I don't. I have the reading. I fake my way through it. I have to think about Daisy. I must think more about Sam. I'm wasting my life. Who's going to believe me? They'll say I asked for it. I can't get pregnant; I have an implant in my arm. But I know I should get a blood test asap and have swabs. He may have an STD. Shit happens I tell myself. That's how I block it out. Redacted. Done. It didn't happen. Like so much history.

Lincoln's Inn Hotel
London

31 March 1924

My dear Daisy,

I hope this travels swiftly, in some sort of linear way, to reach you in Aden.

Not a day passes when you are not in my thoughts, and dear Charlotte too. How is her health? I do hope the sea air has been to her liking and conditions agreeable. The steamers leaving Calcutta in March can be dreadfully overcrowded. Remember to take care in Aden; should you leave the port be sure to travel with companions. Such a bleak, arid town. I have a parting memory of its sharp, barren peaks and flat-roofed buildings as the steamer rounded the Red Sea towards Suez.

How do you like the British clock tower overlooking the slopes in Steamer Point? A replica, of course, of the prototype in Westminster! Across the city there are copies like my mantle clock in its red wood casing and mother of pearl face which has only just chimed the eleventh hour. Very sweetly, very melodiously, with hypnotic regularity – governing the day.

I'm planning a short trip from London next week. Off to Brighton to stay with the Ramsays. Further away from you, I suppose, yet by the sea. My dear, I'm a serious old fool with a penchant for philosophy and science, and habitually crippled in my romantic imaginings, except when it comes to this. How good and relaxed is this? . . . Coming, as it does, so easily, so entirely. How little I want to lose the memory of that lingering kiss, insensible of the driver in the Strand. No reason for me to hide among the vegetables, like a rough, bronze statue in the moonlight. No need to feel clenched, to break down and weep. No ridiculous scenes, no melodramas! The tears we shed after parting in Calcutta were tears of joy. I think about you all the time. I'm taking your letters with me. Those cream envelopes, your hands.

I have been so riddled with jealousy merely at the thought of my rivals, a random suitor you may have met on the voyage, that I could stab myself with a pocket-knife I like to keep myself fingering. Flick, flick. Clasp, unclasp. That sort of thing. I should never have let you travel alone, and so on, as thinking goes. I know it is rather odd.

Clarissa thinks it is a weakness of mine, an Anglo-Indian trait. We've only spoken half-a-dozen times or so in the last ten years, but I can read her thoughts. Our minds touch like the sea rolling from harbour to coastline. Her ego, however.

The parties, fleeting royal tours, mysterious little friend-ship notes. I don't mind admitting that I've tried my best to open her mind to other possibilities. When we were both much younger I gave her my copies of Shelley, Emily Brontë. I suppose she kept the books. By all accounts it has made no impression whatsoever. She's trapped herself in an unhappy marriage. Then there's her desperation for society, for people of importance to surround her: celebrities, VIPs, politicians and Richard in the parliament. All those years ago at Bourton, she called him 'Wickham'.

Where was I? Oh, you see, that's what she does to me with her finery and her digressions, a decay falling short of delu-sions, rumours or conspiracies. Being back in London, in her proper British world, and with India eclipsed in the news, I try not to be petulant. But about us – where was I . . . ?

I am discovering that love is an unwieldy feeling seeing as I couldn't bear to lose you. What does a man do with this peculiar type of fixation? Half-a-dozen letters to ponder over is a clemency. I drink tea and read the newspapers, take a daily walk, a turn through Regent's Park, the museums, like one spellbound. Write to me. Your promise catches my heart like an evening flower quivering. Your words alter their shape like clouds ahead of an English storm. India has fat droplets of monsoon rain, while here in England it is bewitching to see hoary lines of lightning soldering the sky. To see the leaves vibrate and the plane trees blanch, the light dim and the sky become a dark curtain.

Half-a-dozen letters is all I can rightly claim for now. I should like to read your words a few times over. Your descriptions of Madras usher back a wave of fond memories: the esplanade, the marina, Mowbray's Road, the advocates and samasthans and Moslem dewans, those rare bird species and intellects from the south.

My dear, I'm rather desperate to see you. London has become so permissive it is almost dull; mixed weather, occasional parties, random pedestrians, a spot of tennis, a jaunt in Hyde Park, whereupon one observes the day's vagaries: children with nannies, the homeless drifters and hallucinating partisans, the charms and effronteries of Tory socialites, buses and trolleys, ambulances and sandwich men. Everywhere in evidence the style and speed and modernity of a city grinding its way forward after the war, even while it drags its feet in labour strikes and minor uprisings in the outposts. Ramsay MacDonald has a minority lead against the conservatives in Parliament. It was splendid to hear your thoughts on the Gopinath Saha trial and the young Sikh revolutionaries, but all that turbulence lies behind you. London awaits. Here, there is fine art, Chinoiserie and opera, the grandest of museums, with precious collections from the antiquities and rare botanical species (if one cares to look them up) and biological anomalies. I wonder how you picture our future together? Not in the least bit do I care what other people may think, not a straw.

I might have a chat with Richard Dalloway, see what he's got: a personal assistant or a teaching position, perhaps in algebra or Latin. He's a very nice chap, Dalloway – sensible, a little dull, but an awfully good sort. Let's see what Clarissa can do. A cottage in the country, two rooms in London would do nicely for us. Tomorrow, I've got appointments all day. And luncheon with the ghost of Sally Seton. Only now she's Lady Rosseter, with five sons and a fine house in Manchester. Not bad, considering she once pawned her French royalty ring to pay for the trip to Bourton. I remember it like it was yesterday. I was sent down from Oxford because politics sometimes serves the weakest needs of one's character. Those exquisite flourishes a woman glimpses before a good marriage. Grand passions she calls degrading desires, and the faintest strain of resentment for gaiety that is natural and irrepressible. All the chaos one witnesses as life swerves this way or that way, and our paths bump up against each other's.

There we have it, Daisy, there we are. Moments of gorgeous resistance colliding with innocence and insincerity, while there is a cholera epidemic and all the wheelbarrows in India, the darling flags of Empire . . . And who am I then, and what does this make me? An exception, waiting on a word.

Yours,
Peter

Lazzaretto
L'Isolotto, Malta

18 May 1924

They offered burgundy with our evening meals last night.
I drank two glasses, using the Egyptian currency I had
acquired in Port Said. The wine floated in my veins, as
the hours lapsed into nightfall. I dreamt of where the dead
children go after fever sucks the body dry. Charlotte came,
her hair bouncing around her bright eyes, and I was a young
mother feeding again.

We are being held in the lazzaretto, an island hospital
nestled in the harbour facing Valletta where the ship was
supposed to coal. The port authorities have quarantined the
ship and ordered that it be fumigated to prevent the trans-
mission of cholera. We were told there has been an epidemic
in Alexandria and Port Said where new passengers boarded.
There was much confusion among crew and passengers, and
a good deal of frustration when the yellow flag was raised
on the ship and we were bundled into groups and rowed

in boats across Marsamxett Harbour to the Health Office. Most of the Europeans were in a state of disbelief, as they had been preparing to disembark. Clothing, portmanteaus, all our foods and cottons, and other cargoes were confiscated. Captain Findlay warned us that we might be waylaid by forty days at worst, though he is hopeful that he will be able to negotiate our release soon.

I have been listless, dozing off to the sea's lapping and rhythmic fathoms. It is almost noon, and the little blond-haired boy follows me from the main dormitory. The beds are aligned in rows, almost touching. People's belongings are tied in bundles or covered with a shawl. Some of the adults and children are asleep. They lie with flannels on their fore-heads, their mouths open, jugs of clean water by their cots. Radhika and Prem are washing undergarments with water drawn from the well; our quota checked by the matron. I have seen how the boy accompanies her on her rounds. She takes temperatures, checks the skin, gums, and dryness of the tongue, writing it all down. He stands barefoot by her side. Sometimes he tugs at her dress, his neck pulled in. Sometimes he brings her a jug of water to sponge the sick, or a file tied with string, or a thermometer. Each morning she arrives two or three hours after dawn, except for today. Today being Sunday. Roosters crowed rudely, unperturbed by the church bells.

A few more girls are outside the cattle sheds collecting grass to feed their goats. Jane and Mrs Squires and a group of

Englishwomen are playing shuttlecock on the asphalt square. The boy's shadow is thrown behind mine as we walk past a few men in singlets. They sit languidly on sacks, a chess-board resting on a crate between them. They keep their gaze fixed on the board, except for when they are not considering turns. Then, as if the harbour holds the key to their next move, they watch the flotilla. Rowboats come and go, carrying cargo, mail and supplies for the sick.

We enter a long corridor that leads to the terrace. A sign hanging from a wooden door reads VIETATO L'INGRESSO. It is heavy to push open, but I manage. We have been warned there are penalties for breaking the restrictions and curfews.

The best way to describe the room is that it's like entering a disfigured cathedral: cracks in the partition wall, the stone-work discoloured and in disrepair. From one side a grassy slope leads to the enclosed courtyard, railed off, and beyond to an assortment of buildings and stairwells. From the corner side peeling archways afford a breathtaking view of the sea.

At first, it was easy to lose my bearings in this rusting, sea-washed labyrinth which until recently has served as a naval hospital. It has also been the chambers-in-exile for notable dignitaries. There is a storehouse, the stanza profumo, where all incoming letters are destined to be smoked with vinegar, the envelopes slit open. We are told there is a small chapel and a cemetery. Swallows nesting in the eaves have left their droppings. Their cries are echoed in the harbour as they make passage. Fringed clouds hug the sky, stencilled by the golden light, and the waves surround us, lapping and crashing against the soft stone of this long atrium.

The boy polishes an apple against the cotton shirt he is wearing under his braces and with a shy movement he offers it to me. I catch his nervous brown eyes. They sparkle, without a trace of sadness or fear, as if they are acquainted with strange apparitions. When things go missing here, they say it is the work of poltergeists. These buildings are haunted by the ghosts of those who have died and are forgotten, buried in the sea or shot by the quarantine guards, those whose names are etched into the soft stone.

The boy runs away. He disappears behind a buttressed wall.

I twist the stem of the apple and bite into it, hungry for the sweet, juicy flesh. We have not eaten much fruit in the last week; the food is very poor. We are given bread, cheese pastries, oversalted stews served like porridge. My teeth tingle as I chew the crisp apple and my mouth pools with saliva. It runs, dribbling from the lower lip. I wipe it off with the side of my hand.

'E buono?' the boy asks, smiling. Has he been hiding in the lemon tree? He appears between one of the arches with a mischievous look, his hair teased by the wind. I notice for the first time his thick eyelashes.

'Bene, grazie,' I say, but then he disappears again.

He plays this game with me, appearing fleetingly then disappearing between the archways on the garden side of the terrace. The lustre of sunlight and the wonder of his laughter ease my feelings of indignation at being kept here. I, who am broken and almost childless. Have I forgotten what it is to be a mother? So soon, with so little remorse?

Bells are chiming from the Valletta side of the harbour, from a chapel where a Catholic mass is being held. There is a fine dust in the humid air and the sweet, sickly smell of the baked earth rises from the ground. The boy returns. He squats on a slab of stone, his elbows on his knees, his face cupped in his hands, the way Joseph liked to squat. Once, when he was tired of walking with me after shopping at Cuthbertson's shoe shop, he squatted just like that until I bought him macaroons from the bazaar. As the boy watches me, that memory returns.

I begin to curve my body into one of the alcove windows. It feels like I am floating in the turquoise sea, luminous and rhythmic, lapping at the soft, rusting stone walls. It seems like a lifetime has passed since I took up the pen to write. Strange how we devote a lifetime in dreaming and in waiting for what is often beyond our reach. England is not so far. I believe this journey will end, the way that when a woman conceives there is such a stretch of time and patience that the pregnancy feels infinite, even though birth is inevitable. One way or another, dead or alive, the birth is destined to happen.

I steady the nib of my fountain pen and write: 'I have been waiting so long for this separation to end when it seems now to have been a rather futile wish. The sea teaches us nothing that is permanent, not distance nor landfall. Nothing. Only death and love.'

Lazzaretto

L'Isolotto, Malta

19 May 1924

Yesterday, when Mr Carmichael fetched me from one of the alcove windows, I had fallen asleep. Quite alone. Sleepwalking, he said. I must not come back here! The terrace is off bounds and it was almost supper time.

I had been dreaming of the strange boy who offered me fruit, to whom I want to remain indebted. There is no trace of him now, though his laughter rings in my mind and I expect he is fossicking in crannies along the cove for sea urchins. In matters of the heart, Mr Carmichael has been a delightful and loyal companion. He understands my grief, how deeply it courses. It is as deep as history, I wanted to tell him, though perhaps there is no need. These days there is a sickly aura about me, as if I am not here, where I should be; as if I am blind and deaf to things in the real world that, for all their vibrant detail, for all their smells, their colours and their tastes, seem to deceive. I am beginning to understand that I am slowly unravelling. Everything that I had ever known before this journey was merely the torn remnants of a dream.

The sunsets here are singed golden, as if for the inmates' benefit, and the fine dust of the Sahara lingers in the air. There has been little rain in recent weeks. Mr Carmichael obtained special permission to take me out on our third afternoon. We tramped across the arid scarp of the garrigue, where the scent of wild fennel and thyme carried by the breeze is truly intoxicating. It is something I will not forget about the Mediterranean when we leave this captivity, I told Mr Carmichael. He said that he expects that our departure will not be long as the ship and its cargoes have been cleared of disease, the taxes paid. I must write all this down. I told him I once believed that writing repels death, but now I understand that life is preyed upon by other kinds of instruments and contagions. Then he turned askance, a little wistful, and I followed him back to the old convent for supper. Without the boy, this time.

I have not the least desire for his courtship. Mr Carmichael is a dear soul. Very kind. He asks nothing of me, though he is attentive to my condition. When I became sick, he had the doctor called. He checks on what I eat, and he enquires after Radhika. Yet I am reminded that he knows only of me and my dead daughter. He has never met my son, Joseph, nor my cousin, Nora. He has not danced with me at the gymkhana nor seen me dressed in a white tasselled gown, nor did he partner me at the Anglo-Indian Charity Ball in Ballygunge – memories I cherish. Nor has he given me E.M. Forster or Dostoevsky to read. And I remember Christmas in Calcutta – how Joseph loved the train set Peter bought him. Bless him.

The letter he sent to the poste restante in Aden has infected me. It reads as a lover's caution, every dry anguish crumbling, sinking into the very marrow of my bones, for it is true that a sea voyage may be the occasion for two people to fall in love. Islands are somehow intended for reflection. On this island there are many lizards. Small dragons with bearded skin that is green and yellow, a mottle that changes colour but only on the outside. They are a species of chameleon. A clever device of nature to change the skin according to stress and heat. There are one or two who live in the trees by the well, and I have seen a shy chameleon scamper off, hissing, when they were found in the dormitory.

I must have memorised his letter. I remember going over his words after we left the port and entered the Bab el-Mandeb Strait. This juncture connecting the Gulf of Aden and the Red Sea was so narrow, and the water so shallow, that many vessels have been wrecked on its reefs, but all was misty, and we could not see beyond the outline of the coast of Somalia, Eritrea on the west, and Yemen to the east. I remember thinking that love was like that, invisible and treacherous.

By the time we arrived at Port Suez there were seven more cases of cholera on board and we were forced to stay in an overcrowded, stinking and humid station, everything covered in dust and the sun setting over the Red Sea.

From there on, it was a slow queue with several other steamers – French and Portuguese and Italian – through Suez, with its mosque, to Port Said and thence to the wide, busy handsome ports of Cairo and Alexandria, where we were anchored off the Viceroy's palace. It was here that the Earl and Duchess of Guildford boarded, arriving on a luxurious barge furnished in damask and with generous awnings. They were greeted with a fanfare and hosted in the VIP suite, after which time we rarely glimpsed them. We think they were chaperoned to and from the lazzaretto, having been granted exemption on the same day that we were confined. The sea's barriers and gates can be navigated freely for their kind.

For the rest of us how slowly a week passes in such a remote place of ennui. No one to complain to except the local staff, whose powerless apathy has been somehow contagious and placatory. The irritability of all my setbacks and anxieties has settled into a melancholy, like a deep current that could not be resisted in which many thoughts and remembrances drowned. I do not think of my parents. I forget scenes that only a week before had intrigued me, like the vast arid plains of the Sinai Desert. I forgot that Mr Carmichael had pointed out to me the Italian naval vessels heading for Somaliland, the presence of their artillery and their flags hardly competing with ours. These were things that I wanted to write about in my diary and remember to tell you, but our thoughts and memories, like our deeds, rarely progress in straight lines. One can map the journey from Calcutta to London in sections, but to travel the distance it feels more like convergences. Too sad and strange to ponder how circumstances have changed my course; how sudden and annihilating loss can be. I had expected to be a mother of two boarding the steamer from Port Said to Tilbury, but fate has permanently altered my world. Charlotte lies deep at sea; Joseph may never forgive me.

At supper, we are twenty-five or thirty at a table, serving ourselves the weak watery broth and jostling for the best bread, wine, salt and pepper. There are salt pans on the islands but what we have on our tables sets like adhesive. We expect a dispatch from our captain anytime, with good news. We have been given the all clear and will be leaving the island any day soon, rowed out to our ship in the small boats that conveyed us here, and not without much confusion, I expect, over cargoes and monies. The announcement may come this evening that we are to pack our belongings in scarves, cases and carpetbags and be ready. I wonder how the weather will be when at last I arrive in England with Radhika. I pray for good weather to steer our passage.

Gravesend

26 May 1924

My dear Nora,

I am writing from England. We arrived at the Tilbury docks yesterday after being quarantined for ten days in the Mediterranean. I had sent a telegram to Peter, but he may not have received it. I looked for him among the crowd but he was not there to meet us. You cannot imagine my disappointment. For weeks at sea and before, I had prepared for this moment of reuniting with him. The journey has been exhausting and I am wretched, though life does not pause for consolation. The clocks continue to chime, and it seems not a single beat goes amiss. Every day seems to me like an entire life.

When our steamer docked, spouses and relatives came, but they do not have coolies here. From what I observe the workers have a different attitude, I would say, though I am not complaining. Even without Peter, I felt my heart skip. It was a thrill to behold the jetty, the liners and steamers with funnels and masts and the docksides; the sight of church spires, public halls, sunlight on the oil-slicked Thames as we crossed with hundreds of arrivals on the ferry. Quite a different scene from the muddy brown Hooghly with its wooden barges, Tilbury's docks are lined with warehouses, inns, pontoons and platforms, a belt of industrial water, the colour of lead. West of the Thames docks, I am told, there are parklands, deer parks and castles, and rowing is a popular sport. Gravesend has its ordinary charms. There is a first-rate bazaar with a fishmonger, a fruit vendor and live poultry, and on the corner of one of its cobbled lanes today a man is selling violets and cornflowers. It was nothing like the thick ropes of marigolds and sunflowers one sees in Mullick Ghat. The houses are rather dull, without variety, though spared of the overcrowding, the sheer chaos, we are accustomed to in Calcutta. Radhika is very thin and quiet. When we arrived, she felt the chill in the air lifting off the murky river, so I gave her my shawl. I suppose she misses her family. It is thoughtless of me, but in my distress I have not thought to ask if she would like to write to them. She can barely sign her name and I doubt that her parents can read. I must take care of her.

The first officer, Mr Carmichael, knew of a reputable inn at Gravesend where we are now staying. It has a crest above the doorway, its front wall overgrown with ivy. The room is dry but cold at night. I had to ask for an extra blanket. A scrawny ginger cat has been crying outside our door, and when I opened it the mangy creature ventured inside and seems to have made himself comfortable on my quilt.

This morning Mr Carmichael accompanied me to the exchange, so I could telephone Peter. I left a message for him at his hotel with my address. Perhaps it was fatigue or perhaps I felt nervous, but I didn't mind not speaking to him. There was a pang, too, of guilt and insecurity at not telling Mr Carmichael the whole truth. I have not forgotten that our teachers encouraged us to love the truth and certainly it is not in my nature to lie. But what if people in society are already suspicious simply because of your appearance or your means? Any unusual or untoward circumstance in your life could be misinterpreted. I have learned this on our voyage, travelling without a husband. Better to say you are a widow, or that your husband is confined to an infirmary, than to leave a gap open for speculation. Besides, it is awkward to admit to a man who likes to serve you that somebody else is waiting to provide. Men are tender creatures, to be handled carefully when they are falling in love. Mr Carmichael invited us to dine with him this evening. He is staying in Essex for a few days on business. I do believe he would help me get on here.

It is a dangerous condition to travel alone, unanchored. Though I believe that women should be at liberty to come and go as they please, it is never without consequence. We must sew our own wounds, dear Nora. I need some strong protection from Durga nowadays. Do you remember that afternoon we ventured out to Jagannath Ghat to pray with the Hindus?

That driver purposefully took us the longer way. I sometimes pray to Christ, but Durga and Shiva are powerful enablers to our lives. Does this make me an heretic? Remember in the third grade, when we took our Holy Communion in those white frocks? I was always a little cynical about the church ways and that hurt Ma. I remember once cornering Father Paul and pouring forth all my doubts about the Resurrection. I put it to him that the East India Company had seized our land and squeezed most of our people into railway towns that, for all their charms, lay on the fringes of the sacred maps. I told him it was the missionaries who took from us a certain pride and confidence in our actions which now are conditioned by guilt or judged by the laws of God.

Travel has opened my eyes to the wonders and oddities in strange, distant lands and I have seen humankind in all its complexity, its weaknesses and its unexpected bursts of courage. Twice a week on the steamer there were dances and bands playing with quite some romancing and conviviality. It was sad to break up with fellow passengers. Such a range of individuals I would never have encountered in my former domestic life: widows, retirees, news reporters, judges, administrators, bankers. Does it sound very defiant for me to say I do not regret the journey? And yet, I do. But one cannot alter destiny. I have missed a few people dreadfully, Joseph and you especially. Now, my dead daughter haunts me. I have seen her ghost appear at the foot of my bed. Her hair is braided with a few loose strands falling awry. She is thin-limbed and has a young sweet face as I remember. This type of ghost is not disturbing. She holds out her hands for me to carry her; she sits on my knees and turns her mouth to my dry breast as if to feed. I have felt no panic, not even the first time she appeared.

Pray for me, Nora. I must take care of Radhika; she is my responsibility now. I will write again soon, when we are more settled here in this grey, pigeon-infested city.

Love,
Daisy

Taviton Street

14 August 2017

Days when I forget everything: my mother, the assault, the violence of loss that turns my body to panic. I wake to the smell of soil freshly turned and a hole in the ground. By mid-morning I am often in tears, needing to lie down. I feel the little bones and facet joints in my neck creak. Living on fruit, tea, sandwiches, dhal and rice, I endure the hunger and the cold of this city. I lose track of things, messages, undulating moods that are difficult to ride and impossible to record, EFTPOS withdrawals from my dwindling bank balance. I keep my receipts in a small untidy pile. A strange feeling overcomes me when I catch sight of the photograph of my mother on a table in the room where I write. I can't accept this beguiling artefact, how partial the image seems. Look closely. The nose is a little flared; there are floating grey hairs and puckered skin. And yet her smile radiates from the frame. Her smile induces a pain that is numbed, recognised as the grief I take with me each day before I leave the flat.

Harrowing scenes of racial violence in Charlottesville are replayed in the news. It is sickening and distressing the way Trump responds to endorse the white supremacists. People of colour, and white allies are quick to demonstrate their dissent, demanding a final solution, a change to structural racism as #BlackLivesMatter rallies are organised and staged around the world.

Alarming also is climate emergency. Along with infrastructure in the Himalayan belt it's caused erratic flooding in Nepal and Bangladesh, leaving a million refugees hungry and homeless. It is the women and children from partitioned territories who are dying, abused, disenfranchised, buried under layers of fake news, vested interest media. Are we numbed into social passivity by popular trends? Do the media barons induce our complicity with regressive politics? Things get easily conflated and polarised. Minorities lose. Somehow, the truth makes headway, tangentially, in remote or parallel worlds, where it is freed from social norms, or by the flotation of tandem facts. Each truth is a difficult battleground. Yet truth as a spectrum is born of our collective subconscious.

A hopeful thought. I need to trust my detours and digressions to write Daisy's story, to fill in the sketches. I tell myself: at least here is a beginning. In selecting details, in texturing language something else is sacrificed. Gradually, a writer has to die a certain death, for what kind of person dwells in infinite possibility?

Everyday gestures, interruptions, painstaking uncertainties, sentence by sentence, the prose will find its measure while the keys tap away, a cursor marking, backspacing, pausing, cutting, pasting. On and on it goes until a paragraph is written and then another, the subject being tackled at different moments, unevenly over time spent, cast with ambition, complexity, during sobriety or when partly drunk, from various angles, and vantages. Like wind gusting through Gordon Square. Or like waves breaking, nearest to the shore while at the same time from a farther current, the sea sucks and swirls in pools of rocks, each break overlapping the last, till the ocean's ink becomes a hammer, striking, smashing, throbbing against the sand, and a wave drumming upon the ear's membrane, against the page: this is how writing happens. Our dreams and desires are made visceral, sinuous in writing.

So it is with grief – being harder to talk about, one talks around it. Having lost my mother, I am failing appallingly in my duties of motherhood. Partly to blame is technology and social media, depleting my authority as a parent, it made me vulnerable to narcissisms of my own making. This started when Sam got an iPhone and wouldn't let me view his Instagram account. As he withdrew, I fell gradually under Luke's masculine influence, drawn towards his shining orbit. There was a magnetism that connected us, a chivalry that was safe because Luke was unavailable.

I try to ring Sam every day. The phone rings five or six times and I feel the excitement, the anticipation. It is like having an affair. A Do Not Disturb setting, the recorded voice saying *the person you are trying to contact is not available.* No voicemail. I haven't been blocked but am fully aware that I could be. The time difference is unlikely to be the only reason. I send him texts. Vodafone does not always deliver them. I use my Skype account. Still no answer. I sent him an email eventually and after a week he replies. A single sentence to say he is well and has been busy. He is living with his father, Doug, who has bought him a motorbike, a ProBook, a workstation and a 4K Blu-ray player. When it comes to our son's welfare and education there has never been a dialogue, and it worries me. Consistently oppositional parenting. Payback for my unconventional life as a writer. It makes it hard when you are trying to do your best.

Treading water.

The bonds between parent and child are fragile and delicate and the ensuing silences can last for months and be suffocating. My travelling has made it worse. If I let myself focus on this, I'll end up fretting, and yet still time funnels away, escaping me like the story, or I escape into the idea of the story. The story becomes me. And it is like swimming out to sea in flippers, carried by strong currents that chop and change, wave after wave, swallowing salt.

Drowning.

There's a ten-hour difference between London and Sydney.

Drowning.

Between border checks, airports, quarantine stations, every journey becomes a different configuring of time.

Yesterday, at sundown, I thought I saw time curling like the wind through Russell Square. There was my father, wearing a woollen scarf, chasing me around the fountain, the squirrels darting away in the sober light. There was the metronome ticking rhythmically on the piano as I practised my scales. Time stretched. I keep myself immersed with correspondences from the literary community in Australia and emails for the workshop I'm teaching in Islington. I have a seminar to prepare with BAME writers on Politics and Writing at London University, and, not counting the odd cancellation, a short story prize to co-judge and a slow trickle of invitations to launches and readings. I print emails and enter dates into my tablet. With a single click my hesitations and my uncertainties can be indulged by taking sides on social media forums.

Still, the habitual worry gnaws away. What are the power dynamics in a mixed-racial romance? How does it feel to be a Eurasian woman in London? Does Clarissa find Daisy charming because she is coloured? Does Peter encourage her merely to make himself feel superior?

Sitting at my desk I turn my damp socks on the radiator. I gaze at the sky, watching pigeons fluttering and brooding in the attics house. Designed in the style of a manor it is now leased as prestige office space. The sky is absorbing in its swirls; I watch the motion of a crane carrying slabs of concrete. Wondering what has brought me here when my son is in high school?

Berndt emails to tell me he'll be in London later this year and could we catch up. What about his girlfriend? I don't like to ask, but I don't expect she has entirely vanished. No prizes for guessing there's a smart, sassy woman behind the most impressive, formidable post-Marxist, post-humanist existentialist thinker! A woman who is in the background in Berlin, who provides him with domestic stability while he squanders his energies into research risk and philosophy thrills and peer-reveiwed publications. I never really knew for sure if they were in a relationship because he didn't say, and now he doesn't mention. It suits him to be ambiguous, to have me guessing. So why meet him, here in London? I haven't forgotten his habit of changing his mind. The affair with him almost broke me. At least I had not observed him behaving weirdly. He doesn't make odd, involuntary movements or have sadistic tics. Not like Peter Walsh, pulling out his pocket-knife and thrusting it around at inopportune moments.

Mrs Dalloway is really a novel about moments accruing, which makes it rather marvellous. The little girl in pink who pops into Clarissa's mind could have been the same Elise Mitchell collecting pebbles for the mantelpiece; the girl who runs from her nanny into a lady's legs and makes Peter laugh. But such larks, coincidences and correspondences do not seem to happen for Daisy. She cuts a lonely figure in the novel. We are never privy to her home life, which makes her vulnerable to a suitor. But, thankfully, I am not like Daisy. Safely independent and remote from Berlin, I definitely don't want to be the other woman in Berndt's life!

33 Tavistock Square

6 September 2017

I no longer keep a blog, instead saving little notes to self as they come up on my phone. It occurs to me that I exist somewhere between these jottings, my Twitter account, my selfies, my social media posts and messages, revealing to my self and to others who I am.

The new chapter is proving difficult and I am struggling with Peter's voice. Paragraphs stare back at me when I pick the page. A stick of incense burns, the smoke streaming into the window before it ribbons, circling over my laptop screen, thinly, breaking and suffusing the room.

When students ask me about writer's block, I tell them you have to expect to be derailed. In theory having space away from a manuscript is a beneficial thing. With all the distractions of daily life and the occasional meetings, I have drifted, muddled a way through grief, through flurry, and London traffic. On Twitter, someone wins a lucrative prize, someone is pregnant, a politician is shamed, a celebrity is scandalised.

I walk to the grocery store, while scaffolding Daisy's voice in my head. (Daisy, here in London!) I need ingredients for a vegetable soup: leeks, potatoes, stock, mung lentils, bay leaves. I cook it on low heat and use half a cube of stock and a sprinkle of dry oregano. Lucille sent me the recipe. Her messages arouse me, which is not a bad thing when I am feeling glum. Something else cautions me today. Texting can be thoughtless. A sentence or a paragraph can be a writer's demise. One can never be too careful with words, or with their mood, especially when it concerns a lover. It is rare for a lover to interpret a message correctly.

Reading about Woolf's suicide note I discover that members of the British press used it to cast judgement on her. Without fact checking, they presented her suicide, in 1941, as cowardly and unpatriotic. The critics were not always kind to her, either. It makes me appreciate that there will always be media spin. All these notes about Woolf I share with Lucille; despite her age there is an understanding and a chemistry concerning us and our texting is intimate. Strange, because in real life, I hardly know her. But does it matter? And does this feeling for Lucille have anything to do with Woolf's sexuality? I read the diary entries from 1920–1924, during which time she was writing *Mrs Dalloway*.

On 3 November 1923, she wrote: 'It took me a year's groping to discover what I call my tunnelling process, by which I tell the past by instalments, as I have need of it.' Woolf's characters dialogue and interact through the mind; the erotics of her writing, its vivid layering of ideas, political and feminist intensities surface in language. They fuck in the struggle to find form. So, she dared to break with prudish boundaries, and she took risks causing self-torment.

I think about her writerly despair. After rain and floods in Rodmell on 6 January 1925 she writes:

My heroism was purely literary. I revised Mrs D: the dullest part of the whole business of writing; the most depressing & exacting. The worst part is at the beginning (as usual) where the aeroplane has it all to itself for some pages, & it wears thin.

That she went on to finish somehow gives me hope.

The hours, the weeks pass, and I'm not sure what I've been doing. One of my recurring qualms concerns ethics. What is the right form for each piece of writing? Should I start with these exercises? Am I with Virginia Woolf or am I against her? Her repertoire of choices cast from privilege is bound to exceed mine, and yet I think I am more on her side. It is, ultimately, not who I am but what I do as a writer that matters. True, she stands for the establishment, she is the darling, the doyen of British feminism, yet she is also a site of experimentation and cultural questioning, subverting the idea of what self is, the gender binary and the patriarchy. Her famously photographed profile taken by the artist George

Charles Beresford in 1902, does very well selling postcards for the National Portrait Gallery.

How else does India feature in her world? By filamentary and filial connections to an imperial past. Beresford had been employed as a civil engineer in India and returned to England after he contracted malaria to study art. Virginia's mother was born in India; her aunt, the photographer Margaret Cameron, too. There was a whole cast of extras who served in the British East India Company. Her great-great-grandfather, Chevalier Pierre Ambrose Antoine de L'Etang, a French aristocrat who loved Marie Antoinette had fled the guillotine to become a horse trainer in Pondicherry. Did Virginia travel to India, or the Far East? Her husband, Leonard, had spent seven years in Ceylon.

She was perhaps one of the first to attempt the novel–essay. In *A Room of One's Own* she invents Shakespeare's sister as a character to argue a place in fiction for women. Like Virginia I'm not blindfolded by the trick of narrative. Maybe it has to do with its emphasis on symmetry being predictable in some way, how it suppresses the malleable nature of experience we encounter in our lives. Colonialism is part of our history, a fact that cannot be altered. But is it right to assume that a story alone can liberate Daisy of race and gender? Without an argument, without a history, Daisy's story is exotic, or historical fiction. Or it might be a fable.

I want Daisy's voice to convey the randomness of her thoughts, her intentions, instincts, emotions, the chaos and serendipities of her selves. A part of Daisy Simmons lives in Calcutta while another Daisy walks the streets of Madras and post-war London in a way that Clarissa Dalloway cannot appreciate. The emergencies and transitions in my own life, through which voice has been a running thread, speak a story that refuses to be contained by a beginning, a middle and an end . . . Africa, England, India, Australia. Fragments of the past are channelled into the present, like wind doing its work, sculpting the world shapelessly.

33 Tavistock Square

3 October 2017

Mornings are a time I tend to observe the weather, leaves rustling in the wind like a swell. During working hours, the noise of trucks, brakes and machinery can be a distracting sound garden. I watch women pushing prams, I hear couples playing tennis, the laughter of children. These everyday sounds fill the lapses in writing. Heels click on the footpath, the ambulance sirens. A particular noise catches my attention. It is the almost obsessive undulation of suitcase wheels over pavements, kerbs, tarmac, and over drains as students arrive – some for the first time and others returned from trips back home to Asia or to the Caribbean – a sound of passage, of transit, loud at first then fading, leaving me to imagine its destination. Rarely is our destiny anticipated. We could slide into the calm mouth of a deep, black river, like an otter, and be sucked down into its currents. Suppose we meet our hallucinatory fate by falling through a shattered window of the mind, veterans of war like Septimus Warren Smith? Or tunnelling back to Calcutta, we could be on the very balcony of the Writers' Building on Dalhousie Square where, in 1930, the Inspector General of Prisons, N.S. Simpson, was shot dead.

The suitcase rumble never really stops. This endless traffic of bodies moving perturbs me on returning to Bloomsbury. Yesterday, I ventured outside into the chill, overcast evening. It had been raining. The lit pavement was shiny and slippery, and I noticed how beautiful the old drains are in this borough. Walking in the direction of Holborn, I passed a family carrying their luggage: small children with what seemed to be all their personal belongings in suitcases, parents with backpacks, large canvas bags, a basketball, even a yoga mat. They had disembarked from the Tube at Russell Square or maybe they were making their way to St Pancras. I felt glad that my own suitcases and possessions have been stored away. One suitcase is under my bed with the foldaway ironing board, the other on the top of the closet. I have unpacked both now, though not immediately after arriving in London since living out of a suitcase is appealing. Not sure how I'll manage to squeeze in the extra books I have bought, the dresses and a woollen coat.

Berndt has arrived, and today, we are meeting for coffee. I tell him it has been a strange month. We are lucky to find a table in the bookshop café, which has already started to fill with students and intellectual types. Outside there's a drizzle.

Unexpected, refreshing, as the gardens have been dry. We plan to spend the day together. Already we have taken a turn in the British Museum, getting through two halls of Egyptian exhibits. Berndt is more intrigued by the Assyrian depictions of battlefields and date palms. Still, it's hard for me not to be awed by those gargantuan gods, their vessels and sarcophagi, their hieroglyphics.

Berndt asks about my novel, so I tell him about the main character.

'Daisy Simmons – do you remember her as a subplot, a series of sketches in *Mrs Dalloway?*'

'No. Hang on . . . wasn't she the free-spirited beauty with French blood who arranges flowers and talks philosophy?'

'Oh, you mean Sally Seton. There's definitely a suggestion of female seduction, a cool excitement and the catastrophe of marriage – all repressed, of course.'

He wants me to refresh him; the dark-eyed woman with two children who is married to a major in the Indian army. She isn't anything like me, at least not how I have become, a little abstract, a little brittle. And perhaps, I am less prone to romantic folly than Daisy.

'Am I playing a dangerous game, turning myself into Daisy, through the narrator? Clearly, she needs a life of her own. It's a bastard really; a subtle bastard of a thing that fiction does to your life!'

He sips his tea and bites his lip.

'But it's more interesting, more vivid for you to write as Daisy, precisely because she isn't you, so your angle is different. You are adding something new.'

He affirms the choice I have made to write in the first person. It surprises me that he is drinking tea but since giving up cigarettes he has quit drinking coffee altogether. I notice that he looks younger than the last time we met. His hair isn't receding quite as much. He appears to have gained weight, which suits his lanky frame. I notice that he isn't checking his mobile phone.

We pay and leave the café. Berndt goes downstairs to use the bathroom in the basement of the shop. I stay to browse the books then decide to use the bathroom myself. There is only one cubicle. I wait my turn in the narrow hallway. Berndt's eyes burn rapaciously when he passes me.

'Would you like to walk to the canal?' I ask, when we leave.

The towpath provides a tranquil diversion from the shabby atmosphere of Bloomsbury. Besides, I can't invite him back to my flat. The idea of Berndt entering the space where I've spent so many hours alone, frittering away the hours at my desk feeling all at sea, is quite appealing. Anjali, the Nigerian housekeeper, will be cleaning the building most of the morning, changing towels, mats and toiletries in the second- and third-floor bathrooms. I've bumped into her in the stairwell a few times and we've ended up talking. She has told me about her children and their father, who drives a bus, and how she lived in Berlin before she came to London. Berndt appears hesitant but doesn't reject my suggestion.

As we make our way along Gray's Inn Road the rain gets heavier and the traffic more congested. People are walking in the opposite direction to us, many carrying overnight suitcases. The crowd here seems rougher than the Russell Square set. A group of boys bump into us as we walk under Berndt's umbrella. I tried not to worry about the rain but forget how much the Germans hate it. Regardless of the weather and his inscrutable moods, a suppressed panic compels me to stick to the plan I've devised. Berndt's politeness means I need to play host and make decisions. It didn't occur to me that he might want to reach the obvious and unavoidable conclusion of intimacy at a much faster speed than I anticipated.

The link to the journal I am trying to open isn't working. I have boiled the jug and poured tea for myself, cold water for Berndt, who is sitting in a chair. He grabs my arm. Now I'm sitting on his lap and we're kissing. I am so much smaller than him. I can feel the bulge in his jeans and it excites and terrifies me.

I wonder if he's carrying a virus or if he's been sleeping around. In the restaurant he'd said he hadn't slept with a woman since Lorna. A condom slips out of his pocket. I'm uncertain if I can do this. I know it will hurt because I am tense. When he touches me I want to cry. I hold him close, my head on his shoulder as he fondles my thighs, my curves. I guess he may have read my blog where I've written about the dissociation of the body one experiences as a writer going deeper and deeper into the text.

'I don't think I can, it's been too long,' I say as Berndt leads me to the bed, undresses me, but it doesn't stop. I'm not assertive enough. My body, his body have conflicted minds of their own. It feels tender, raw. It hurts like I knew it would and I am worried that my body is tensing again. I'm worried that I'm too old to relax. That my cunt juices don't flow anymore.

When he goes down on me I feel nothing. But it isn't unbearable and at least I am letting him do it. For a few weeks I haven't been eating well. I have lost the extra weight I'd been carrying so I should feel like making out.

'We should have used a condom,' he says.

'I don't like them,' I say.

'Nobody likes condoms,' he replies.

Afterwards I cry a little. Berndt is lying on his side, the weight of his legs over mine. He is stroking and kissing me.

'Maybe we should get married. Then you can live in London and we can live in Australia,' he quips.

'Yes, if it were that easy. I mean with Brexit. They have to accept me first.'

We talk a little. How did I become like this? When my husband touched me I would flinch and he would tremble and pour sweat all over me. We only ever did it the missionary way and I couldn't wait for it to finish. I never had an orgasm with him. Not once. Or maybe once, if I thought of someone else, something else. Afterwards I used to get out of bed and piss and watch the stringy, watery secretion leak out of me. I would squeeze it out and wish it would stop. I started to think I would never enjoy sex again.

Berndt tells me he is easily turned off these days. He has tried a few online dating services, but most people are crazy or dysfunctional. One woman brought a suitcase to the first date and wanted to move in with him. Another woman was a heavy drinker and they drank two bottles of wine on the first date. He has tried to apply for a job as a lecturer a few times now and quite given up. He is teaching fine arts in a technical college. When we met – at a conference in Auckland – he was surrounded by nubile young arts students. It was easy to date. He tells me he goes to dance clubs and parties, but he doesn't have many friends. I know better than to believe everything he says.

We shower, separately, then dress and catch the Tube to Waterloo. He is stroking me as we stand together holding the rail in the stuffy, crowded carriage and I think I could die. He has bought us tickets for a play at The Shed, but by the time we get there we are five minutes late. It doesn't surprise me that the usher won't permit us to enter but Berndt is pissed. In Berlin, he tells me, we could bribe our way in, but the English are so proper about things such as punctuality.

The usher takes us up a flight of stairs to watch the first act on screen. I ask Berndt if he's tried to have his play about the Hamburg Riots performed. It was too complex, he says briefly, then changes the subject to my own work, to Daisy. 'So, what happens to her? Do you take the story to London?' he asks.

'Not yet. It's hard to find time to write. The teaching is sporadic, but it takes so much preparation, and then there's marking. I'm hoping to get a grant or something, a top-up. London's not cheap. I did apply for a permanent position. Didn't even get an interview. Now I've used up my referees.'

'Yep, I know how it is. You should think about living in Berlin. London is so expensive. I guess there are other drawbacks.'

I don't say anything about the incident in Hyde Park. I've normalised it, telling myself I was jet-lagged, exhausted; that's why I walked with the guy in the first place. It was shit, but it happens, I'm telling myself.

Instead, I speculate about how it might have been for Daisy when she finally arrives here to meet up with Peter. Can she survive as a woman separated from her husband? It's curious how a brown woman's life vanishes into the shadows of *Mrs Dalloway* when she could have all the intensity of Tess Durbeyfield . . . Did she have the same desperate passions? Will her son die as a result? Will she destroy herself and be financially ruined? And what of Peter – what might eventuate? I don't know, but I'm disturbed . . .

'What else have you been researching, Mina?' he asks.

'Oh, exciting history like the shipping routes from India to Britain in 1924. The history of opium traded with China and spices and the violence and racial hatred that was used to suppress the Bengalis.'

'Yes, that was kept hushed up. But why China?'

'Good question. It sounds odd, I know, but there was a vase that I saw in the entrance hall to Charleston.'

'Ah, the Bloomsbury connection? Is that where Vanessa Bell lived with an artist?'

'Right . . . yes, with Duncan Grant. She lived with him in a bisexual relationship. In a farmhouse in Sussex. I took the tour, with a woman I met in Lewes. It was spring, and the gardens were ablaze with colour and form; and all the furnishings, walls, covers all hand painted. It is quite something . . . Quite an alternative life they led. Their daughter never knew that Duncan was her father, and she ended up marrying Duncan's long-time boyfriend.'

'Well, that's kinky, or radical, depending on how you look at it, I suppose.'

'They were gender fluid. Not a bad thing! To have no boundaries between art and life . . . Imagine! But this vase from China had me curious. The guide said it was brought back from Wuhan by Julian Bell, Vanessa's son. He died not long afterwards apparently. Vanessa and he were especially close, and she grieved for him for the rest of her living days.

He had taught English literature at a university there in China, and had an affair with the dean's wife, Shuhua.

'Ah, so possibly a parallel, with your Eurasian character, Daisy Simmons and Peter Walsh? Could that work?'

'I love the tangle. It could be a thread for my novel . . . But this woman, Shuhua, they called her Sue, was already there, as a writer, I mean. She'd met Rabindranath Tagore when he travelled to China. I've been reading a biography about her, and letters . . . it was all a bit colonial and racist the way she was pigeon-holed. They did a number on her. Mind you, Hogarth Press published her memoir after Virginia Woolf died. But here's the point: she had to present herself as an accomplished Chinese gentlewoman in England to get published.'

'She had to be exotic. That's fascinating.'

He doesn't ask about Sam and how he is coping with my absence. He is staring into my eyes, but I know he doesn't really get it; he's not a parent.

Berndt goes to the bar. He buys us drinks now that intermission has started. We observe the other audience members: they seem relaxed, interesting without appearing pretentious.

This is what I like about London: such a diversity of stories. In the nearby college there is a Lithuanian economist who plays saxophone on Sunday nights; a black playwright from Camden; a Harvard-trained neurosurgeon who loves opera and is a health fanatic. Amazing people, really. I am going to miss them when I go back to Sydney.

On the way back it is raining torrentially. The pavements and driveways are flooded. Over the river there are fireworks to celebrate the anniversary of the National Theatre. I would like to stand for a while, watching them in the rain, but Berndt follows the crowd back to the Tube and I follow him. We are both thinking about the inevitable parting at Russell Square. He kisses me wistfully and I tell him which way to walk back to his hotel. Then I set off, hands in my coat. I take the long way at night along Gower Road past International House and Coram's Fields. I used to play here as a child. My kindergarten was across the road from Mecklenburg Square. Among the photographs in Mum's album there is one with my hair in a short bob reading books and colouring in. In another photograph I am standing beside Serena in a woollen skirt and stockings. Sheets of snow lay caked over the parked cars having fallen in the square, so that when I look at the photograph, I remember snow melting in my mittens and beneath my anorak, and the dampness against my chest. I remember crying from the cold, which was harsh after Nairobi's pleasant climate. My mother seemed happiest in Kenya. Ayah coddled me in the evenings because I was afraid of dust devils and thunderstorms. At bedtime in the evenings she sang in Swahili. I still remember a few words, my third tongue.

The rain is a drizzle now and there are puddles in the gutters. Two skip bins outside the flats are filled with rubbish from the refurbishments. The old facades are being pulled down as new money is injected into this place. The borough seems more affluent, more gentrified than when we were children. Often, I see students gathered smoking in the evenings outside Mecklenburg Square. Usually they are talking about money, but tonight there is only a couple making out in their car.

I want to tell Berndt that I love him, but I don't. I know I am simply a diversion to spice up his life. I don't even know why I agreed to see him. Unfinished business, I guess, or possibly desperation. But just in this moment, walking back to my flat alone in the shiny, flimsy rain, it feels life changing.

Westminster

30 May 1924

Peter, my dear,

How heavenly to see you in Bath. Hugh tells me that you have brought your fiancée from Calcutta. Please do call in as soon as you get back from the docks in Tilbury. Has the matter of her husband been sorted yet? Imagine. I've been talking to myself. Got back from playing bridge this morning, mending my dress, and said to myself, There he is . . . in love! And about to be married again! So, Peter is in love, after that hasty marriage aboard the ship on the way out, and after all that happened in Bourton that ghastly summer. You do remember? Well of course you do, I have only just been saying to myself. Not to go back to the past, you understand, that would be agony; but to see what it has made of us. And what exactly is that? What has it made of us?

Anyway, we absolutely must have your company at lunch on Friday with Lady Bruton and my aunt Helena. Both of you, of course. We're simply desperate to meet her and hear all about what is happening in India. Lady Bruton's been terribly concerned about the Armenian refugees; wants to write a letter to the editor of *The Times*. Well, you know how she likes to talk on matters of importance: immigration, the disintegration of Europe and so on. It's very distressing. I think Lady Bradshaw might be coming, too. They've taken on that poor Italian widow, Lucrezia Smith, whose husband jumped from a window a year ago and on the very day I happened to throw a party! Such poor timing, though I suppose it is a sign of the despair so many ex-servicemen have felt; all that horror of the trenches comes out in voices that can't be repressed but acts radically upon them. Well, she's been homesick apparently, but has been talked out of leaving London, what with all the skirmishes in Italy. Very kind of them indeed to offer her a position. Shall we expect you then?

Midday will do nicely.

Clarissa

Lincoln's Inn Hotel

London

16 June 1924

My dear Clarissa,

Thank heaven for all you've done! Presenting Daisy to Lady Bradshaw was a stroke of genius! She's been invited to stay at Cornwall Gardens tutoring the Bradshaws' children, Evie and Lachlan from the orphanage. This will ameliorate the situation immensely for it just wouldn't do to have her stay here. So very young. So very ripe and pretty. And with her it comes so easily . . . but it won't do – not until after the divorce. On that subject there's the matter of earning one's keep. I am keen to direct my energies to some commerce or scheme, if either you or Richard can hatch a plan. Rumours do fly! Not least about her divorce, I dare say – assuming that they can be managed. But I ask myself, does it matter? Do I care? For just to be sitting on the sofa with you yesterday with your scissors and silks, reading Pope or Shelley, or walking the promenade in Brighton with the smell of the incoming sea adrift, or enjoying the summer sunlight in Regent's Park, every instant of it seemingly as our lives intended, at the ripe age of fifty-seven! It all impresses me as being utterly pleasurable and complete. And perhaps now one has no need for another, though she is – and I'm glad you approve – a rare bird!

One never really gets over the first love, Clarissa. I often think that you sapped something from me permanently. No quarrels. No tears or confessions necessary. Nothing prudish or horrible or odd! Simply the essence of each moment releasing its joys and ecstasies, a sumptuous interlude that will always return to me, unfolding its wisdoms and pleasures like the scent of pink and yellow frangipani fallen on the pavements of Madras. Something to be taken hold of, observed and turned over in the mind for years to come.

Like a dead soul brought to life – such is the wonder of seeing you.

Peter

33 Tavistock Square

9 October 2017

Berndt took the train back to Berlin from the Eurostar terminal in St Pancras. 'I'd like to catch up when you live permanently here,' he said. His tone apportioned blame to my temporary status. Then he corrected himself, 'It's been lovely seeing you.' Romantically, I didn't want Berndt to leave, but the situation was impractical. When I got back to the flat there was an email and a photograph from Sam. He has grown tall, his hair thick and curly, tied back. It catches my breath how much I love him; his email is a reminder of my other life.

Daylight passes and darkness comes too quickly. Rain beats against the windowpanes like fingernails. The leaves are fusty in the square. I fret and fidget. My daily cleaning ritual involves sweeping loose hair, dandruff and paper dust from the carpet under my desk. The writing is slow because it is squeezed into routine, so I get maybe three sentences or a paragraph done. Dull pages stare oddly back at me from the screen. Serena has sent me an invitation to her wedding in Sydney, a plush event which I feel obliged to attend as there are so few left in our family; I like her partner, Mike. At a peer assessment for my sessional teaching, I am questioned on my 'wellbeing'. Two of my students are late in submitting their master's theses. I have missed a symposium at which I was meant to give a paper. Student emails are piling up unanswered and I have to force myself to mark their essays or read their manuscripts.

'I guess I may need to take leave,' I tell Brogan, the head of department responsible for recruiting staff.

They are talking in a very condescending way to me, as if to indicate that the faculty are not a charity, not designed to accommodate the burnout, anxieties, obsessions and praxis of a writer. For some reason, as they speak, I keep staring out of the semicircular windows, framed in red brick and stone dressings across Wyclif Street. Light and shadow play through the leaves of the beech trees. Bicycles are being parked and secured near the railings. A string of students walk from St John Street, where the bus to Moorgate stops. I feel exhausted; wanting to say something but mentioning nothing about the disconnected paragraphs and sketches that I have been slowly attempting to transition into a novel. Nothing about the swirling feelings of lesbian devotion, having been in relationships with men for most of my life, and how distracting that has been, how overwhelming. In a flash, I understand that this may simply be conflated with the desire for meaning that comes with writing, or the hunger for love that comes with grief. One of the panel, a tall, suited professor of literary theory, asks again why I have applied to take twelve months off, and I reply that it is hard to shift from one discipline to another. (I may have intended to say 'country'.)

What remains undisclosed is that I worry for my son and how this time away from him is damaging our bond. I am quite sure I haven't missed the security of my Sydney neighbourhood. If I am honest, I have enjoyed escaping from most of the rest of my family.

The professor turns away from me sternly. It seems we are speaking a different language. He doesn't understand the lame excuses I can barely comprehend myself. How to explain what is happening? This unravelling? A freelancer, feeling like a fraud and now a failure. Somehow, the breaking point has been my mother's death, and writing this novel.

Queen's Gate Mews

13 June 1924

Dear Mrs Smith,

A few of our friends are coming to afternoon tea on Friday next, and there will be a little singing and music. We have a new governess living with us now, all the way from Calcutta. I should so like for you to meet her. Perhaps you may be able to look in for half an hour? I should be very pleased to see you and Mrs Filmer.

I do hope you will both come along.

Sincerely,
Lady Bradshaw

Princes Bridge

27 October 2017

Nuptials and funerals. Coming home for Serena's wedding has felt distinctly relaxed compared to the last time my Australian passport was stamped on arrival. Still, after twelve months abroad Sydney seems a world away from London, or Calcutta. The sunlight is far too bright, but my little courtyard garden delights me with colourful spring blooms, the straggly daisies and obscenely pink azaleas. Nothing has happened to my house though the gutters are filled with leaves. The rooms seem small and cluttered. I notice the prayer flags that Susan has sent me. I unwrap them and tie them to trees.

Sam lets me visit. We drink tea and talk for a few hours. He appears relaxed; emotionally something has shifted. He is dressed in baggy pants, his hair swept back into a ponytail. We order pizza. He doesn't show me the assignments in his bedroom; what every mother is curious about, if only to glance. I miss that intimacy so much although it has been deteriorating for years. Our conversation is awkward because it lacks the familiarity of daily life, but it is also strong and natural in the invisible love bond between mother and son. I can't convince him to spend even a few nights with me. Some good news is that grants for conference travel to China and New York have been approved.

Emails keep pouring in. There is an event on memoir at the Wheeler Centre that seems interesting. I make a special trip to Melbourne. This is an excuse to see Lucille. After all the texting, I'm wondering if she'll be warm, or aloof.

My flight is delayed so I get to Tullamarine later than planned. She is waiting outside the National Gallery, reading a book, as the Uber driver pulls in. She just hugs me, withdrawing into herself and I sink into her. We amble through room after room for an hour, admiring the photographs and installations. I notice she is fidgety. Neither of us wants to say we are bored of seeing the paintings.

When we leave there is a brightness in her smile. Her voice is like cream I want to dip my finger into and lick. She is tentative, pressing strands of hair behind her ears, talking almost with terror about her ex. I feel like she is holding back, like she is unsure; she is too caught up in her head. Point taken. We are more than a little absurd with our gaps, our differences. So, I say we should get a drink and we find a pub. There are straight couples sitting at tables, but we sit at the bar. It is a little awkward. Just her and me. My hands are tender turning her mouth towards mine. My tongue remembers how to kiss even when her eyes are not closed. I go to the bathroom and coming back see her from across the room, sipping her drink, legs folded. There she is. Gorgeous. Fragile. What is the perfect vantage point, I wonder? A boudoir? A writing room? Nothing else and nobody else in the bar catches my attention. The waiter likes us and offers us a plate of olives. It gets to be conspicuous. We leave, and I can sense her mirth over the whole situation. *Lucille, Lucille,* how amazing the feeling of holding her hand, as we walk bumping shoulders and legs in the street.

On my lips I wanted Daisy. I wanted to write her exquisitely, as I had begun to before losing my mother, before the assault, before Berndt, or this clash of being racialised, or placating a writer from a different ethnic group, or that writing deadline. And maybe, because it is impossible to write Daisy, though it might be a phase, I am here with Lucille. We sit on the banks of the Yarra, near Princes Bridge, the bars and the rowing club at a comfortable distance. Dandelions, river birds, cyclists, skyscrapers. It is a perfect day, so warm that the sky could burst.

Wynne Avenue
Kharagpur

14 July 1924

Dear Daisy,

I cannot express how I felt on hearing your news from London. We have all been worried for your safety. Only this morning when I walked with Esther, Papa and Mama to the Church of Don Bosco they asked if I had heard from you. Rest assured, dear cousin, that I will keep your confidence. Bishop Lefroy gave a moving sermon on gambling. We prayed a novena to Our Lady, and dedicated prayers to St Francis to protect you through sickness and storm. I'm encouraged that you are coping, managing the burden of grief. (I am struggling to accept it, too. I pray for Charlotte's dear sweet, departed soul.) I haven't told the rest of the family. There's no need to cause any more grief to your parents, I agree. You should only tell them when you feel ready, and only then.

My hope is that Radhika is of some assistance, as I imagine that being in a different home and a European climate must pose hardships. I am glad, too, that you have a kind protector in Mr Carmichael. The sailors and pursers we meet, those who come from the coastal trade to the Anglo-Indian dances, are mostly fine, strong and good-looking men, so I do not doubt his positive attributes, even though the sea can be a hazardous environment for a lady, especially one of our ilk. Your Papa always spoke with a great respect for mariners. Do not be afraid to lean on him, Daisy, if necessity demands. Don't be fiercely independent. Allow him to arrange a carriage or a car. Let him write a bank draft. Perhaps he can help you to find rooms to stay, should you get stuck.

Life goes on here in much the same way. We have dances at the Bandstand on weekends, the hit parades, Radio Ceylon, Sunday school for the youngsters, Mondays and Fridays, badminton. Aunty Bea and Mama say that I am preparing the groundwork for marriage in sewing, cooking, overseeing the household chores, buying mutton, fish and vegetables from the bazaar. We are all very sensitive these days, even the AI girls who get drilled in the Methodist missionary schools. A date has been set for our wedding: the third week of September, after the rains. It is not for me to presume that the stars shall so favourably align as to bring you home across thousands of miles. God willing you will have returned by autumn as Mrs Walsh.

Remember the pledge we made to ourselves in the seventh grade? How protected our lives were in boarding school. What a gift it would be to have you back here as my bridesmaid with Violet and Catharine.

It sounds as if you are settled in the mews. Lady Bradshaw is blessed. I am sure there could be no better tutor for Evie and Lachlan. And tell me what news there is of your intriguing friend, Lucrezia. Very beautiful and inventive, she sounds. Tragic to have lost her young, brave husband to shell shock in a foreign country. She must be homesick for Italy. Is she missing her family? It's tremendous that she has consignments to make hats and a new apprentice to coach. I suppose it is good for a widow to have independent prospects. Will she have to relocate closer to the factory in Stockport? I hope you find comfort in one another's company. I know only of the hardships you describe through the children from the orphanage, and the poor and destitute of our parish. No state of mind that I've encountered compares to the distress you and Lucrezia have borne. Still, it strikes me that during times of tribulation in our lives the bonds of friendship and intimacy are tied. You are always in my prayers.

Your loving cousin,
Nora

Wuhan University

3 November 2017

Leaving the airport, the first thing that assaults me is the pungency of fuel in the dry air. We are tired and our bodies are stiff from the long journey. At the taxi stand there is no one in attendance so Meiling and Ching haggle with drivers for a car, but then we wait in line and I'm assuming that this is how the locals negotiate; talk with the drivers first, fix a price, then join the queue. Meiling's suitcase takes up half of the back seat. We squeeze in, Daniel sitting in the front seat because of his height. Indra, Wei and Zhuqin follow in a second taxi. Meiling is excited because this is her hometown and her parents are travelling from their city an hour to the north to spend a few days with her. She hasn't seen them for two years. They will stay in a nearby hotel.

A long low bridge carries us across the Yangtze River, cloaked in darkness. The traffic streams over flyovers in orderly lanes, passing stark grey facades and then approaching the ghostly, untenanted skyscrapers that loom above like a scene from some futurist dystopia. A vast and sprawling city is laid out before us like a bowl of blackness and light. The road slopes into an underpass funnelling back out into medium congestion. Traffic signs and neon-lit script in Mandarin dazzle and perplex my Western eyes. Approaching East Lake we pass plazas, food halls, cinemas and designer stores. Now the traffic crawls. The driver takes a right turn. To our left is the campus of Wuhan University, Meiling says.

The buildings are obscured, blurred in darkness, the silhouette of trees drawn on the night's canvas.

I'm aware of the pollution but I notice the absence of third-world slums such as I witnessed a few months ago driving from Dum Dum Airport towards Kolkata – the city of joy and love and heart-breaking poverty. My seven or eight kilograms in cabin luggage belies a cargo of historical curiosity, or the lovers tugging at my heart, or the suppositions of a British feminist novelist to tackle. By whatever means are at my disposal this has been my purpose, so that for a trace of Daisy Simmons, Kolkata lured me. Now, here I am, hurtling into the past as frantically as the future.

I am more than a little unprepared for China. The sleepless night I spent before leaving has left me a little delirious. It strikes me that door to door the sixteen-hour trip by direct flight is but a stroll in the park compared to a three-month voyage in 1935.

That was how long it took Julian Bell, Virginia's nephew, Vanessa's son, when he travelled east to take up his professorship at Wuhan Normal University. Here he met Shuhua and fell into an illicit affair with her. She wrote short stories. She was a distinguished calligrapher and the wife of the Dean of Arts and Literature, Chen Yuan. I have to admit she is the reason for my visit. There are facts to untangle from fiction. One hopes for small epiphanies. Take the case of the poet Xu Zhimo: I'm uncertain what route he took during his journey from Shanghai to Cambridge in 1926, his belongings packed in wooden crates and suitcases. I make a note of this as something to check in my research. Xu Zhimo carried with him Shuhua Ling's friendship scroll, inscribed with a poem in Sanskrit by Rabindranath Tagore, a passage by Dora Russell, Bertrand Russell's wife, and the poet Wen Yiduo's sketch of Tolstoy. I've been trying to find out more about the friendship scroll's physical characteristics as well as its contents. The search has yielded little, though I have tracked its preservation to the New York Public Library. I may need to make a visit there. But that would mean yet more time away from Sam.

We arrive at the hotel. I stand on the pavement as Meiling talks to the driver at length. I feel the ease of not having to communicate. Daniel explains that the taxi driver is saying he cannot give Meiling a receipt because his printer is not working. The night air is cold, and I'm aware of the flimsiness of the thin shirt and petticoat dress I am wearing over my jeans.

Meiling finally ends her conversation with the taxi driver and indicates that we can check in. As we approach the hotel entrance, Meiling's mother comes running down the steps. I am struck by her thin-boned beauty. She is fashionably wrapped in a red woollen coat. I recall Meiling telling me about her mother's vegetarianism, and it made me think of my own mother. My grandparents kept chickens in their house in Nairobi. Every morning, when the back door was unbolted and the kitchen flooded with light, and the servant girls sweated as they washed pots or swept or ground masala, those hens would peck and chirp, an incoherent ruckus rising up after the rooster crowed. Having lived in close quarters with those hens, my mother could not bring herself to eat chicken, whether stewed or curried, breast or a thigh. It occurs to me that I am thinking of her and in this random way she is part of a book waiting to be written. Like water, the grief is a mystery; it flows along its own gradient, escaping understanding. I sense my reluctance to lose the intensity of grief, as it would mean further loss. I keep her preserved in time, while my peripheral world alters. It sounds clichéd but she loved me more than anyone else in this world ever has, and I was her subject; I was never mutinous.

When my brother gave me a bag of clothes to give away, I was hurt. I said nothing. But as much as I loved her, I could not wear her purple jumper, a garment that belonged to someone dead. Why is it we reject death in this way? More recently, whenever I leave the flat and catch the photograph that my brother-in-law had framed, which is now placed in the hallway, I sometimes feel oppressed. The reproduction is so lifelike that it seems incongruous with death. There is a disquieting ambivalence in my mother's radiance. I haven't forgotten how her eyes shone or her neck strained into the photographs I took on my phone, even when paralysis left her withered. In the last weeks she could not hold even her neck upright as she sank into her commode in the shower.

Meiling speaks to the hotelier at the counter and after some discussion he issues us with keys and meal tickets. She explains about breakfast arrangements then distributes the keys and coupons to each of us. How maternal she is. We wait for a lift to take us to our rooms on the ninth floor. The supportive, convivial atmosphere feels all the more invigorating because we are researchers from different disciplines: Daniel from the history department; Indra from international affairs; Zhuqin from social sciences and Wei from law. Zhuqin and Wei are almost always together. Zhuqin is thin, softly spoken and deferential; Wei is curvy, young, bright in her demeanour and confident, so they complement each other, giggling in the lift the way my beautiful niece might with her friends. I find their voices, and the tones of Mandarin, soothing.

We alight on the ninth floor and loiter on the landing making arrangements for the next day. A few tours have been organised for the group. Meiling and Wei will not be joining us. We agree to meet in the foyer at 9 am, after breakfast.

Opening the door to my room, I'm relieved to have some privacy. The room is spacious and comfortable: two double beds separated by a bedside table where I plug in my phone. I start to unpack some of my clothes and hang them in the wardrobe; there is a dusty and rather archaic-looking fire extinguisher inside, as well as two pairs of fluffy white slippers with wafer-thin soles. On the desk an empty ashtray holds the smell of tobacco. The vertical louvre blinds are gathered open, bunched up to one side. A draught enters the room. The night shimmies, erratic as a wild animal, triggered by what is visible from the surrounding hotel windows: the spot-lights, traffic signs. There is a cool breeze not quite hitting my face. I take a shower. My ears have not popped from the compression of flight. There is a wall dividing the room made of intagliated glass so I can see the bed as I shower. The suitcase is open and my belongings are strewn. A water jet streams down, catching my upright body as though it is about to plunge. I feel strangely wired, not quite joyful.

There are no new messages from Lucille. From yesterday morning, counting the five-hour difference, there's the message I received in the taxi as we sped through the M1 tunnel and then the harbour tunnel: *Hope things go well, safe travels. And yes, I will download WeChat right now xx*

Wuhan University

4 November 2017

My phone reads 5 am. Excitement of waking in another country, in mainland China for the first time. Intrigued, because of Shuhua Ling. And, of course, Julian! Exuberant, wild, quixotic Julian. In 1935 he travelled here to teach English literature for two years. He called Shuhua the Anglicised 'Sue'. He also used the appellation, 'K', for her, his eleventh lover, K, being the eleventh letter. Very logical, that! He wrote openly about the affair to his friend, Eddy Playford, as well as to his mother, praising Shuhua, recommending her work but also exposing commonly held racist attitudes towards the Chinese and towards Indians. His letters to Vanessa, describe Shuhua's heartbreak in almost forensic detail. They betray a borderline passion and colonial thinking.

These private correspondences are intimate notes regardless of their tone. Shuhua's writings appear to stand in for all of China, as 'Sue' does. With her help Julian translated her stories while at Wuhan. She was a bilingual foreign experience for his restless spirit to navigate. After he broke off with Shuhua, Julian dated Innes Jackson Herdan, a poetry and calligraphy student who was on exchange from Somerville in Oxford. They returned to England together. He soon departed to fight in Spain during the Civil War where he was killed while driving an ambulance. Shuhua wrote letters to Virginia Woolf, also to Vanessa. Before her death Virginia had read Shuhua's chapters and sent English novels for Shuhua to read and emulate. She was given another shortened anglicised name, 'Sue Hua,' for her book, *Ancient Melodies*, which Woolf's Hogarth Press finally published in 1950.

And how does history remember? When I run a search on Shuhua Ling, I find a link to the story behind how Julian Bell named her, 'K'. Other links take me to a legally contested novel concerning their affair but there is almost nothing about Shuhua's correspondence with Virginia Woolf, or the memoir she had planned to write about Virginia Woolf.

There is little interest in her as an artist, a short story writer, a translator. Naturally, there's no shortage of references to this miserable affair.

To think it happened right here! Darting to the window, I am excited for my first daylight view of the city. China lies beyond the dark, wallpapered room. Orange-yellow sunrise spreading over the East Lake beyond the tower blocks, the pagodas and the silhouette of Luojia Mountain. I take a few photographs to send Lucille. How surprising and addictive it has become to share my travels and adventures with her.

We spoke a couple of times over the phone before my trip. She flaunted her caramel voice, laughing, flirting recklessly and I felt turned on. I suppose it was just fun. Perhaps Lucille is a distraction I need to relieve the tension of writing. I printed my travel itinerary while deep in the fantasy of being her girlfriend. *Slut, slut, slut,* I was saying in my mind; that's how badly she'd teased me. No amount of Taoist philosophy on reining in pleasure was going to stop me. I felt lousy and ashamed when I thought about it. Lucille had captivated me, that's for certain. I hadn't been writing and there were gaps in the paper I was supposed to be presenting at the conference.

She wanted to Skype the night before I left and suddenly that seemed more urgent than packing.

Now that I'm here, after all that has happened and all that is ahead, and she is there drinking coffee and cider in Fitzroy, I'm not even sure how I feel.

Strange to be awake so early. I figure there is enough time to play my exercise video, the fat-burner I've been taking to maintain a semblance of fitness, but when I try to play it I can't: the firewall has blocked it. So I run through the routine from memory; front squats, dead lifts, forward and backward lunges, hamstring raises . . . Afterwards, I read a few pages in one of the reference books I've packed, then go down to enjoy a leisurely breakfast.

People are queueing up outside the dining hall. Steam drifts and sharp smells waft out into the lobby. To my Western eyes, few of the other guests appear to be foreign. When it is my turn at the buffet, I plonk some porridge, vegetables and a pork bun on my plate. There isn't any coffee on the servery, but there is a sugary drink like Milo with sweetened condensed milk being rationed in very small paper cups. I am annoyed with myself for forgetting to bring coffee sachets as I had intended. Irritation is buffered by a headache and foggy thinking, which I attribute to caffeine withdrawal.

After breakfast, the other members of my party and I meet Frank in the foyer. Frank teaches in Wuhan University's Department of Foreign Languages. We remember each other from a conference we have both attended recently. His manner conveys a palpable warmth that cuts through formality. Brogan has quite likely sent him a recommendation. Academia can be a space that offers refuge from the hardships of the writing life; it can be a haven of intellectual curiosity and respect. Subtract the toxic narcissism and one can shelter in academia's almost Confucian neutrality and rén. Writers of colour are under pressure to write about identity and to do this in a particular way. Or to write about assimilating. It never occurred to me to see myself as some white people do: dark-skinned and diminutive. Gatekept, always at the pointy end of industry and barely recovering. Seriously, don't they realise we are a dying race? Quite literally. If we hope to tell the stories of our families, our elders while our families are still alive? We stand up and write while the stones are being thrown. And this is how I have lived my life as a writer of colour.

There were misreadings of Shuhua Ling's work. The stories she wrote about women's lives and about domestic repression were adapted into memoir. Her feminist rage was described as strange and charming by Virginia Woolf, by Vita Sackville-West, and by English critics. From the beginning of this Bloomsbury–China exchange Julian and Vanessa Bell discussed Ling's stories in letters they wrote to each other, comparing them ever so slightly in a patronising way to English styles. Years after Julian's death, and after Virginia's death, when Shuhua came to England, Vanessa introduced her to Vita Sackville-West as well as to China scholar Arthur Waley, and historian Margaret Strachey.

So there it is like a bird's nest: strands of biography and history entering a novel. And looking back, my coffees in Gordon Square were like the unclenching of creative reserves festering within, frustrated by their fringed and partial flowerings in the mind, contracted as fragments on the written page, yet capable of sparking like a private display of fireworks.

Frank divides the group into two. I am to go with him in his car, while Daniel, Indra and Zhuqin are driven in another car to the Yellow Crane Tower. As we drive, Frank talks on the phone with Paula, another academic, who is not sure if she will come out for the day. He takes a leafy route winding through the Wuhan University campus to the other side of

East Lake. From here it is a short drive to another, more plush hotel. He parks his four-wheel drive outside and we enter the lobby to collect two more visiting academics.

We meet up with the other group at the Yellow Crane Tower and spend the morning there. A delightful tree-lined walk leads us to the reconstructed barbican. We climb the rebuilt staircase to the galleria. From here we can look out over the pavilions and bronze statues of the tower complex on Snake Hill to the Yangtze River and its bridges, teeming with traffic. A sepia filter stains my photos with nostalgia. I take some interesting angles. A Chinese woman wants to have her photograph taken with Daniel because he is a handsome white man. I imagine this kind of attention from women was amplified for English lovers like Julian and Peter.

The Literature faculty host us to lunches and dinners in plush private rooms before and during the conference and we are treated to a selection of regional cuisines. At one of these meals I meet Wendy, a Chinese sociology lecturer whose paper is on transnational divorces in same-sex couples. She tells me how she left Singapore with her same-sex partner owing to the political repression, despite the fact they enjoyed the protection and privileges of academic life. It strikes me that this was all meant to happen. I was meant to talk to Wendy about Lucille. I have never felt so passionately about a woman. On the surface, we don't have much in common; we live in different cities, she is younger than me, and she doesn't have a son. How did she get under my skin? Before my divorce, I had one or two fleeting encounters with women, but living as a single parent for so many years has led me to question my sexual preference.

'Fiction is like a spider's web attached ever so lightly perhaps, but still attached to life at all four corners,' wrote Virginia. Hers was a pragmatic feminism. She argued for the fiction of the poor woman, who in real life 'could hardly read, could scarcely spell and in real life was property of her husband'. For weeks, for months, I have neglected writing about Daisy, but she is never far away. Hauntingly, she dissolves my boundaries. She has turned me inside out. Daisy has made me untrustworthy and erratic. She has made me a deserter. It may surprise a reader to learn that this is how a character can take hold of a writer, even to the extent of thriving at the writer's expense. Daisy passively consumes me, even when I am not writing her story. Admittedly, it has taken longer because of interruptions, and therefore not having lived the writing enough. Writing becomes an act of translation. Fictional lives are swapped for the real which threaten to collapse under the scaffolding of our inventions. Meanwhile, I persevere with research: reading archives, pouring over maps and understanding history. I've been reading about modernism, the bridges between China, India and England. I've been reading about independence, the end of indentured labour, the flourishing of Marxism and socialism and feminism. My research prepares me to mediate the historical past tense into the fictional present.

On the last day of the conference we all meet for a drink later that evening; everyone is there except for Meiling, whose family have planned a small farewell celebration. There's a bar in the hotel where we order lychee martinis and mango liqueurs. Daniel talks a little more about his month-long sojourn in Wuhan last year to research Australian emigrants residing near the treaty port of Hankou. He is hoping for a post-doctoral scholarship, so he can return to research the lives of these expatriates. Daniel is gentle and tall; he has a kind intelligence. I'm impressed by his study of Mandarin. He knows about the wide shady streets of Hankou, the colonial architecture with slat blinds and colonnades in the days when British warships sighted the flashing lights of signals, when telegrams to England would take up to two days, after the Wuchang uprising in 1911, before the revolution that would eventually see the overthrow of the Qing dynasty shifted from the Pearl River Basin to the Yangtze River Basin. Wuhan, he tells me, was a centre of world communism in 1927, when Mao stayed there for six months. Isherwood and Auden visited during the Sino–Japanese war in 1937, when they co-authored *Journey to A War*, a book of poems, travel memoir and photographs. It was a time when the repercussions of the Great War left writers questioning nationalism. In 1941, after the streets were bombed, when Virginia Woolf would take the Tube from London Bridge to the ruins of Temple, the buildings 'gashed; dismantled' and the red bricks turned to a suffocating residue of white powder.

My mind is drifting from the first and second world wars (. . . which shattered Virginia, which shattered Septimus and Rezia . . .) to mooncakes, to orchids and to jade-green leafy bamboo shoots. Immersed with Shuhua Ling, her biographical fragments floating through my thoughts, bumping here and there into imagistic shadows of her and memories of my own, unpicking their seams into threads so I can almost visualise her ghost. She is thin, spectacled, fashionably attired. This woman who was suicidally in love. This woman who fled to Shanghai for a few days to be with Julian, even when the affair was no longer clandestine. Such desperation. The kind that leaves you humbled. That is what desire does to the soul, whatever its engine may have been. She would be possessed, know this folly, joining our table at this bar, in a slim-fitting printed dress, carrying her reading glasses, neatly folded. Shuhua appears and then fades like the mystery I've been trying to piece together, impeded by the exotic, Orientalist defect in my Western process. Thought is like a stain which is too stubborn to remove. A brilliant Chinese poet, on giving a reading in Scotland, confessed that she sometimes questions her own work as being Chinoiserie, and I wonder if that is why Shuhua appeals to me; her privileged Peking childhood and the quaintness of concubinage, but without the violence. Yet there have been women who drowned because they displeased their husbands; women whose husbands drowned them.

In London, I read a biography written by Shuhua's great-niece, the American scholar Sasha Su-Ling Welland. Sasha spent more than ten years visiting China, teaching English there, as a way of acquainting herself deeply with her inherited culture. In *A Thousand Miles of Dreams* I read about how Shuhua grew up in Bejing (then Peking) with many half-sisters and brothers and servants in an aristocratic house, flowing into courtyards on GanMian Hu Tong. Her white-haired mother was handpicked by an illustrious scholar, Ling Fupeng, from a ship docked in the harbour of Portuguese Macau. She was one of eight concubines. Imagine. But this is part anecdote, part myth. Somehow, it is telling of the way women are often objects to be possessed, as Daisy is possessed by Peter Walsh. After all, 'dark and adorably pretty' is how she is presented to us by Virginia Woolf.

As readers of *Mrs Dalloway* we come across Daisy in a dog cart in the fragrant, sweaty dusk one Calcutta evening, with her maid and her lapdog, weeping at the crossroads, an Englishman having irretrievably altered the course of her life. And I can't help wondering if women like Daisy and Shuhua control their own destiny – or does that depend entirely on narration? That obligation, that responsibility to a singular history which had fallen some years after the war (not by mere coincidence) in the quaint village of Rodmell to Virginia. Does it now fall to me? Rodmell, with its water meadows and muddy paths leading to the River Ouse, where Virginia Woolf put an end to her harrowing mental suffering. Along the banks of that tidal river there are white stones with yellow daubs, the size of a man's fist. I lay there on the wet grass under the spell of April sun, the blue-sky aching like the gaps in my life, my bones unbroken. 'Women have been regarded tacitly in much the same way as colonial exploits, to be the conquests of history,' I thought. As so many queer, bi and transwomen succumb to the violence of a homophobic, cis-gendered world. All this was interweaving, discerned with hindsight in the process of writing it as I am now, but also no less was it the ghosting of Shuhua's real life.

Red Cottage
Snakes Lane, Woodford Wells
London

12 July 1924

Dear Lucrezia,

Thank you for attending our workers' meeting. It was a great
pleasure to renew our acquaintance, and to meet Daisy. Quite
a journey she has made from the shores of married life in
India to South Kensington. So bold! Despite the grief and
misfortune of our lives, the slings and wrongs suffered by
some women, I read in this a sign of the times. The angel
of freedom sounds her trumpet everywhere – in prisons and
well beyond Lady Bradshaw's parlour!

How fortunate that you've found solace in each other as
I have with Silvio. He escaped Mussolini's politics of hatred
and silencing. Still, Gramsci is in prison and Matteotti has
been murdered. Perhaps you've heard? Stabbed by a carpen-
ter's file. He was found in the forest two weeks ago, stuffed

into a suitcase. When I studied painting in Venice, I saw for myself the cruelty of the Fascists. Anyone who speaks against them is silenced, brutalised by their secret police. Here in England, we are utterly disillusioned with Parliament. The only true resistance is outside the institution. That is why we should continue to support the exiles. Persist with our pamphlets. I am not always in agreement with the Communist Party; I think we align more closely to the socialist movement. (Mr Lenin, it seems, is dismayed with me . . . but nevertheless . . .)

So kind of you to design my boater. The tricoloured grosgrain looks super. Perfect for the rally we're planning for Bow Road in August. We hope to enlist many young women. They are not limited to a particular background. Some of our Irish nurses and dailies will come, Elisa and Margherita, whom you have met already. Also, some other workers: weavers from Spitalfields and Bethnal Green (mostly these women are French and Italian). Each of their stories makes a singular contribution to our cause.

After the march we'll have supper. I hope you and Daisy can come as there is much more to talk about! I'm curious to ask about land tenures in Bengal and if they liken to the Punjab for my book on India. There's every possibility of a lecture tour as well with the publisher in Bombay. Before British arrivals, the panchayat was a village council similar to the Russian mir. Perhaps Daisy's mother knows our dear friend, Mr Keir Hardie. He was a delegate in Calcutta after the separation of Bengal, and he wrote quite a lot about this.

And so, my very best, until soon,

Sincerely,
Sylvia Pankhurst

St Thomas' School

Kidderpore House

4 Diamond Harbour Road, Calcutta

17 September 1924

Dear Virginia,

I hope this reaches you in the best of health. My heartfelt thanks to you and to Leonard for your generous gift of books. I am overwhelmed with gratitude. They will provide me with many hours of joy and pleasant distractions.

Last week we visited the outlying stations. Each time we set up camp preparing to baptise converts; mostly chamars to whom we teach bhajans and the gospel stories. Occasionally, we are invited into the houses of Hindu women. Many of the Indian catechists are taught bible education or they train as nurses. They learn handicrafts, they help with all aspects of teaching, serving the diocese, and as the Church involves Indians, the mission is reformed.

We have three hundred children, many from the village outskirts, Christian boys and girls, Anglo-Indians – or

Eurasians, as they are often now described. In Calcutta, there is an alarming number of poor white orphans. Were it not for the school providing salubrious conditions for their nurturing, they would otherwise be left to loiter the streets. Inevitably, these sad souls would succumb to profligacy. For it is lamentable how distressed the common European, the poor and the elderly, here become. A great many escape from their impoverishment by drinking spirits or smoking opium.

Which brings me to the case of the young boy about whom you enquire, if I may venture to guess, for the purposes of fiction? A more unfortunate circumstance I cannot recount! His mother gone on a mail steamer bound for London, eloped to live with a high-ranking Anglo-Indian official, and his father is ruined; depressed, dismissed from service with the army. Apparently, the father served as a major, but was a drinker and the household of servants and chattels have been evicted. The poor boy hardly spoke to us for some weeks. He was in such a state of shock that he did not speak his own name. We have called him George. Thanks to God our perseverance has been rewarded. Now he makes progress and shows a remarkable natural aptitude in arithmetic. The boy likes to fix things and will do well. We think he will go far. An apprenticeship would be just the thing! A clerk in the railways, possibly, or in transport.

It worried me to read in last week's news about the Sussex floods. I do hope the waters have receded and the debris cleared. I expect the swallows and martins are leaving the marshes for their journey south, and the wild ducks have arrived for winter.

Does Leonard plan to sojourn in India after Hambantota? Will he be travelling with the ILP? He is very welcome to stay as our honoured guest. Reverend Fletcher would be pleased and humbled by his company. The Reverend assures me that a trip to Srirampur to visit his spiritual friend the Mahatma Gandhi could also be arranged.

Yours most affectionately,
Winifred Myra Dean

Chemin des Oliviers, Aubagne

6 November 1924

My dearest Nora,

I'm sorry that I've been so slow to reply. Until now words failed me. I am staying with Lucrezia on a farm in Provence. Our genial host, Madame Amélie Chaubin, is a patron and a suffragist; and her husband is a notary. We are sojourning here on our way to Italy. The windows in this old stone cottage are open. Autumn has been pleasant, and there are bees humming in the French ivy.

So much has happened. I have not seen Radhika for a month. It truly upsets me. I feel partly responsible. I searched for her along the cobbled streets of the mews, in Kensington, where I had been living with the Bradshaws – an area filled with splendid shops and museums; public inns which are popular in the evenings; estates and royal parks. Of course, it was kind of the Bradshaws to take us in, but I had my reservations, and they proved right. From the day that we first went to live there, I slept comfortably, while Radhika shared a cramped room under the stairwell with the English maids. At first, I went to check on her each day and we spoke a little. But as the days passed it seemed as if she had less and less to say, and I was forgetting my Bengali.

At some point, it may have been a week after we arrived, I forgot to check on Radhika in the evening. That day, I had accompanied Evie to the museum. It was my first experience of the grand establishment, its sculptures and domes and Gothic arches. Breathing the dusty light, the atmosphere seemed to inhabit me for some hours, dissolving all sense of my responsibilities. Evie's restless personality drew from the springs of my attention more than I could anticipate. I seemed to forget more often to check on Radhika after that day. When I did see her we had very little to say to each other. She barely responded to my questions, answering in mono-syllables. 'How was your supper?' 'Did you sleep well?' Our one-sided conversations started to feel like a chore. Before long, my neglect had become a habit.

She had been my sole companion. Too softly the echoes of doubt had whispered in my mind that something was not right. Why did I not listen to my intuition? Radhika was my responsibility. What made me place my trust in an English household to adopt her and substitute my care? All that time during our voyage, while I was preoccupied selfishly with my own grief, she had suffered. She had worked hard, slept little, eaten less. She had grown feeble. The cold weather gave her chilblains. Lily, the housekeeper, told me the old farrier's son had taken to mistreating her. So she ran away. But what did I expect? Too late! One should not dismiss the twitches of conscience and minor stirrings of consternation in our lives.

What dark ironies I must live by. What folly! There were fluxes in my state of mind as each day brought its own trials. I expected the love I bore for Peter to be returned. It was infatuation, sparked by dreamy anticipation. I suffered from a hastening of the heart; this came and went almost every day. Sometimes it was difficult to breathe. I had pains in my chest as if the slender muscles connecting my ribs had been torn.

From one day to the next I could not remember the state of my feelings or preoccupations so the present moment took hold, and everything I experienced overwhelmed me. Some mornings I was so mired in disappointment and confusion that I had to convince myself to eat breakfast, to dress, to prepare my lesson for Evie. I had been reduced for the sake of love. I remember feeling disconsolate day after day in London, because I'd stopped hearing from Peter. His excuses and post-ponements were politely delivered. Sometimes, what seemed to be messages from him came through others.

I received an invitation from Lady Bruton to afternoon tea, and there he was with the well-bred residents of Westminster, administrators, landlords, the sons and daughters of admi-rals, one or two rivals. Did he mean to test my behaviour for suitability or was I simply an embarrassment? Clarissa is his fixation. What was I? Little more than adornment; not a sapphire or a ruby, perhaps, but nevertheless a semi-precious stone from abroad.

For the visitor, at least, London offers many distractions. It is like a grand bustling stage with mansions, palaces, docks and hubs, with automobiles, markets and machinery. London gives the impression of being organised in its sprawling chaos. The trains and omnibuses run to time, the clocks chime, the clerks are brisk, the Queen's wardens parade. And yet, there are always interesting gatherings: committees, associations and leagues for working women, communities of immigrants, charity workers, socialists, anti-Fascists, suffragettes from the factories in the East End.

My new friend Rezia is acquainted with Sylvia, one of the Pankhursts; she's not at all an elitist. She dines with ordinary women who sew garments and make lace. Her de facto husband, Silvio, was conscripted to serve in the Italian army as punishment for printing pamphlets. He fled from Turin. They are good people, the kind who make life tolerable. Running a kitchen for the poor. Keeping friends and associates from all walks: liberals, Catholics, Protestants, Jews, Theosophists, those who do not believe in a god.

In Marseille, there is a great variety of people; I have seen more lascars, Africans and countrymen in the narrow streets along the docks. Some loiter outside taverns, a little odd and doleful. There are many by the fountain and in the church squares who perform colourful acrobatics to the beat of drums. They attract crowds, and passers-by offer coins. Others seem cheerfully employed in industry in the hotels, in transport as drivers and porters, and in construction. Many of the houses are several storeys, made of pink stone or sandy yellow, and there is a quaint old church in the town, which wraps itself around the shimmering Mediterranean. Fort Saint-Jean is a barracks by the sea, facing Africa, where the French military are shoring up influence. On the day we arrived we saw Berber soldiers in their white pantaloons and fezzes, and at first I did not see them as colonialists. But then it struck me that many of the slave merchants were from these countries of Africa. Rezia says the Italians are just as culpable, that Mussolini has been using poisonous gas in Libya and that he has opened camps in Somalia. I thought once more of the oppressions the British have inflicted on our people and how it has affected us. I thought of my son: what news is there of him? Am I no more than a shadow in his past?

Oranges and clementines are ready for harvest in the orchards. The plums, peaches, chestnuts and lemons are ripening. Twenty barrels are sold in the markets each week in Marseille. We see many immigrants working in the country-side, gypsies and refugees from Italy. And we've heard there are Poles and Ukrainians working in the coalmines.

I am uncertain how long we will stay before travelling on to Italy. My stipend has been locked and I am waiting for a cable from the bank. I fear you will pity me, but do not. I have found in Rezia a healing companion. The changes life brings remind one of the weather: now sunny spells;

now curtains of rain. Some days, after walking through the field, returning to the house by the chemins, or what they call the donkey trails, it occurs to me that sorrow is as delicate as the wildflowers, the phlox and the dandelion. I can hold the thought of Charlotte without misery. I do not like to tell my story if someone asks, 'Do you have children?' or 'Why did you leave India?' as it feels as if I am not speaking. It is a narrator who is uttering the words, miming a kind of conventional wisdom: 'My son is at boarding school, his father is a drunkard, my daughter died from cholera on board the SS *Ranchi* on our voyage from Calcutta.' Only rarely do I think of her. Sometimes, before dawn, when there is barely a streak of light in the sky, before the birds sing, or a stag may appear to have stopped still in the mist, then I feel the horror of my life, like a blanket covering me. Tears fall freely. I am skilled in abandonment by now. I believe that if you abandon those you love entirely you learn to miss them less and less. Peter was surprised that I stopped being in his thrall. Nothing came of our mutual plans, my divorce was not filed. But do not pity me. He was so full of himself, so assured of his control, pulling the strings of his dark, adorable Daisy like a predictable marionette. A trifle. A miscalculation. Never mind. We had not counted on loss, and how it has altered me. I find myself drifting. Confused by love's algorithms, priorities shift. I need to prepare for contingencies, a passage back to India.

I cannot speak for Rezia, the lessons of her journey, except to say they are inevitable. These days I seek only to be happy.

Write to me soon, Nora. Send me news, a word of Joseph.

Ever your loving cousin,
Daisy

West 29th Street, New York City

3 April 2018

They say April is the cruellest month, breeding lilacs. It has been snowing bitterly in upstate New York. From my hotel window a shaft of vacant space walled in by window frames towers up to a dark sky. A fine, cold drizzle eases by after-noon. I boil the jug and make peppermint tea. The room's charcoal wallpaper is soothing, the double bed hugs me to sleep, the retro furnishings are easy on the eye. Half dressed. A few of my clothes are hanging. Like the blue woollen coat and the Paris Atelier jacket which I bought in China.

Having packed my books in Sydney and saved my work to the cloud, and having backed it up to a USB. The files include chapters from the novel. I packed a book of essays on race in literature, including notes on gatekeeping and reduc-tive criticism on Anglo-Indians. I brought Nora Scott's *An Indian Journal* and *Memoirs of a Bengal Civilian* by John Beames.

There is something hopeful about standing on the porch under the cobwebs and turning the key to the lock for the last time in weeks, possibly months, not knowing how long it may be before you return. The life of a writer is erratic and unstable. You can't look back; you can only look forward. Dust particles adhere to my shoes. Then, off I go.

Taxis and Uber drivers nearly always miss my end of the street, because it's divided by the railway in one section and by an arterial road at another section. Sometimes, if I'm travelling to the airport, I'll wait and wait and then, when the taxi doesn't appear despite phone messages and GPS navigations, I'll end up carrying my suitcase down to the station, my handbag weighing on my shoulder, rubbing against the collar bone. I'll drag my luggage past the taxi stand, where a driver may or may not be waiting for a random fare. I've had rides with Pakistani drivers and Afghan drivers, but mostly they are Indians. We talk sometimes about what it's like to be an immigrant. When you're about to leave a country and there's a stranger at the wheel, you might talk about life in candid fragments. There's a risk, a burst of exhilaration that via this unpremeditated conversation you may come to understand yourself better.

Ours is perhaps not the most beautiful railway platform on Sydney's North Shore line, but Wahroonga station boasts an attractive show of potted plants. Opposite the track there is a park planted with dense shrubbery and magnolia trees. What the station lacks is a lift. It is suitable for commuters and students travelling to and from the city, but those needing transport to the airport must rely on spouses to drive them in shiny cars or taxis pulling into their gravel driveways and quiet cul-de-sacs. During my marriage, that was how I travelled. My psychologist said it is good to normalise, but is it advisable?

I admit it bothers me, but it doesn't matter what I forget to pack. Incense sticks are a necessity for me. I'd brought some sticks to fragrance the long, often purposeless hours of thinking about but not writing, for hotel rooms like this one, as well as power adaptors for the UK and India, just in case I happened to return to Kolkata for research. It doesn't matter that I forget my umbrella or my hiking boots, or that I haven't written the paper I plan to read. What has slowed me down? Why have I spent hours each night not knowing where to begin with my subject, how to address my reader? And who *is* my reader? There is industry, government, the tax department, university . . . and then there is you, patient reader. I fill you with my writing and I empty myself. I, who am asked to be silent. Am censored. Because nobody really gets to read the truth. But who am I pleasing? Who am I least failing? There are matters I've long neglected: tax returns that may lead to a refund I badly need, having not registered with Centrelink in Australia, which would entitle me to a student card for discount pharmaceuticals, car rego and rates. In my Sydney townhouse the floor is covered by islands of books, piles of folders and papers, a sink of dirty dishes, a laundry basket load of clothes waiting to be put away, cat fur snarled across the rug, books I have earmarked to read. I am altered. Writing has altered me. Has it been the industry that has altered me, or has it been writing? This is not how I want to be, and it's partly because Daisy is a slippery thing. Because Daisy cannot be pinned down, with her arch ways, her twists and turns.

But it is not entirely the responsibility of the novelist. Some readers will not allow it. Which readers? The industry readers, I say . . . the average reader on the street, the she/he/theys, the very readers that Virginia Woolf called the 'common' readers, the laydies and gentlethems, the Browns and the Smiths, want more. From their iPhones and their hot desks, they are demanding more. And right now, an industry-busting Daisy is stepping forward, emboldened and illumined from her invisibility to take hold of me. The Daisy whom I see taking Peter Walsh's hand in hers in the tea shop, turning the band on her finger, weaving her fingers through his, until his eyes cannot avert and until later he stoops to kiss her neck. And later, the industry Peter . . . will ask her if she contrived to take his hand like that, so fast (like a character from *Poldark*) or if it was spontaneous. As if something sinister is happening invisibly, exhaustingly. But hasn't this always been the case? Lift the layers and there is misogyny blended with racial scorn, racial infantilism.

And after all, it is depleting to be one whose work is critical. You're seen as an activist. The industry is siphoning away from the Daisy the novel deserves. The one who must leave her son behind for the sake of her daughter; the one who must choose her family or her life and discover the consequences of these catastrophes at sea, a few hours away from the coast of Africa. Later (. . . meaning not then, but now, as I'm writing this, meaning this now, this then-now . . .), I'll think about my mother, and how calm she was, how quietly spoken, despite the migrations and upheavals, how she managed to make the cycle of the day a routine to live by, to sanctify. Each day a prayer; a decade of the rosary. Drawing the venetian blinds so the neighbours could not see. Closing her eyes in the late afternoon sun, by the window in the commuter's train carriage; the men drinking their beers. How generous she was to me, and yet how parsimonious with expenses she could be at other times. As if motherly love was never about power but about economics.

Emails arrived last week to inform me that I didn't make a shortlist and was knocked back for a grant. Maybe what I write is not what they are 'after'. Who are 'they'? Not the readers, the industry. My moods have been altered by social media; if I'm honest, I'm addicted to at least one platform, Twitter being habitual. Something to fill the emptiness, the boredom, when I feel frustrated or creatively blocked; when the ending to a chapter eludes me or when I fail at tidying the structure of the manuscript. The time it takes to write a novel can surely be measured in the things you ignore: the dirty clothes in the laundry; the mawkish reek of compost, attracting ants by the kitchen sink; the ants that have drowned in the sweetened condensed milk. So many losses. In my numbed state of mind, I somehow managed to drift into JB Hi-Fi, where I purchased a new laptop with eight megs of RAM weighing just under a kilogram. It went into my hand luggage with a copy of *Mrs Dalloway*, the pages loose. Does it matter that the story I am writing keeps being interrupted . . . ? And although it is spring in New York, autumn in Sydney, I feel in my bones the fragility of mist hugging the bare oaks. I am dying to see the squirrels scampering in Russell Square; to shoot sidelong glances at the cats of Brooklyn.

Up the hill I lifted my suitcase over grassy tufts and then carried it along the Pacific Highway for fifty metres as the cars and trucks whizzed past, then turned down a quiet street, passing the construction site for a nursing home car park, past pleasingly landscaped units, leading to the commons surrounding the post office, where I had been that day to arrange the holding of my mail. I see Kirsten from the bookshop and tell her I'm on my way to New York and then back to London, to write, to meet an agent. She looks a little tired but could not be as sleep deprived as me; she thinks it all sounds awesome and we laugh about the real fantasy life of the writer. The writer.

There are no taxis. In the train on the way to Kingsford Smith I think about what has stalled me for the last two weeks when I should have prepared. Quizzical correspondence from Jonathan arriving just at a time when I was about to burst free from domesticity. How trapped we are by the gaps in meaning, how we search for completeness, explains how I have felt since being struck by his words. But is the one who wounds a true lover?

Having finished another chapter; while planning my trip and sorting things out in the house. Perhaps that is all love is: nothing beyond the catch, the chase. So what happens when one is caught? My lovers elude me like my characters, like writing. Maybe love is a story one needs to speak with private whispers, the way Peter Walsh toys with the idea, assembles Clarissa, mending her dresses, walking to and from the House of Commons, entertaining guests, and the monologue within him saying, *and there she was, and there she is* . . . and nobody, scarcely even him, noticing Daisy . . .

(So my thoughts drift as the train chugs on and I am forgetting my grief about the job I no longer have and the grants I did not receive, or that I haven't found time to invest the small inheritance my mother left me in short-term accounts, having run a quick mental check and, not least importantly, here is my passport, credit card, my phone . . . and now the screen on my phone is broken, yet the camera still works) . . . And now I am tasked with giving this narrative to Daisy: her own internal monologue, of what is to pass and what has been erased. Station to station, Warrawee, Turramurra, Pymble, Gordon, Chatswood, Artarmon, St Leonards, going over and over thoughts, I make the interior jottings. Changing at Central. Thinking of how Daisy would have taken the toy train to Darjeeling to meet Peter Walsh in the summer of 1922; strange that I haven't observed until now how tenses in my letter writing or my emails do not conform to a standard. There is a plasticity about our grammar; our tenses slide with our desires from present to past continuous or to future subjunctive as we petition those we adore: for instance, what is the difference between saying, when expressing devotion, 'I want you to know,' or saying, 'I wanted you to know'? Is the difference politeness, or is the difference a distance created as if to observe the impossibility of such a devotion? When love is unlawful, as it is for Peter and Daisy, when it crosses the correctness of matrimonial law and Englishness. (And here is Luke, and here is Jonathan . . .) And here is Peter Walsh, one moment calling Daisy some younger woman, then displaying Daisy, the wife of a major in the Indian army, as his Daisy, becoming lovelier as he tells Clarissa about his romance. As if he, Peter, had been somehow decorating a plate. As if she, Daisy, was adornment and he has properly planted a tree in the sea-salted air of his intimacy with Clarissa, the wife of an English Tory parliamentarian.

Such are a single day's happenings in the life of an English socialite, yet it begins in the past tense: 'Mrs Dalloway said she would buy the flowers herself.' Only then does it slide into present participles, 'winding', 'rising', 'falling', 'standing', 'looking', 'musing' and so on. The past tense is like a frame for the picture. The picture is Clarissa. No sign of Daisy. Zero referencing in the literature searches, which highlights to me the Eurocentric bias of academic frames.

On the plane, I am in economy. Seated next to Mark, a slender bespectacled American with a kind appearance. He sleeps most of the way to Honolulu, while I read. The movies are not appealing. I get a few hours' sleep, and so does Mark. Over breakfast we talk, and he tells me he is a geologist researching a project on one of the rural islands. He asks me about my trip. I mention the conference, and Daisy, and talk about history; how history not only forgets the minorities but mangles their history, the way Clarissa is appallingly ignorant of the Armenians and the Albanians, how in the midst of her queerness she creates a grading based on a cross-racial fantasy between the English and the Anglo-Indians, between Anglo-Indians and the so-called 'Eurasians'. The borders of the unwritten past are muddied like rainwater coursing through a steep valley, like a creek or a river bubbling and ringing across bracken, leaf beds, stones and sandy sediment, absorbing and spilling in dirty light the composite tannins.

As we descend into Honolulu, a safe distance from the Bellows Air Force Station, we see Diamond Head and Waikiki Beach, the lush green valleys filled with high-rise development. It is the escarpment of US occupation and investment, a para-disal sovereignty. From this aerial view, beneath the clouds, the island is like a military palimpsest; Pearl Harbor written over native title, over Polynesian land, Polynesian names.

'To see this,' I tell Mark, 'the whole escarpment has been colonised. In the same way colonial powers like Europe and

America haven't merely occupied the countries of the developing world, they have shaped our stories and remade our history. They have completely inscribed the developing world.'

I'm suddenly aware of a kind of fluency in my thinking; an understanding, which is simply the result of travelling, working on my subconscious. In a micro way, movements like this, however modest, can shift history and politics in the mind. And all this turquoise water is washing across the divisions and barriers of time like nature's unguarded purpose. 'If only we could be like water,' I say. It seems unusual for anyone to accept this, or to understand as Mark seems to. Easier to be blinded by the first world bias in books. In novels, even in non-fiction, the voice of whoever speaks determines the storytelling, its consistency and evenness.

We land. As I go through customs, I turn on my phone and read a message from Katharine. She's happy to write a reference for a grant application. I type an email, but it doesn't send. Between terminals I cross the road finding it pleasant to walk in the Honolulu heat, under the breezy palms and a canopy of tropical sky. There are no adaptors on display in the shops but pineapple-shaped chocolates are hard to resist. Perfectly sized for my hand luggage, I buy some as a gift for the conference host.

At Kennedy, the cold polluted air relieves my cabin fever and I catch the air train to Jamaica. Gazing out there's something seductive about the exterior world: first the pylons, the aircraft buildings, then all those bare trees and the bleak, pasty sky. I've had lovers out there and in the ether, but they are not on my mind. Perhaps it is the paranoia of the writing life; one feels hurtled and manipulated. As women we must be arrows flying through a world that is often determined and increasingly monitored. We dream up ways to cut the puppet strings. The publishers might be women but behind the industry gates are the men whom one needs to get beyond, simply to survive. Some of my on-line reviews have vanished, or my URL links have been variously cloned with spelling mistakes and other careless errata. This is how whiteness and class maintain symbolic value, by bullying others considered less. The spin and the play and the dance is exhausting. If it is not the industry chewing me up and spitting me out, it is the alpha males.

I take the Long Island Rail Road to Penn station, walk down to Twenty-ninth and follow it across Seventh and Sixth avenues to the hotel. It isn't as cold as I thought it would be, but it's raining lightly, and I don't have an umbrella. I try to flag a cab but in the end I just keep walking; it's only ten minutes there if I walk briskly. On the way I stop in at a small shopfront on Broadway selling suitcases and umbrellas, staffed by a young Bangladeshi man. He looks tired and is plainly dressed in a flannelette shirt. I show him the mismatched plug and my phone cord. 'England?' he says. I say, 'No, Australia.' 'We don't keep many,' he says. He pulls out a plastic bag filled with an assortment of adaptors and rummages through it until he finds one for my iPhone.

'What about the power?' I ask. 'Okay, wait,' he replies. Then he leaves the glass-topped desk and dashes outside, returning with another bag. He pulls out a yellowed plug with a red, half-torn price label and the still-sticky residue of older labels on the side and bordering the socket. I am happy with these used pieces, like recycled soup bones. They will nourish my cyber hunger. This man could be a vendor in a shelf-shop on the streets of Dhaka or Kolkata. I ask him where he's from and pay the ten dollars as we exchange on terms that put me at ease. In Dhaka or Kolkata, it might have been quite a different experience. But here, as two South Asians in America, we recognise our fragments as affinities, rags of belonging and history.

I arrive at the hotel before my room is ready, so I hang out in the darkened lobby, a transformed nightclub, already infiltrated with young start-ups and freelancers working on laptops. The desks are illuminated by Art Deco lamps. I make a nest for myself near the bar, under panelled walls, soothed by the graffiti artwork. I plug in my laptop to recharge. There is another email from the agent. He wants to meet me, but he is leaving for Paris next week. We chat by email for a while and then, finally, there is a window when we can meet. He sends me the address. Is it a rejection? I wonder? Bracing myself for the worst, like the winter trees I watched from the train, their buds swelling at the tips like pins. There is a brittle fatigue inside me but, however exposed, the mind is working.

There is one day before the conference. One day in which to prepare. But I cannot focus on my paper: this software is taking time to learn. Then there is Luke. He knows how to get my attention by hurting me, by pretending to lose whatever it may be that we have. This rankle, this festering, always seems to hook me, just when I am beginning to feel I am free to write. Free of him, of any man, even free of Lucille. For Daisy's sake, I may have to get over Lucille fast. Right now she may be in a bar, drinking cider with her friends. I may need to surprise myself. The rawness of losing Mum, the grief still overwhelms. When things became intense one day I had pleaded and begged Lucille, making myself mad. My life was a mess. Writing does that, like rust in damp, salty air it erodes the metal of the writer's mind. For a couple of weeks, I was quite erratic. It occurred to me that I have to pull myself together or let the novel and its cargo sink. For Daisy's sake. For the sake of her children; they are real to me. What becomes of Joseph, and all because of Peter's desire? What about my son? The Buddhist monks teach that letting go of attachment is simple. That is not always so. The violence of war, the violence of adultery and manipulation prove this. Let the mind be still and after a few days, a few weeks even, it passes. So why am I succumbing to this? This intrusion from Luke, these emotions tugging at my strings, trading something unclear for something even more unclear. It is a folly! Deals are not done this way, on the hint of a promise, an expectation that may or may not be fulfilled.

But I am more vulnerable now. History passes through me like the coldest of winds. There are days when I feel so exhausted that it scares me. It feels like I have no control. And outside in the park there are spring daffodils. (My mother is dead. She lies in the ground, or she is framed in the picture, or she is enclosed in the parentheses.) This is what happens when your story is not autonomous. You are the stargazer. You and her become as one; as the other.

I turn down the air conditioner and open the window, so the cold New York wind slaps my face. I would have it enter my bones. The sky still thick and pasty. Theresa May and Trump are talking about bombing Syria. I turn on the radio: an interview with Junot Diaz. The PowerPoint slides I format have a purple background. I stare at them and try to write my paragraphs because I don't want to sound stupid when it is time to deliver my presentation. Then I send an email to Luke. I tell him that I have only heels and it is snowing in New York.

I stay up all night, still writing. I don't dare check to see if Luke has replied. It may upset me, and I want to finish. Sending a letter or an email feels like losing but is better than holding on to hope. Receiving a letter or opening an email reverses the situation. For then, one must nurse the feeling as response, mulling over it, pondering the feeling until it is ready for discharge. Silence is beautiful. Either it is rebuff, or silence is the most patient contemplation. Writing, however, is freedom and address, and that is what I want for Daisy.

There she is, after all, unfairly cooped up in Virginia Woolf's novel, without so much as an alcove of interior space to move about in, to express her ecstasy or to vent her grief. She suffers without family or society, swallowed up in Clarissa's language, and only seductively on the outskirts of social space. So, Daisy appears on the verandah, or at a crossroads near some coach stop, or perhaps close to the dockyards (. . . why do we not even know?) as Peter Walsh leaves (. . . which Indian port?). Daisy trapped in the past, in a moment, a vignette, but not the kind that would enter a room, open a window, to a life inside, a life in the mind, as it does for Clarissa with a squeak of hinges on the very first page of *Mrs Dalloway*! Not a real girl, Daisy, too arch perhaps, the air not stirring for her, seeing as she has no present tense.

At about 4 am I shut my eyes and rest. I have not been sleeping well, but it hardly matters. I have the charcoal eyeliner; the pale pink lipstick. I have the best Lancôme concealer. Somehow these trivial things matter: to have my hair and my nails done, to cleanse and moisturise the skin as my mother always taught me.

Next morning it is raining again when it's time to leave. A taxi pulls up outside the hotel. The driver gets out and says he is taking a break. I walk up along Broadway skirting the puddles; now my hair is getting drenched. There is a shop selling handbags and scarves. I ask the Chinese attendant for an umbrella. She is middle-aged and wearing a green cashmere jumper with a boat neck. In my tired state I am enjoying the dampness and cold, the sound of pipes and eaves dripping, and car tyres squelching through puddles as I turn into Fifth Avenue and walk uptown for a few blocks to the New York Public Library, where people are already queueing to enter. The daffodils are trembling in the morning air. I can smell bagels and roasted coffee beans. I enter the university building and take the lift up to the fourth floor, where I sign in at the front desk then find my way to the lecture theatre.

Jonathan arrives late, during the first plenary on refugees. Based on a memoir written by Behrouz Boochani, a Kurdish-Iranian journalist detained on Manus Island, the presentation draws from footage taken with his iPhone and produced as a film. It screened at the London Film Festival. The Manus Island Detention Centre was officially and traumatically shut down in October 2017, while the refugees live tweeted and the conscience of Australian citizens haemorrhaged through social media activisms. Over seven hundred detainees were moved to holding barracks. Under a resettlement deal with the US rushed through before Trump was sworn in as president, some refugees would be accepted in exchange for Australia accepting Central American refugees.

The presentation articulates trauma and witness with chilling sensitivity.

After the professional tension and exchange of work-related emails between us, I try to avoid Jonathan, but we bump into each other in the corridor. He embraces me. 'I'm sorry about . . .' I begin, unsure of what I am regretting.

The academic disagreement? He responds in a tender voice, 'You need to do what's best for you.' After all these years of acquaintance and correspondence, I barely know him. Though he is slim, there is something firm about him, and I am the elusive, nervous creature. He allows me to move closer, move further away, to evaluate him, to photograph him, and most of the time he is very still, and I am trembling. He tells me it has been snowing upstate. The shock of seeing him makes me dumb. Then another colleague approaches – a woman – and he hugs her too, so I have to assume he does this with everyone. A warm and gentle soul. I slip away, but from then on, I'm confused, and I'm not thinking about Jonathan. It was not Jonathan. It was always Daisy. Daisy, Daisy Daisy . . . and only the women or the men who can help me recover her vibrant and courageous voice, deleted by the record. Like any author, I am ruthless. I will betray my heart and my soul. I will do whatever it takes.

But there is Katharine, the editor of a journal I wrote for. She is rather beautiful and pregnant, and I have lunch with her, sitting behind Jonathan who sits alone, until some friends join him. And there is Josey, who wears exquisite clothes, and we hang out together. We take the M train downtown to Fourteenth Street, then the L train eastbound to Brooklyn. Here, in the laidback streets that run like a grid around a park, we walk to a bookshop where we are reading. We are talking about our lives, the writing life, men, female friendship; we talk about how the industry doesn't encourage us to be experimental or to be aesthetes, instead we are restricted to writing about ethnicity, as a domesticated migrant. Because if you're too complicated, well, that's challenging for them and a threat to their superiority. I couldn't agree more with Josey. I tell her about my son. About my divorce. The difference between myself and the male writers I know is that they can complement their artistic lives by the marital arrangement: it provides security and legitimacy. But partly, I also know, it is simply an excuse.

Friends arrive for my reading. Chloe is here from New Zealand with some students, travelling for a month. She is jet-lagged but as stunning as ever. We have time to talk in a little corner of the now crowded bookshop. We have time to spend a few hours together. Roger, who is convening, is also here. It's teamwork. We take it in turns to read our poetry and prose. We pull apart the thickly layered cheese pizzas. With greasy fingers, we pass around antiseptic wipes as there are no napkins. Eric talks to me. He is heading back to Adelaide after the conference. I know he doesn't even notice his privilege. The very mention of racism or whiteness seems to jar on his nerves. So many white girls around me. The gorgeous, blonde American college girls. I feel like a bit of an outsider, but it is probably because I am tired. I may be the only one who notices that Jonathan is not here.

We go back to our hotels in different groups. Josey leaves early and kisses me goodbye. After the conference, she is going to spend a week in Boston, and she invites me to join her. Might be fun to do some writing together, poke around a bit in Massachusetts. I'm tempted. Jen and Nikki and Lorne are going to party on at a nightclub. Chloe is exhausted and staying in Brooklyn. I walk back past the brownstones and the cafés, past the park and the vibrant graffiti, to Jefferson station with Richard, one of the poets. We talk about how there is no money in the arts, how the universities are all scaling back in humanities. Science wins. We talk about a colleague's gorgeous children and his young wife. We catch the train to Union Square where we take different lines uptown. I get off at Twenty-Eighth Street.

The hotel is lit up and a group of people are queued outside. The lobby is pulsing with dark, cool energies, music and people. A couple of tall, cheerful men catch the lift with me and ask me what the rooms are like. They are checking me out, peering at my body, and the effect of the wine I have had makes me relaxed about it. I am giggling. I could invite one of them to my room. I feel chronically sex deprived, but it's okay, and the fact that I haven't been watching porn for a number of weeks is a good sign. It's just the vulnerable, lonesome life you lead as a woman and a writer. In some countries you are judged severely for travelling alone without your children. Once when I was at Heathrow, an immigration officer wearing trousers, shirt and hijab stamped my passport with a black mark because on questioning me she was suspicious that I was a writer arriving to take up a fellowship. She asked who was looking after my son while I was away.

I was about to reply that his father would be taking care of him when instead I blurted out that she was overstepping the mark. 'That's not really your business,' I declared. She was a pretty woman, going by her thick eyebrowed eyes, but her jaw clenched and her lip curled into an unpleasant smirk as she stamped my passport emphatically. She had been questioning me for so long that I was the last passenger to pass through immigration. But it was not worth making a complaint. She was baiting me, hoping for a reaction. There's a faint pang of remorse because I haven't emailed Sam since I've been away; it strikes me that I am less anxious.

I pass Jonathan again, the next day, in the corridor and there is desire, I'm sure, in his greeting. How can I know? So unsure. The male gaze intersecting the bisexual gaze. He sits behind me and Josey during the reading and I can see his legs tremble. The longing I feel surprises me and holds me hostage. But as the reading deepens, he relaxes, he succumbs to the abstract. Words do that to your impulses: they choke you; they colonise desires and what ends up suffering most is the body. The body forgets how to talk sex; it forgets how to respond. The body folds back on itself like frost flowers.

I am not sitting as close to Josey now. Josey, Jonathan and I form an equilateral triangle in a far corner of the lecture room. Josey notices the geometry.

'That felt to me like walking through a forest,' I say, turning to Jonathan, when the reading finishes.

'Washed by poetry,' he says grimly. Neither of us is smiling.

Slumped over the chair is my blazer. I pick it up. I collect my bag and walk to the doorway. For a moment I look back over my left shoulder. It matters how bodies are positioned.

Jonathan has moved to the opposite corner of the room. How different he seems; in his gait, his slumped shoulders.

The city is glorious outside, the cold air crisp, the pedestrians window-shopping or lining up for tours. The Black Americans have an agency, a voice, and a history of suffering and survival, which is foreign to me. I don't want to assume a shared experience of racism, assimilating differences I don't understand and I can't express. But I'm glad to hear their voices, to walk this city on Lenape land, to enter their shops, to buy a coat, to walk through their subways and tunnels and to get lost in the connections, further and further away from Jonathan, and nearer to him again, thinking, If only . . . If only we could have sat in the park and held hands.

But it surprises me. In my hotel room, I open my laptop and compose an email message, then I press send, breaking open my heart, knowing the wound will never heal. Who is Jonathan? A writer I can properly admire? A man I can turn to for advice? One who provokes my audacity! A stranger! Like glass, like a mirror! After all these years! Like Peter Walsh hovering in the mind of Clarissa. Who knows the hold each has on the other? How queer it is, the language of two minds, denying their bodies. I am crying. I am weeping. But I make myself dress for dinner.

Open bar, a smorgasbord. Conviviality. Two glasses of champagne. Two emails: one from Jonathan and one from an agent, saying he is looking forward to our meeting. We eat and drink merrily, tired from the conference. The professors don their coats and gloves and a few of the young researchers are hanging about. Outside, the night air pulsing in New York, a cluster of people, the subway stream is almost endless, the joint we share, doing the rounds. I take a little puff, thinking that rich Americans can be very charming. A bubble, a little spark, it pops into my thoughts, a sentence from 'Mrs Dalloway in Bond Street', the story Woolf wrote in 1922. Do I really want the kind of man who seems perfectly charming; or do I want a man like Peter, with his impudent comments, which really are a little odd? I check my phone. Nothing more but the waiting, something in the air, perhaps a little triumph to anticipate. Don't want anything bright.

April is the cruellest month, breeding lilacs out of the dead land. It has been snowing bitterly in upstate New York. I am mulling over 'The Waste Land' and the weather forecast as I take a few turns in Washington Square Park, where the fountain jets have not yet been turned on.

My eye catches the soft blue irises and violet crocuses bursting out of leaf mulch. They make my heart sing. Dry, caramel-coloured leaves are shivering on thin wands, as if at any moment they could snap off from their saplings. A few squirrels scamper into balls along the grass.

Students are sitting on park benches, smoking joints, talking about the planned air strikes on Syria, young couples are wheeling prams. Wrapped around the lampposts and swept beside the base of trees there is something that resembles large clumps of snow, but on closer inspection they turn out to be the feather down from the spectacle of a colossal pillow fight. I wish it would snow.

Snow, with its fresh canvas, helps us to forget – unlike the buds and icicles of spring, bursting from branches, or churned up from the twisted dry roots of desire. There are gullies of rainwater coursing through this city, through its drains, across its streets and the stormwater, the seepage beneath the ground. If I put my ear to the cold earth and close my eyes, I know I will hear this gurgle streaming into the rivers. The water never stops flowing; it carries Daisy to London by a circulation, by the connections to port cities from Calcutta to Ceylon to Port Said to Tilbury, as in 1941 it swept Virginia Woolf's heft of melancholia, her hat and her cane to separate landings, downstream.

Tomorrow I am flying to London.

Porta Ticinese
Milano

8 December 1924

Dear Sylvia,

Travelled by train to Milano, along the French Riviera – a journey that took the better part of two days, because ahead of us an Italian train had collided with a French train and several people were injured. Then snow caused delays. Felt elated arriving at Milano Centrale just after six a.m. Chill in the air, the frost was melting. Had not told my family when exactly we would be arriving.

Mama was sitting on her chair outside the house in a cone of sunlight, dressed in black with her shawl and pinafore. She started crying when she saw me. Papa hugged me. Simona was baking panettone, our dog Pepita, yelping, kicked his front legs high and was rewarded for keeping a good watch over the street. He licked us to death. Within an hour my aunt Michelina came to the house with her daughter Vanda and her son Francesco. We ate bread soaked in oil, we ate cheese and drank wine; there was much talk and laughter and tears. My family were all very sad about Septimus, so it was hard to explain the feelings of being freed from a husband's controlling delirium and anxiety. I don't even wish to remember. How joyless it was to be living in that room in London, with his wandering, deteriorating mind. I literally had to drag him off the streets and keep him from hallucinating in Hyde Park.

But I have missed my people, this city, the convents and campaniles. Daisy says the taste of oranges could not be sweeter and she had never tried gelato. When it snows the aperol spritz keeps us warm. We've been out and about to view the fashionable shops and bars in Via Sammartini. I couldn't wait to buy some felts, ribbons, velvet and other supplies in Piazza del Duomo: I found the softest purple straw!

We had to be quite careful with our expenses in France. Here we can relax for a while. But sooner or later, it will be awkward to stay, sharing a bed. Family life brings its own prospects and complications. Perhaps you know how censuring they can be. A widow is expected to remedy her conjugal status or remain cloistered. I wanted to bring Daisy here, have her spoiled a little. We have been to Chiesa di Santa Maria del Rosario. That pleased her and reminded her of the churches in Calcutta. And there is plenty of work; the cloche hats are all the rage. Change is everywhere, the centre seems cleaner, more organised, there are housing developments and socialist posters. But further out, in the suburbs, we've seen more poverty, refugees, factories and smokestacks. There are new laws, apparently, and people are talking in quiet tones about the squadristi.

How is Silvio? Send our love and thanks to Ethel. Keep me updated on your news and the meetings, and if there's anything we can do from here.

Yours,
R

Calle Ghetto Vecchio
Venice

4 March 1925

My dear Nora,

I may have missed your letter since we have travelled to Italy. We stayed for Christmas and through winter with Rezia's family in Milano. Her father is an innkeeper; he speaks English well. Her sister is a milliner also. She has the finest gift for patterning roses, threading straw and feathers, cutting buckram and shaping velvet, stiffening silk.

Italy has appealed to me very much, and Venezia has been a baptism in art, in light. How is it possible to come here and not want to describe, or draw, or paint? For those who do not speak the language, who are not direct descendants of western civilisation, estrangement brings its own private joy: one feels sheltered here, oddly, on the shores of memory, like history's castaway.

Watery rhythms mesmerise the soul; the horizon is opaline, a welcome change from London's chimneys, its grey and brown brickwork and its smog. Early every morning by the Grand Canal at Rialto the boats and barges bring in supplies for shops, for constructions. The canal-facing arcades come to life, bustling with traffic before sunrise, then coathanger stalls open. Rezia and I buy most of our vegetables, fish, fruit and herbs here. I try to remember some phrases, or I simply let the language fall on my ears and do not strive to understand what the words mean, much as a child learns. We see people walking to their places of work, dressed in smart clothes, the ladies elegant, well-heeled, hair pinned, the old men with tanned skin and snipped beards, dressed in waist-coats, slightly stooped, carrying a briefcase entering the amber frescoed light of the sotoportego; the elderly women in coats with shopping baskets.

In the calli there are porters crossing the bridges with two-wheeled carts and trolleys. By morning, the postman winds through the labyrinth of the sestiere and later the firewood seller comes, water carriers return from the wells, and then the refuse man.

Detail catches the eye: the craftsman's swirls and intaglios, the inscriptions of time, pediments, peeling plaster, Moghul-inspired window frames, watermarks, knotted beams, scarified rotting timbers, split, cobwebbed varnish, graffitied ruins are glorious under the blue canopy of evening skies. One spends the day watching from the wooden shutters, down, down, down, into the narrow cobblestoned calli. And having fallen into the habit of gazing across the rooftops, the eye scans the campanile of San Marco, where the bells toll. This is how the day is spent, sewing the silk flowers which Rezia has gorgeously cut, watching a family gather for supper. I may overhear as a wife argues with her husband in one of the nearby houses, her accusations; and his short, sharp replies incoherent to my ears. Always the seagulls circling above the rooftops and the cry of swallows at dusk, when the light turns rose. Sometimes, I will tune in to the radio and listen to the sound of the broadcaster to practise my speaking Italian. I turn the pages of a dictionary and teach myself a few words and practise with Rezia. Last week, I surprised myself when I asked someone in the street for directions.

I can think of nothing as sweet or refreshing as the juice of Venetian oranges, grown in the orchards of Mestre or on the island of Sant 'Erasmo. We squeeze the fruit by hand. The hours slip by. Rezia takes orders from the buyers, Mrs Chiara Longo in San Marco and Borsalino in Padua. Gondolier hats, ladies' straw hats with sashes, ribbons and flowers. Like maids, we live simply, the difference being that we have no master. I prepare meals and wash our clothes. If I wash in the morning our laundry may dry before mist falls and the sky darkens. There is still enough daylight for reading, sometimes a walk, or a little drawing. Early mornings and evenings are best, with so many churches, domes, towers and palazzos to sketch and a constant stream of pedestrians from Piazzale Roma to the lagoon. It is better to leave early. On my way to the market, I will stop and pray at one of the churches, crossing myself the way Ma used to whenever we walked past a church. I light a candle. Reflecting for a while on the silent pools of my soul, I shed a tear for my past life. My failings, my penance. What kind of mother thinks she can live in this world by her own rules? My past is a memory that I cannot speak; a story that is governed by others, those of whom are not very significant and quite peripheral to my life, yet they try, with the best intentions, to interpret or to elaborate my journey. This dressing up is a masquerade they do not mind because my story gives them power. What they make of me becomes original. But if I were to speak for myself, it would deprive them of the deep satisfaction that the telling of a story brings. Trust me, there is no shortage of imagined histories and past lives imposed on the likes of a dark, immigrant stranger. The anger and pain one feels on being silenced is like a death.

Living with Rezia has made it possible to evict these ghosts. They are no longer my inevitable companions. Still, I pray for dear Charlotte's soul, and for Joseph. For Mama and Papa, for Bunny and Radhika, their unreadable trace. Anyone who comes to Venezia feels destined to arrive in this floating, frosted city, as if the journey could not have been a fault. Despite misgivings, and although our tenancy here may be brief, the city is time's crucible. Timeless and fleeting, from our single attic room, the city goes about its rhythms and routines, with the traghetti and the vaporetti ferrying people back and forth across the canals, with the birds swirling in the salt air and the chimes of the bells tolling every hour from every basilica and chiesa on these islands. Gazing outwards from this room, I have felt what every exile longs for. Not that we are permanently stationed, but after leaving a city like Calcutta to arrive in a city like Venezia, I understand that one never loses the past, one is always destined to return.

Love,
Daisy

Brixton Markets
London

12 July 2018

At the New York conference I met an academic from Seattle who runs a small press and was interested in my novel. He wants to see more, but I have only written fifteen thousand words. Money has been tight and kept me spinning in overdrive, in dizzying circles. I haven't revised the essay on Shuhua Ling that I had pitched to the *London Review of Books*. Somehow, I keep getting side-tracked by issues like racism and immigration. One feels responsible; one feels like part of a community resisting media control, misogyny, the alt-right configuring and harnessing our brown bodies for labour, trafficking us, manipulating us as 'free trade' tokens. Even as writers we can't escape being an identity – it can stultify your life, but these are the issues we engage with daily.

Boris Johnson has resigned as foreign secretary and a host of other resignations from the Brexit think-tank have swiftly followed. At the Brixton undercover markets, I bump into Celine, and we sit down and have coffee. She looks as amazing as ever. She is pregnant, all baby bump, and eager to hear about my travels, the novel and how I am managing with being a parent across continents. Appalling news. Her dad's deportation order came courtesy of the Royal Mail. Al-Jazeera ran a clip from the protest march yesterday at Whitehall and there's a march being planned in Birmingham. Theresa May's Tories have voted not to disclose secret documents which disappeared years ago relating to the beleaguered Windrush citizens.

I just feel tremendous sadness. Celine has been talking to immigration lawyers in the city. There was a caring sense of community when we all lived in the rundown house in Tavistock Square, in our separate flats. Jeremy and his wife Suella visited on weekends; I had met them a few times in the lobby. They are softly spoken, gentle folk, supportive of their daughter. They had arrived from Jamaica in 1968. Jeremy's medical bills are no longer being covered by the National Health but Suella's residency status has not so far been questioned. Such a shambles! The number of people detained and deported because their landing cards had been destroyed not being accounted for, and the targeting erratic.

Opposition to the far right is increasing in parliament; there is as an overwhelming sense of public outrage and calls for a second EU referendum. Almost every day there is a protest on campuses, outside Westminster or online. The pound has dropped in value. Rents and the cost of living are noticeably more expensive. I have coffee with a colleague near Waterloo, trying to reconnect. Another friend invites me for dinner in Surbiton. The seminar I am teaching at City, University of London has finished up, and aspirations for my contract to be renewed for the new academic year have not materialised. The head of department has taken early retirement and two other senior colleagues have found positions elsewhere. One is moving to Reading, the other to Kent. Partly, it's the economic uncertainty caused by Brexit. There's always an elsewhere, and I am overdue to stop trying to pass through the revolving door that separates past from present.

For some of us home is nowhere, or it is in the past, however broken or wherever that may be. However demeaned and depleted. I have to be in so many places to inhabit Daisy's life, which means abandoning my own. I am falling into crisis but can't stop myself. The price you pay for looking too deeply into the past, for trying to correct history, for even believing that you can try, is that you lose your fixture in the present. Like loose threads in a fine fabric, I am easily torn. Pulled apart. Yes, my mother had died. But I had not guessed how distant my son would become. (How possessive it is for me to even say 'my son'. And yet, how often I have taken this liberty in my work.) Very like Clarissa, self-important, sitting in her drawing room with Peter, on his return from India, the morning of her party. There is Peter, rushing upstairs past Lucy in the hall, his hands trembling as he kisses hers; her hands histrionically dropping the scissors and silks draped over her dress, and all the intimate exchanges between them that follow in spasms, intensely, leading to her asserting with pride, 'Here is my Elizabeth.'

That morning, on leaving Westminster, Peter could muse about how insincere and cold that was of Clarissa, and how it irks Elizabeth, while he has told her everything. Everything! Like a fool! It makes the blood boil! Calling on her like that unannounced on the very morning of her party! For two years I had mistaken my son's coldness for independence. Perhaps he needed more when there was less and less of me. They have been using gender neutral pronouns and changed their name to Sinéad but I didn't know. Sometimes they wear mascara, sometimes a skirt loose over leggings. They have written a poem while sitting on the Juliet balcony that connected our rooms, perhaps before dawn when the moon is a crescent and the rainbird sings, mysteriously, multi-toned. A poem about time called 'Waiting for Tomorrow' in which they write: 'I will not fall.' That line alone made my heart glad.

Lucille and I are texting. Hearing from her makes my travels seem to flow between each surprising incident with a spark and serendipity. London, Calcutta, Sydney, Tathra, Wuhan, Melbourne, New York; there are so many departures, arrivals, guesthouses, hotels that it's hard to be settled anywhere. What does settlement mean for those of us like Daisy, or Lucrezia? Are we destined to belong in the liminality of harbours, rivers, airports, social media? I am restless for work. Self-esteem has crashed, money is burning. I don't want to dip into my meagre savings. Several days are wasted applying for an Arts Council grant. Believing in the project and garnering references, all of it, so much energy. Very likely wasted time! Have to be thick-skinned, these days. It's grist for the mill, character-building and so on, but inside I feel I'm unravelling fast, and it's more than a bit scary.

Returning home to my townhouse in Sydney, I know the fridge will need cleaning out, layers of washed clothes will be draped over the sofa. Two days later the mail will arrive, bundled up in thick brown elastic. Among the invoices and journals, a hand-made card from Lucille. It will be her way of telling me she's done, and she can't possibly go away to Italy with me.

We talked about a trip to Venice, staying in one of the monasteries. We talked about the lives of Eleonora Duse, Peggy Guggenheim and Thomas Mann. We texted flirtatiously on a daily diet, and feverishly when I travelled from Sydney to Melbourne. We talked all night, that first night, after the poetry and the beer, and that second time after the Yarra River at sunset. She offered me a twist of vowels, birdsong drifting from her mouth, pure and elusive like a heady scent.

I could spend hours tasting her, turning her words on my tongue. Like 'dazing', or 'Daisyed'.

Pleasure, she said with confidence, was there to be had. She reminded me of a lotus, violet-tinged, tight-bloomed petals, languid in their disclosures, then curling afterwards.

The Grand Hotel
Venice

25 May 1926

Dearest Ape,

What a splendid time we are having here! I do think the pavilions at Giardini look marvellous, the gardens have a leafy,
quiet atmosphere apparent from the vaporetto. Have become
a huge fan of Degas, who has four paintings here with the
French. Splendid to be with Matisse – and his eleven master-
pieces – no less! To think it's been almost fifteen years since
Roger hosted the post-Impressionists at the Grafton Gallery.
Our company is modest by comparison. I believe Duncan's *St
Tropez* has been quite a success. My *Coppa d'arancie* seems to have
garnered a few compliments too. All pleasing! Are you back at
Rodmell, Billy, scrambling about along the riverbank? Do be
kind to yourself, especially if it is raining and muddy. Roger
says he fancies sketching me in gouache and pencil. Let's see.

We lunched today in Campo San Stefano, near the
Accademia. Duncan and I have been poking about in Castello

behind the Arsenale docks where the locals seem to gather. We are making time to paint; feeling waves of confidence now and then, absorbing the light and the shadows. Have been walking in Giudecca to escape the crowds. Madness, as usual once you step into the calli. I keep an eye out for leisurely vistas, stray scenes of intimacy between couples, or a mother's gestures as she walks her children. By the way, I encountered two outsiders in Padua whom I thought would be perfectly suited for your outsiders' society. Daisy – an Indian woman, or she might be Eurasian, very pretty, approachable – and her lover Lucrezia, a young milliner. I was coming back from Giotto at the Scrovegni Chapel. They were taking in supplies to a shop owner, exquisite hats that piqued my curiosity. Thought of you, Billy, seeing as you have a touch of India in *Mrs Dalloway*. Might be a story there you could use?

Some of the warehouses in Giudecca are being renovated as studios. They're going to make it residential. I think it'll become a desirable address. I guess it might be costly with construction here, everything on barges, even the scaffolds and cranes. Mario and Astolfo have been hosting gatherings. We attended for a little celebration, prosecco and cicchetti. He has wonderful views of St Mark's Square. Very memorable! We all went to Ravenna to see the mosaics, which are really something. Spent a few days in Roma. Roger accompanied us to the Hotel Ambasciatori to see the frescos painted by Guido Cadorin. Stunning work, and he's got Mussolini's lover in it too, Margherita Sarfatti, Grassini's daughter. Old, old

Jewish family, I'm sure you remember their palazzo on the Grand Canal. Her biography on him is going to be published before long, in London, so I'm told. Rather a dare, I think. Not sure how that will go. Anyway, should be interesting. We have noticed the presence of Blackshirts and there have been strikes on the mainland at Mestre. Posters too. I'm not a fan of Mussolini, he seems a bit of a bore. Tell me yours. Are you writing furiously? How is *Mrs Dalloway*?

xxx Nessa

Calle Ghetto Vecchio

Venice

29 May 1926

Certain things concerning my present circumstances oblige me to confide, though what use is this? I do not know. Surely, nobody will discover let alone want to read this journal. I have spared my cousin, Nora. Her letter to me this week is full of sweet hope for our reunion. She sends news that Joseph is in a good school, though apparently not the boarding school where I had him enrolled. They want him to take up a carpentry apprenticeship.

Nobody but Rezia knows of my current employment. In Venice, it does not feel sinful to be plying my trade on the streets, or to share a bed with a woman. Men are mostly respectful; some are even kind to me. Nora would be horrified to know the depths to which I've sunk. It is my hope not to dwell on the dramatic moments in my life, the ones that altered things forever and led to sorrow: Peter Walsh, losing Charlotte. But these memories are masters of themselves, they seep and seep. I've tried to see the changes more like reflections in water, a gradient flow, a current against which it is useless to flail, as if it is witchy for this story that two women be here in ink, in each other's arms. How is it possible that our real lives can alter the story being told about us? No, I cannot trust my addictions, the force of will or my skills any longer. Accepting what my story makes of me is not defeat. On the contrary, I've felt joy. Neither Kali nor the Christian deities of the Serenissima is more evident.

Others might construe this as blasphemy. Nora perhaps. But I have learned that people change, and women are strong. They know hunger. They know when to swallow waterbrash in their mouth and when to bite. I remember our parish priest and the convent nuns saying it started with Eve, but that's Catholic guilt. Nora is no stranger to the bitter fruit of married life. This is what crossed my mind today on my way to the Ghetto Nuovo. The leaves trembled in the rain, coloured prisms of light reflecting off the facades. I had come to meet Rezzie. She was modelling for an artist. Had set off early. Along the way, in a rather plain, deserted campo, a large, middle-aged Italian man approached, regarding me with desire. He offered me fifty lira then took me to a third-floor room. I sat on the edge of the bed. I felt the scrape of his rough hand down the front of my dress, the hairs on his upper arm. His body pressed into my backbone, his breath heaving. He squeezed my breast. Tugged my nipple. I felt him pull himself and I heard him groan. He turned me, shoving his penis between my lips. Swept my hair to one side; the way men like to do to watch a woman choke on fat. Then he pulled my thighs, pushed into my legs. It was a little rough, but quickly over.

I felt the familiar chafing I had suffered with my husband. Afterwards, he gave what he promised. I took the notes and stumbled down three flights of water-damaged steps. I stood in darkness in the damp vestibule and turned the heavy doorknob. Outside, heavy black clouds had tangled the sky in dark swirls. I walked in a daze, soon part of a throng, telling myself it helps me if I can save what I earn from these encounters. Rain fell, cold on my bare arms, and it washed my tears. People began to open umbrellas, but I did not have one. Fortunately, I was wearing a hat, which kept my hair dry. It didn't matter that my dress was soaked.

Some of the Jewish residents had gathered under an alcove near the synagogue and were talking to each other in soft tones. I stood with them, shivering, waiting for Rezia and for the rain to subside. We could hear bells chime; perhaps from Chiesa della Madonna dell'Orto in the sestiere of Cannaregio, which is close by. It was a relief to walk in the shadow of opulence with the beggars and tourists. It occurred to me that I felt no shame. I felt careless and mildly exhilarated by my resilience over the turns of fortune and fate. Like a dolphin, I felt utterly free. I could not be hunted. This strange, addictive feeling of independence, of being exiled from my shame as much as my grief, was discernible to me, standing there with the folded notes in my bag. For what woman is rewarded in marriage for chores and how often does it feel to her as if she is being gagged and raped? It may shock my cousin, but the profession is very well accepted here in Venice. On the whole, it is rife.

As I stood there, sorrow seemed to have loosened its hold on my body. I heard the bells chime again and I saw Rezia walking out of the mist. We recognised each other from across the courtyard. We walked to an osteria for refreshment, and I was able to pay with the money I had earned. We spent a good hour and a half, enjoying the wine, the company and the cicchetti.

The rain had paused, and a deep stillness enveloped the canal as it coursed under bridges between the tenement houses towards the horizon. Sunlight broke through cloud in skewers, enhancing the reflections of a convent and the stern of many boats that dipped and swayed on the surface of the water.

Varuna, Cascade Street

Katoomba

9 August 2018

Light breaks through the black silhouette of trees in pale streams. The sky above is a dark blue drift of separating clouds, the scalloped sugar-brown leaves of the maple tree scraping the windowpane become distinctly visible. Minutes pass. I am awake and at the desk in the main room out on the verandah. The noise of a plane overhead strikes me as unusual, then a burst of kookaburra song, the cascade of branches outlined, small birds calling from, and leaving, their perches. Frost on yellow tufts of grass covering the track towards the driveway.

Within twenty minutes the horizon has turned pink and the verandah is flooded with light. The blanket warms my thighs, my shoulders are aching. There is a humming noise in the void of silence that surrounds me, and I can hear the distant acceleration of cars along Cliff Drive. And now there is a rose light suffusing the tree line.

I wrap myself in a blanket and write a few lines. More minutes pass. I scan and search parts of the manuscript, thinking through my travels, my reading, the address of letters, diary entries, their tenses, digestible and slippery, as if lived now in the present moment, on a winter's day in Katoomba, on stolen lands of the Gundungurra and Darug nations. Daisy meets Rezia Smith for the first time at Dr Bradshaw's home in Chelsea. She tutors the Bradshaw's children. They go to a gathering of anti-Fascists in London, led by Silvio Campo. Here they meet Sylvia Pankhurst, Campo's lover. Sentences almost take the shape of paragraphs. Then I feel stuck. I make tea and keep trying to write. Finally, unable to resist the temptation, I pull on my boots and go for a walk down Cascade Street, past the fibro cottage for sale. There is a path leading down into the steep overgrown ravine, a log crossing over a cold stream and a walkway down through tall pines that line the Kedumba River into the reserve. The camping sites are empty and there are no caravans. An elderly man wearing a beanie and duffle coat is cooking a hot breakfast. His ute is parked by the picnic tables. I walk past him and through the Falls Reserve. A web of frost covers the grass. It is crunchy underfoot. I cross the road over to the old, derelict kiosk and lookout. A wire-mesh fence has been erected to protect walkers from subsidence and the view opens out onto the garish Scenic World complex on Violet Street. I turn back, hesitating near the steps leading to the Prince Henry Cliff walk towards Echo Point. It's tempting, but I want to get back and write. I'm not here for the world-class scenery.

Something always yields when I stand on one of these precipices gazing down, mist licking the canopy, shrouding the Jamison Valley. A spiritual experience. It's like falling from the edge of the plateau into the canyon, the wind buffering between bluffs, currawongs winging from the trees to feed. It's like hurtling towards death and not moving at all. This is the best time of day, before a swarm of tourists arrive with walking canes. A group of hikers have crossed Katoomba Falls Road, their backpacks full of gear. A pair of hawks are small, blurred wedges in the photograph I stop to take with my iPhone.

One has to carve out some writing space. Can I use this line or is it a random thought?

As I walk, I ponder the weight of demands that I am failing to meet. My body feels heavy, the muscles tight as it blunders along. This reprieve from the writing scene with its maze-like subterfuges and spins is not nearly enough. If I'm lucky I'll write a single chapter. I'll get Daisy and Charlotte as far as Colombo. How badly I'd lost my way in grief, after Mum died. A delusional grief; not seeing, not sensing that Sinéad was also grieving.

One way or another, we get recruited, derailed. Social media takes a deceptive grip over our lives, the FOMO and clickbait weirdly demanding. Apart from being blocked there are no visa requirements in that world. No barriers like the ones encountered when I try to talk to Sinéad about school, their friends, their world. The intimacy we once shared when they were in primary school is now replaced by social media, Instagram and Snapchat. Technology is the parent. And though I've sensed the beginning of the drift and estrangement, I've missed the chance to get counselling. On the four nights a week Sinéad spends with me we have dinner together but they sit with eyes averted, headphones embedded. The bedroom door is always bolted, and I am not permitted inside. My guess is that they're gaming, messaging, on chat lines, while I've spent the day with disruptive anxieties, such as trying to cancel my Telstra account via a call centre in the Philippines. Emotionally in turmoil, making slow progress with my novel, I haven't perceived the extent of resentment for the times I've travelled overseas. Success, they say, comes at a cost, and is apparently selfish. Strangely, though, it doesn't even feel like success. The artist, the writer, is always an outsider.

Berndt was mistaken that morning in the café. I am like Daisy, taking risks, leaving everything behind for the idea of tomorrow. Daisy's story.

Writing is dangerous. It may sound overly dramatic, but time after time I have felt its gravity flex and fracture me: the fusion of two worlds, and the schisms. Strange movements and rumbles are heard. Hints and forewarnings. No way!

gives way to dread. One can scarcely believe it is happening. To write is to dream. It is also to birth (the verb, not the noun). Writing is like entering the narrowest portals of a rich intuitive world; one cannot leave unmarked. One travels an imaginary geography where the boundaries separating the real and the created, the Orient and Europe, the past and the present are always shifting. I was naive. I wanted to believe that love and fiction are accessible destinies. But if I'm honest about it, there's a part of me that is restless and cannot suffer complacency or being ruled. There's a part of me that wants this challenge to happen, this unpredictable journey.

So, I'm here now, following the currawongs up from Katoomba Falls. Beneath this blue plateau there are layers of silt, sand and mudstone buried in time. They were formed more than two hundred million years ago, pushed up from the vast deposited sediments of a shallow, inland sea. Turbulent streams and rivers flooded. They spilled carbonate and karst and, afterwards, when the earth's plates shifted, volcanic lava. Deep valleys and gorges have been undermined by the collapsing seams of shale and soft coal, carved by gravity and water. There's a prehistoric story of transformations written into the rock. Indecipherable. The land is timeless and I'm a speck of dust walking across it. I'll return to my room with the radical hope of another chapter, and another, leading to an ending. Walking through the reserve; it is now ten minutes to seven. The elderly man cooking himself breakfast smiles as I approach. He takes a step towards me.

'Morning! Have you had breakfast?' He has a stubble, bright blue eyes and pale skin, the capillaries branching on the surface.

We begin talking, as happens sometimes with strangers. He introduces himself as Neil and invites me to join him for a cup of tea. He has water boiling away on his portable stove.

'Oh, thank you! My name is Mina. I'm going back to where I'm staying for breakfast,' I say. Breakfast time at Varuna is a quiet affair: cereal, yoghurt, a pot of hot tea, the sound of the clock ticking and the floorboards creaking as fellow residents wake and dress. It's curious and pleasant to speak to this man, Neil, like this. Not something I would normally do.

'I used to live here,' he says, 'but I've come back from overseas and it's out of my price range. The real estate is so expensive around here now; I can't afford even to rent a place – and Sydney is worse, of course. So I've been camping. Every few days I take a shower in the public blocks or a swimming pool.'

He has a cultivated, English sounding accent. His van is packed with stuff, which I can see through the rear window. It strikes me how inconvenient it would be to live without the essentials: a hot shower daily, an internet connection.

'I've been living in India most of the last twenty years,' he explains. 'In Varanasi and Gujarat. I lived like a local; I speak Hindi. You used to be able to stay on a visa for five years but now it's a tourist visa that only lasts for six months and then you have to get it renewed. Sets you back about two hundred dollars, and it's getting more expensive to live there too . . .'

He raves on for a while, telling me that India has lost its spiritual way and has grown corporate. People like him have become exiles, without a home.

'But India is no different to any other nation,' I argue. 'Don't you think Indians are entitled to benefit financially from Western tourism? After all, the British and other colonial countries exploited India's wealth. India has its own debts to pay. And isn't it a good thing that a city like Mumbai has fast food, five-star hotels, 4G cellular networks and outsourcing?'

'Yes, but that's globalism and it's everywhere, and Indians were honest, trustworthy people twenty years ago when I first lived there. What brings tourists to India are the temples and the gurus, the Tibetans in Himachal Pradesh and the Dalai Lama.'

He starts a kind of rant about India, melding philosophy, astrology, Sanskrit and the Vedanta. He's a writer, apparently, and has self-published books on healing and philosophy.

'But don't you see?' I say, seizing my chance to inter-ject when he pauses for breath. 'Your whole view of India is exploitative; it's typical for white men, colonialists and missionaries to be expounding on and educating India. You're centring yourself, with your own viewpoints on India. Maybe, too, instead of talking at me you should be listening to me, because *I'm* Indian. Isn't it time that white people started listening to people of colour!? Even this land that we're standing on was stolen; it belongs to the Aboriginal nation.'

'Oh no, Mina. No.' He starts talking over me, repeating things he has said with a kind of affable pomposity.

My blood begins to boil and I decide I can't listen any longer. I want to go back to Daisy and write about this.

'I have to get Daisy and Lucrezia from Marseille to Milan,' I told Viv last night as I steeped the peppermint teabag in my cup.

Viv has steady eyes, a strong, tanned face. We had driven out in the wind to the bottle shop earlier that evening. The wind was so strong that it blew my car door open. We settled on a South Australian pinot noir and a pinot gris. Viv is from the Adelaide Hills; she knows about birds and she is writing a novel about feral camels.

I want to write about the Neil incident before we meet for dinner. It's so quiet in my room, framed by the trees, the variations in light. Yesterday, I spent a lot of the time alternating between escaping the sunlight streaming directly through the verandah, then feeling the cold. I moved my laptop and books from the east-facing window, looking out on the front garden, to the desk which overlooks the neighbouring house. Two boys were kicking a soccer ball. Their father was chopping wood. My thoughts drifted with the smoke curling up from their chimney and the clock keeping pace.

That's where I want to be now. Time is running out, and if I want to find Daisy's story it will be on the page. Writing can be an impartial space, where binaries and polarities are neutralised, a surrogate ethics for our lives. I miss the evenings having dinner with Sinéad; I miss them coming home from school, walking towards the door, past the garden I have tended. The old photographs speak a story I am not ready to fold away. Sinéad hates those I've had framed and displayed as if they are trophies, no longer part of their value system. It hurts, of course, but it also feels bewildering. The signs of coldness in our relationship are almost casual.

No matter the cost, I say to myself. No matter. But it's too late. Daisy has left the mews at Sir William Bradshaw's house in Mayfair where she has been staying because she is in need of a new family. She has met Rezia and the women from the East End. Clarissa simply wouldn't help Peter to find lodgings. That was his excuse. It was well within her means and would have freed him up to haunt and hover, to taste variety, the companionship of women, the loyalty of men in games rooms and smoking rooms, while beholden to Clarissa. Somehow, always. She has been the singular predicament of his devotion. That rendezvous at Bourton is an imprint for every subsequent romantic – or otherwise – failure in his life, when what he's wanted more than anything is to succeed. Bourton, like an hourglass, stretching and refining the measure of his emotions into an inevitable and unattainable thread of fine sand.

Radhika doesn't like London at all. It is cold and gloomy, this London she has heard fine people talk so much about!

The houses are not well spaced as they are in Garden Reach. The buildings are drab and very much the same, side by side, sharing walls. Most of the nurses she'd travelled with on the journey to England have ended up destitute, waiting for a passage on a steamer back to Ceylon or India. One girl, Anna Gonsalves, went to the ayahs' home in Hackney. It's hard to find bed and board in London if you are not European, though there are other orphanages and refuges for the poor ayahs and lascars. Perhaps it is fanciful for Daisy to think of returning to her home in leafy Garden Reach, to Joseph and Mrs Burgess and Bunny, but she does hold a mental picture of Joseph asleep in his cot the day she left India. Her plans for his education – boarding school and being sent to Oxford – will never eventuate. Still, the boy has coped admirably well. His new life with the Jesuits is not at all bad. Tactfully, he never speaks of his mother or his sister, and Miss Myra Dean now has a new scheme. He can do better than carpentry. She might send him to Kampala to work as a cashier in the clerical services.

In London, Lucrezia is thrilled to make a boater for Sylvia Pankhurst. Sylvia wants a grosgrain ribbon around the crown in suffragette colours. Because it's vital, and not too late to petition, to march and write on behalf of the multitude of poor women, each with their separate life. (Women who must pay taxes yet cannot vote.) They meet in a stable in Soho, furnished with chairs and workbenches. Sylvia and Silvio are running meetings here with three hundred Italian exiles.

They organise and publish anti-Fascist pamphlets. Silvio Corio is an exile from Turin, a manufacturing city where a working-class militancy has grown in the post-war decade in the shopfronts, fuelled by Antonio Gramsci's journal, *L'Ordine Nuovo*. London's East End, like the north of Italy, is a hive of socialists, factory workers and dockworkers. Certainly, it is not Clarissa's end of town. It is where the Bengalis and Armenian refugees sell fruit and vegetables out of cardboard crates in the street markets. But it's too late for the politician, Giacomo Matteotti, who has been kidnapped in a car owned by the editor of a newspaper, his dead body dumped in a forest outside Rome. He had just returned to Italy after meeting with the British prime minister, Ramsay MacDonald, unionists and members of the Labour Party who were attempting to defeat Fascism.

Meanwhile, news today about the climate changing, weirdly. A polar vortex has caused New York and London to freeze, while there have been floods in Indonesia, in North Carolina, in Townsville, and the acqua alta has submerged the piazzas and tourist sites of Venice. The latest catastrophe has outdone the last, and clairvoyants are in demand.

And it's too late for Sinéad and me to live together as I had hoped, moving from the suburb where they are schooling, closer to university. A decision to live permanently with their father has already been made and I will be the last person to learn. I've strayed. Too absorbed in writing. Having struggled to distinguish between imagination and fantasy, while the floodgates had long opened, the emotions swirling out of control, the trees that once gave us shade uprooted from our courtyard, the debris and the dead things swept downstream. I'll never look back and not flinch, though I've yet to see the damage. Grotesque and unrecognisable, the remains of my mother, Charlotte, Lucille, Luke.

And further afield, in a place that Virginia Woolf described as 'the floor of the mind', there is Sam, like a dead name, bruised purple from words unspoken, from private sentences in their diary cursing my selfishness, and then my thoughts, which are ropes around their wrists that I have failed to slacken. Like the other remains of this life, they are sodden, covered in mud, like something seized. But I am not drowning. I am standing right here, where the water has reached its highest point. I am thinking of Daisy and Lucrezia dropping a few coins, taking a riverboat to Santa Lucia in Venice, the gentle green lapping of water, the shuttered windows of a medieval convent where they will find a temporary shelter. The sky is mottled, violet and puffy. It is no longer menacing.

Now, I'm in the spotlight. I can smell the acacia, the leaf mulch, the wet sandstone. Neil is standing right in my face, lecturing about Krishna and the ego and possession, speaking with quiet authority, with centuries of exploitative colonial history behind him. He attempts to instruct me. Sublimates and reasons in a proper, middle-class English accent. But I haven't been listening. I've been daydreaming again, and the minutes have turned to years.

'Look, you're not aware of what Indians themselves might be thinking,' I interrupt. 'You're not listening, you don't want to hear . . .' Then I decide it's not worth it. Neil is never going to understand.

I turn and walk away. His tirade seems to echo in the reserve, but his voice gradually fades. Hooray! He is lessening and I can hear the ardent language of Virginia Woolf drowning him out, vividly, through the pages of *Mrs Dalloway*. There are pages I turn, peeling away layers of colonial privilege that have already devoured India. Some I fold into origami shapes that tell a different story: Daisy's rendered home with its semicircular balconies; Daisy's carriage; the SS *Ranchi*; a writing desk, the kind you can lock; a closet filled with hinged leather hat boxes; a gondola for Lucrezia and Daisy. I mark other pages with Post-it notes, releasing Daisy and Lucrezia from a fictional destiny that sees them backed into dark, uncertain corners, disconnected from society in a country that was never their home. In the main room, my laptop will open to this very page, the blanket thrown over the wicker chair out on the covered verandah, the heater beside the writing desk, the jug ready to boil for peppermint tea well into the afternoon as the light smoulders through the ghost gums and the clock on the mantelpiece ticks away until it is supper time.

The light is grainy, rays of it spilled in the gully. With the stubbornness of a brown girl refusing to be silenced, I cross the reserve, the grass damp now that the frost has melted.

An ordinary penance; a woman carrying her private sorrow but not in the grip of anyone's memory, someone like Daisy or even Lucrezia, refusing demise. Nothing to look at in her t-shirt and leggings, her hair in a messy top knot. Words rise and tumble from the floor of my mind as I head towards the creek with a brisk stride, following the scent of the pine trees. It yields to acacia and eucalypt. To dogwood flowering, to birdsong and birch enclosing the sodden, steep pathway, as I climb up to Cascade Street.

Notes

p. 11   'Vainly the dark, adorably pretty girl ran to the end of the terrace;' Virigina Woolf, *Mrs Dalloway* (London: Penguin, 1967), p. 174.

p. 68   'I dig out beautiful caves . . .' *The Diary of Virginia Woolf*, Vols 1–5, ed. Anne Olivier Bell. (London: Hogarth Press, 1977–1982.) Vol. II (1920–1924), p. 263.

p. 70   'Benjamin is a ravenous wolf, in the morning devouring the prey and at evening dividing the spoil.' Genesis 49:27, English Standard Bible, 2016.

pp. 74, 75   Diary entry for 30 April 1926. *The Diary of Virginia Woolf*, ed. Anne Olivier Bell. Vol. III (1925–1930).

p. 83   Quote from Virginia Woolf, *The Waves* (Oxford: Oxford University Press, 1992), p. 228.

p. 118   'Yes, the old ladies . . .' The memoir club contributions: '22 Hyde Park Gate'. *Moments of Being: Autobiographical Writings*, Virginia Woolf. London: Pimlico, 2002.

p. 119   'One feels about in a state of misery . . .' 15 October 1923. *The Diary of Virginia Woolf*, ed. Anne Olivier Bell. Vol. II (1920–1924).

p. 177   'My heroism was purely literary . . .' 6 January 1925, *The Diary of Virginia Woolf*, ed. Anne Olivier Bell. Vol. III (1925–1930).

p. 214   *Leave the Letters till We're Dead: The Letters of Virginia Woolf*, Vol 6: 1936–1941. Ed. Nigel Nicholson and Joanne Trautmann. (London: Hogarth, 1980) pp. 289–290. In a letter to Shuhua Ling, Virginia

Woolf writes: 'Now I write to say that I like it very much. I think it has great charm . . . I find a charm in the very unlikeness. I find the similes strange and poetical . . .' In Vita Sackville-West's introduction to *Ancient Melodies* (London: Hogarth, 1953) she describes Ling's writing as 'charmed' five times and praises its quaintness and simplicity.

p. 218 'Fiction is like a spider's web . . .' Woolf, Virginia. 'Essay Three.' *A Room of One's Own*, London: Hogarth Press, 1929.

p. 220 'So by tube to the Temple; & there wandered in the desolate ruins of my old squares; gashed; dismantled; the old red bricks all white powder, something like a builder's yard.' January, 1941, *The Diary of Virginia Woolf*, ed. Anne Oliver Bell. Vol. V (1936–1941), p. 353.

pp. 241, 250   References to Virginia Woolf's *Mrs Dalloway*, (London: Penguin, 1967) p. 1 ff; p. 173, 'Daisy on the verandah, Daisy all in white with a fox terrier on her knee; very charming, very dark, the best he had ever seen of her . . .'

pp. 234, 255   Riff on 'April is the cruellest month, breeding/Lilacs out of the dead land' T.S. Eliot, 'The Waste Land'. (London: Faber & Faber, 1922).

Acknowledgements

This novel was written on stolen Aboriginal lands of the Gadigal, Gundungurra, Yuin and Ngarrindjeri people. I am deeply grateful for the opportunity to live, work and write here on these lands as an Indian woman. To elders, past, present and emerging, I salute you, and stand with you in your struggle against racism and its crimes, the erasure of language and of stories, which are the threads of our families' lives; I thank you for your laws, your languages and your custodianship.

Historical figures in this novel have been researched through my reading of their diaries, letters, articles, books, and other research sources. To my best knowledge and ability, they are fictionalised with a careful balance of accuracy and speculation. Some dates of events have been altered for the purposes of fiction: for example, the publication date of *Mrs Dalloway* was May 1925, while Vanessa Bell exhibited a painting at the Venice Biennale in 1926.

To Vanessa Radnidge, Karen Ward, Ali Lavau, Alysha Farry, Madison Garratt, Sharon Mo, Emma Dorph, and to everyone at Hachette, my deepest gratitude for your confidence in me; and for the meticulous shaping and making of this novel.

My special thanks to Meena Kandasamy, Patrick Flanery, Hilary Mantel, Beejay Silcox, Robert Watkins, Mohammed Ahmad, Melanie Cheng, Brian Castro, Tamryn Bennett, Michelle Hamadache, Jo Langdon, Lucy Valerie Graham, and Nicholas Jose.

To David Godwin, a thousand thanks for believing in my work.

My thanks to Catherine Cole, Michael Griffiths, Judith Beveridge, Ivor Indyk and Anne Brewster for your invaluable readings.

I appreciate kind support I have received from Wenona Byrne and Joanne Simpson from the Australia Council for the Arts for a Literature Grant to edit this novel. My thanks as well to the Varuna Writers' Centre where I was blessed with an alumnus residency, and to the Arvon Foundation for a Retreat at The Hurst in Shropshire.

Michelle Cahill is the author of fiction, essays and three collections of poetry, including *Vishvarupa*, which was shortlisted for the Victorian Premier's Literary Award, and *Letter to Pessoa*, a short-story collection that won the 2017 NSW Premier's Literary Award (Glenda Adams Award) and was shortlisted for the 2017 Steele Rudd Queensland Literary Award. Born in Kenya, she attended primary school in London before migrating to Australia. She lives in Sydney, where she graduated in Medicine and Arts. She is editor of the online literary magazine *Mascara* and co-editor of the anthology *Contemporary Asian Australian Poets*. Michelle was awarded the 2020 Red Room Poetry Fellowship. Her short story 'Duende' won the 2014 Hilary Mantel International Short Story Award and 'Borges and I' was shortlisted in the *ABR* Elizabeth Jolley Prize.